CRACKER

THE BIG CRUNCH

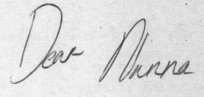

Dear Nanna

I love you

Kyra

XXX

P.S I hope you like this book.

CRACKER

THE BIG CRUNCH

Liz Holliday

Virgin

First published in Great Britain in 1995 by
Virgin Publishing Ltd
332 Ladbroke Grove
London W10 5AH

Cracker © Granada Television and Jimmy McGovern

Text copyright © Liz Holliday 1995
from a screenplay by Ted Whitehead

Cover photographs © Granada Television

ISBN 0 86369 965 0

Typeset by Galleon Typesetting, Ipswich
Printed and bound in Great Britain by
Cox & Wyman Ltd, Reading, Berks

In memory of my mother.
Sweet dreams, mum

With thanks to all the usual suspects – you know who you are. Thanks also to the Friday Nighters – especially Rose E who puts up with far too much; and not forgetting Amber. Almost last, but never least, thanks to my family: Pat and Bob, and Maureen, Edwin, Alex, Christopher and Tristan. And finally, much thanks to Peter, Andy, Rebecca and Kerri from Virgin, for being so supportive during a bad time.

ONE

Norma knew what she would find, there in the woods, with the trees stretching above her like pillars in some great green cathedral.

It didn't bear thinking about, so she didn't think about it. She just clutched the camera in her hand as she concentrated on getting closer to them.

And then she heard them.

Or rather, she heard the ungrateful little slut moaning and panting, even though it was broad daylight.

Closer Norma went, and closer still. She could hear him too, now, his deeper voice counterpointing the girl's with occasional grunts.

It was Kenneth's voice, all right. Kenneth. Her brother-in-law. Her best friend's husband. Her –

A bird rattled up from a nearby tree. Norma froze, but neither of them seemed to have heard her. She pulled a branch down. There they were: the slut sitting in a low fork of a tree, gasping and crying and taking the Lord's name in vain, while Kenneth did –

While Kenneth –

It didn't bear thinking about. Norma raised the camera and clicked the shutter, and clicked the shutter, and clicked the shutter, while Kenneth did *that* with a girl young enough to be his daughter.

'You don't want to leave me,' Fitz said. 'What you want is ritual humiliation: no problem. I can give you what you want.' He drew the razor across his face, watching himself dispassionately in the mirror as he shaved. What to say

1

next? What would convince her. Not promises – 'I'm sorry my life's a mess. I've fouled up. Emotionally I'm incompetent, I know; can't express my feelings, have to cover them up with smart patter and abuse –' That was better. She'd go for that, Judith would. 'Intellectually I'm a hypocrite; able to dissect, diagnose and treat the faults and flaws in every personality but my own.' God knows but she'd said it to him often enough. It was an old counselling trick: reflect the client's own words back at him. She was smart, though, his Judith. She might recognise what he was doing. He moved on swiftly. 'Physically I'm a wreck; someone's corkscrewing my liver, sandpapering my lungs, blowtorching my stomach and, yes, I have to admit there are times when I wonder if Wee Willy Winkle will ever come lighting with his candle again.' It reminded him too much of the terrifying couple of hours he'd spent at the hospital when he'd collapsed at Mark's party. Besides, there was only one thing he really wanted to say to her. The hardest thing. He stared at himself in the mirror, daring himself to look away. After a moment, he dashed some water over his face, then carefully wiped himself with a towel. There was no escaping it. 'I love you, Judith.' It didn't seem enough, somehow. It was too bald, too raw. He had to convince her. 'Those three words, I love you, they're the truffle you find after snouting through the shit.' Better. *Now* if he promised her – oh God, if he could only convince her he meant it . . . 'I'll change. I'll try.' Good. Better not to labour it though. A little touch of humour? Something to say that he was still himself, wasn't losing his essential Fitz-ness: 'A marriage isn't five furlongs on the flat on a spring afternoon at York; it's four miles over fences at Newton Abbot on heavy ground with November mist descending.' That would do it. It would be like old times, when she had laughed at his jokes, applauded his outrageousness, rewarded his rancour. 'That's better, do I detect a smile? So long as I can get a smile out of you I'll know you've never really left me. Not in here.' He touched his heart. It was a little bit dramatic, but

2

very effective, and with any luck it would remind her of the last time they had made love. That hadn't been so very many weeks ago. It had been good. He had been good. 'Now, don't start crying, please – I know we can work this out between us, Judith –'

The purr of a car's engine – no, two engines – interrupted him. The sound died away. He turned to the window and pushed the curtain aside just in time to see Judith get out of her car. A man emerged from the other. They shook hands and headed towards the house.

'Thank you,' Fitz said, looking upward. Just for a second there was no mockery involved. 'I owe you one. Look me up next time you're in the Basketmakers' Arms.'

He hurried downstairs, past the door that stood open, revealing the unmade bed inside it. He hadn't slept there since Judith had left. Down the stairs, ignoring the half-empty whisky glass and the scatter of towels on the landing, realising with a jolt of guilt that he'd forgotten to water any of her plants.

She came through the front door while he was still on the stairs. He saw her wrinkle her nose as if there was a bad smell, and noticed the full ashtray and jumble of take-away cartons on the hall table at the same time she did. Never mind, never mind. It would just prove to her how much he needed her –

The man came in behind her. He had a briefcase and a clipboard.

'The kitchen's that way,' Judith said. She was holding some papers. In the shadowy hallway, her hair was much darker than usual. She pointed. 'That's the study and there's the living room –'

The man nodded and left.

Estate agent, Fitz thought. Had to be. Couldn't – mustn't – be.

He smiled at her. She stared back coolly. God, he loved her for that, for the way she was always so in control. Opposites attracting, he thought, positive and negative, light

3

and dark. There was always the chance that when they met they would cancel each other out, explode in one brief burst of glory and leave behind them nothing at all. But he didn't choose to believe that. He chose to believe that they complemented each other perfectly, fitting together like the sea lapping an island's shore, each defining the other.

All he had to do was make her see it. He forced himself to walk down the stairs slowly, though he wanted to take them two at a time. Had to retain his dignity. Judith would appreciate that much more than some show of emotion at this point. He started speaking as he went. Now, how did it go? 'You don't want to leave me, what you want is ritual humiliation. It's not a problem – I'll give you what you want.' Judith started to say something, but he carried on. Now he'd started, he just had to get it out, make her understand. 'Listen, I can say the words, stick to the script –' God, he hadn't stuck to it at all. What came next? What came next? 'I'm sorry. My life's a mess –' She'd said something. What was it? Even as he spoke, he re-ran it in his memory. 'I've fouled up.' And then he knew, but by then Judith had stopped speaking. 'My life's a mess,' he said into the sudden silence. And then, 'What?' But he'd heard, and now he couldn't deny it: she wanted to sell the house, split the proceeds, leave him for good.

'I'm perfectly able to look after Katie, and I expect you to do the same for Mark.' Her voice was matter of fact. He wondered if she'd rehearsed this little speech.

'What?' Fitz said, still not quite willing to understand. This wasn't the way it was supposed to go, not the way he'd planned it at all.

'I get Katie, you get Mark.' She was having trouble staying calm. Her breathing was rapid, and she was slightly flushed. She brought the papers up in front of her, like a shield. 'That's the deal.'

It was her rationality that was so offensive, as if she'd worked it all out in advance. He wasn't going to be pushed, though. Not this time. This time he was going to keep it together, give her nothing to complain about. They'd laugh about this one day. Him and Judith and Mark, and yes, his beautiful little Katie. That was what he thought. He thought it even as he opened his mouth and said, 'Oh I see, you get the lochs, and the mighty mountains and the glens of the Highlands, and I get the toxic waste dump. Is that fair?'

Of course it isn't fair, something screamed inside his head. How could you be so stupid as to think your life, your wife, anything that happens to you could ever be fair?

Judith waved the papers at him. They were parchment-coloured, very crisp and official-looking. 'If you'd care to sign these papers, everything can be settled amicably –' She was calmer again. Fitz realised that she was back on the script she'd worked out earlier. She let her hands, and the documents, fall to her sides.

Well, two could play at that game. 'A marriage isn't five furlongs on the flat on a spring afternoon at York, Judith –' he said, thinking, Smile Judith. Smile for me. Let me know I can still win.

But he'd fallen at the first fence. 'You're not funny,' Judith said. She brandished the papers at him again, as if to punctuate her words.

Funny? Fitz thought. No, I'm not funny. I'm dying inside, and you dare stand there with those papers as if they hold the secret of the universe written in legal bloody jargon. He took the top sheet and stared at it gravely for a moment. The end of his universe. That was what those strange words meant.

Well to hell with them then. He stuffed the sheet into his mouth.

Judith sighed. She turned to the estate agent, who was busy measuring up the living room. 'Do you think you could come back another time? He's about to turn nasty.'

Nasty, Fitz thought. I'm not – But before he could complete the thought, the estate agent pushed between them. He looked nervously up at Fitz. Go on, Fitz thought at him. Go on you weaselly little bit of nothing, or I'll show you nasty all right. He growled at the man, like a watchdog. The man scurried towards the door and almost threw himself through it. Judith followed him, and Fitz went after him.

The man fumbled the front door open and tumbled outside. He skidded on the gravel, turned and threw a frightened look at Fitz. Fitz grinned and speeded up.

'In the car and go,' Judith said, hurrying the estate agent along.

Go, would she? Wanted a nice civilised little divorce, did she? Fitz thought. God, the anger in him *burned*. He wanted to say something, to stop her being lost to him; but he felt as though if he opened his mouth to speak flames would gush out and engulf them both. He had to try, though –

She looked back at him, and he saw that he'd already lost her. Well damn her then. Repress his feelings? Be civilised? That was for wimps, for estate agents and counsellors – part of his brain noted that little lapse with some amusement, even while it whisked the milk-sop image of Graham, Judith's one-time lover, back into the safe dark closet of Fitz's mental attic – and other lapdogs. 'You're being too civilised Fitz,' he said, making sure Judith heard him as she got into the car. 'Have to let the anger out, express it, liberate it, the only way you'll come to terms with it –' It was counsellor-speak, the kind of thing he used to trot out to his dull middle-class clients until police work had given him a worthier outlet for his talents. He was sure Judith would appreciate it: after all, she'd tried to get him to – what was her phrase? – to 'see someone' often enough.

She stared at him through the car window. She didn't seem too appreciative.

Tough.

The agent's car pulled away. That's it, he thought. Go on, leave me, take my daughter, sell my house . . . his eye lit on the FOR SALE board at the top of the path. They hadn't even asked him if they could put it up.

Good. That meant he didn't need to ask them if he could take it down. He marched over to it and started to yank it up. The action made his fury burn brighter. 'Don't deny anger,' he shouted, to himself alone now, throwing his huge weight against the sign. 'That way it'll turn on you like a badly treated dog.' He pulled it harder, relishing the physical effort. He heard roaring in his ears, as if his blood were burning. 'Take anger for walkies, throw it a stick, give the dog a bone to chew.' He could hardly breath. 'It's the only way you'll ever be free.' He wrenched the sign loose just as Judith backed her car out of the garden past him.

He whirled round holding the sign up like a placard in a demonstration, and followed the car out into the road. 'Bitch!' he shouted. 'Harridan!' Judith swung the car around. For an instant it came almost to a stop. He saw her watching him through the side window, and thought she was going to get out and talk to him. Well of course it was too late for that, wasn't it? Wasn't it? So naturally he wasn't surprised when she accelerated away. 'Harpy,' he yelled at the retreating rear of the car. 'Hag! Witch!' And then somehow the sign was up over his head and he could feel the weight of it on the fulcrum of his shoulder as he screamed, 'Wife!'

And then it wasn't in his hand, it was flying stake first down the road and he could feel the backlash from where he'd hurled it. That would show her. That would –

The stake slammed into the rear windscreen. Glass exploded. Tyres squealed on tarmac.

My God, he thought, I could have killed her. He wanted to take her in his arms as if she had been in some terrible accident, to tell her it was all over, that no-one would hurt her ever again. That he would never hurt her again.

Judith got out of the car. She was incandescent with rage. She stalked round to the back of the car before he could move, and stared at the sign for a second.

Now, he thought at himself. Say something now. Last chance. But for once the words wouldn't come.

Judith grabbed the sign and tossed it to the ground. 'Not any more Fitz,' she said. By her voice she was past resignation, past contempt, perhaps even past anger. And definitely,

Fitz realised, definitely past him. 'I'll send you the bill,' she said, and turned away.

She got in the car and drove off. Fitz watched the car go. The neighbours were out in force, watching the show.

Well, let them, Fitz thought. It didn't matter to him. Nothing mattered to him, now.

TWO

Kenneth Trant stared round at the Fellowship. They were good people, he thought. He had gathered them together by the grace of God, to do His will. Now he stood before them, haloed by the gemstone light falling through the stained glass window behind him, with his family – his wife Virginia, his brother Michael and his sister-in-law Norma – on either side of him, ready to bring them comfort and instruction.

'Out there,' he said, 'out there is hatred and confusion and bedlam.' He watched the congregation carefully, judging the moment to continue. They were God's people, but they were also his, and he held them with his voice and his gaze. It was not pride: he acknowledged that the things that had brought his people to him were gifts of God. He let his voice roll on, bringing to them a small part of the message God had vouchsafed to him. 'People without direction, wandering blindly – desperate people, hungering for certainty in a world of snowflakes.'

He paused to let them think about that, and let his gaze sweep across them. Young and old, rich and poor, all had come to him when he had started his ministry. There was Dean, staring at him as if hungry for approval. A broken reed, Dean; but nevertheless one of God's children, one of those Kenneth must bring into the light of God. And somewhere there was . . . aah. There she was. Joanne. One of the most blessed gifts God had given him.

'In here is fellowship, love and peace,' he said. He felt the mood of the congregation lift, slightly, as he eased the burden life placed on them. Only Dean still seemed uncomfortable.

He made his special sign, raising up his hands and making his thumbs and index fingers into a kind of view-finder. He peered at Kenneth through it. Kenneth had often wondered about that; but he did not need to understand it. The Lord did not demand that of him, only that he treat Dean with compassion. 'The peace of those who have surrendered themselves to the Lord,' he concluded. 'Amen.'

'Amen,' the crowd murmured back at him.

He glanced around as if deciding who to choose, but he had already made the decision. 'Joanne,' he said. 'Would you care to read?'

Joanne stood up. She was willow slim, and as blonde as any angel, with her short hair shining like gold in the light. Kenneth thought of stroking that hair, of his fingers knotting in it as he thrust deep inside her, of the brightness of her eyes as he took her to that place that God had promised them both. It wasn't wrong. It was God's gift to him, God's way of helping to keep the terrible darkness in his soul at bay.

He sat down. There were things it was better not to think about. Not here, in this house of God. Virginia murmured a compliment about his sermon. He muttered something back, but he couldn't keep his eyes off Joanne.

'Charity beareth all things, believeth all things, hopeth all things, endureth all things,' she said, in that clear, innocent voice of hers. He'd known he had to bring her into the Fellowship the first time she'd read in assembly at school – save her, before she left school and was outside his sphere of influence.

He settled back in his seat. For a second he thought he glimpsed Norma staring at him oddly, rather than paying attention to Joanne. He would have to have a word with her about it, later. It set a bad example to the congregation, and he wouldn't have that. He dismissed it from his mind, and concentrated on Joanne's reading.

'Charity never faileth; but whether there be prophecies, they shall fail.' She hesitated, for no reason Kenneth could see. 'Whether there be tongues, they shall cease; whether there be knowledge, it shall vanish away . . .'

She faltered again, and now Kenneth realised that Dean was staring at her through the lens of his fingers. Kenneth would have intervened, but she picked up again. 'For we know in part, and we prophesy in part –' She glanced at Dean, then at her book. Dean stared at her through his fingers. Joanne looked pleadingly at Kenneth.

He knew that look, loved that look. He let the moment stretch on for a second or two, then said, 'Thank you, Joanne. You read beautifully.' She smiled gratefully at him. Dean was still staring at her. Well, there was an easy way to stop that. 'Dean – would you like to finish the chapter?' he asked. Dean turned his flat gaze on Kenneth, then raised his hands up to look through them. 'Dean?' Kenneth said again.

The boy didn't seem to have understood him. Kenneth was about to let it go, when Michael leaned forward and said, 'Dean? Read.' Dean slowly let his hands drop to his lap. It was understandable. Out of his Christian charity, Michael had given the lad a job at the packaging plant. He was used to making Dean understand what he wanted. 'Read the book. Do what Mr Kenneth tells you.'

Dean's hands fluttered in his lap, as if he wanted to raise them in front of his face again; but he didn't. He picked up his Bible and started to read. 'But when that which is perfect is come,' Dean faltered, 'then that which is in part shall be done away. . . .' Kenneth let Dean's voice roll over him. It was one of his favourite passages, for it offered the peace of perfect knowledge to replace the terrible uncertainty he lived with every day. 'When I became a man, I put away childish things. For now we see througn a glass, darkly –'

Dark, he thought. Yes, I do see darkly. Sometimes he felt as if his vision had been burned away by the awful light of his understanding: that the universe was complete in itself, without the need for God. He knew it, but he did not believe it. Not in his heart, where God would look to see if he were worthy. That was his only comfort. He glanced up. Joanne

11

was staring at him. He looked away quickly, aware that he was denying the only certainty in his world of snowflakes.

Joanne hated the get-together in the church hall after the Bible meetings. It was so mundane: the chattering people, balancing cups of tea and sugary biscuits while they talked about nothing very much; the mothers trying to cope with fretful children; the need to think of something to say to people who didn't interest her. She hated having to pretend to be just another member of the congregation. But most of all, she hated having to watch Kenneth with his wife. Virginia, that was her name.

They were talking to two of the older women. Kenneth was smiling at his wife – he said something about their honeymoon – and it was like a knife in Joanne's heart. Then he put his arm around Virginia, making it clear they belonged together, and it was as if he'd turned the knife.

Not that Joanne didn't understand. He'd explained that his vow to his wife was sacred before God; but that, nevertheless, God didn't expect him to live his life uncomforted. She knew that, but she couldn't stop the little worm of jealousy that gnawed away at her.

Dean said something. Joanne smiled at him. He was a bit slow, a bit strange in the head. That was an uncharitable thought, but she couldn't help it. He was standing too close to her. She pulled her shoulder-bag round in front of her, uneasily aware of the way he was looking at her, like a puppy looking up at its new owner.

She saw Kenneth kiss a baby out of the corner of her eye. 'I'm so glad you brought him along,' he said, holding the child up till it gurgled delightedly. He was good with children, Kenneth was. 'Never too young to start, hmm?' That was what he'd said when he'd invited her along to the Fellowship. Even then, she'd known he thought she was special –

It was no good. Dean was still looking at her expectantly. She hadn't really heard a word he'd said. He had quoted the

12

Bible at her, something from Corinthians, the passage he'd read.

'You don't see the world through a glass, darkly,' she said, and giggled. 'You see it through your fingers.'

Dean held his hands up, and made his sign at her, peering through the double 'L' of his fingers. 'I see you,' he said, as if it meant something. 'You see me.'

Yes, Joanne thought. I see you. Great. Virginia had left Kenneth's side, and was taking a collecting box round the room.

Now perhaps she could talk to him. Not any of the special things they said when they were alone. She just wanted to hear the sound of his voice, and know he was speaking only to her. But he walked past with one of the other girls.

'So glad you passed first time,' he said. 'Doesn't that just show the power of prayer?'

He turned back at the door. Joanne knew Norma was watching her, but she couldn't help it. She turned to face him. He didn't smile. Before she could say anything, he moved away. It didn't matter, though. His eyes said everything there was to say.

His sister-in-law, Norma, looked up from the conversation she'd been having, and stared sharply at Joanne. Joanne smiled at her. I've done nothing, she thought at the woman. Nothing.

Michael Trant stood next to Kenneth, saying goodbye to each member of the Fellowship as they left the building. He was proud of the older man, and admired the way he knew the names of all the members of the Fellowship, and the easy way he had with them – never at a loss for words, now congratulating this one's success, now offering condolences for that one's bereavement, now chivvying along one who had missed a prayer meeting or two, all without the slightest hint of strain.

Virginia pushed open the plate glass door of the church hall. The breeze brought her perfume to him, a swirl of rose

13

and musk. She stared at him for a second out of heavy-lidded eyes, but he knew she didn't really see him. All those years of marriage, and she still had eyes only for Kenneth. Well, who could blame her?

'Off on my rounds,' she said, and jingled her collecting box in the air. Sunlight glinted in her white-blonde hair. Kenneth smiled lovingly at her. Then he kissed her.

They were good for each other, Michael thought. He was glad of that. He pushed his floppy black fringe out of his eyes, wishing he were a better person – more like Kenneth, perhaps – so that he could really mean it.

Norma followed Virginia out of the church hall. Michael smiled at her. He loved her desperately.

'I have to take Dean back to the yard,' he said. 'Make sure he knows what to do while I'm not there.'

'Will you be long?' Norma asked.

'Couple of hours.' Michael pretended not to notice that Norma, like Virginia, was more intent on Kenneth than on him.

Kenneth turned to him. 'I'll meet you in the morning,' he said. His voice, honed by years of public speaking and Bible reading, was resonant and clear. 'Eight o'clock. Sharp.'

Instantly, Michael smiled. 'Yes,' he said. He started across the courtyard, to the van where Dean was waiting for him. 'Yes,' he added over his shoulder. 'I'll be there.' To his own ears, his voice sounded thin and gabbling.

He was still smiling when he got to the van. He knew a lot of people found Dean a bit strange, but he didn't mind that. You just had to know how to deal with him.

The boy was talking to Joanne, one of the girls – young women, Michael supposed you should call them – that Kenneth had brought to the Fellowship. Michael was suddenly aware that Norma was watching him. He suddenly felt trapped between her and the girl, and it made him nervous. Still, it was a chance to prove that he could get on with people every bit as well as Kenneth.

'Right, young man,' he said, punching Dean lightly on

the shoulder. 'Show willing.'

Dean started to make his sign with his fingers. Michael grabbed his hands and fought playfully with him for a moment. Then they both got in the van.

As Michael drove away, he saw Norma in the rear-view mirror. She was talking to Kenneth. Michael thought: Charity beareth all things, believeth all things, hopeth all things, endureth all things.

But there were some things that were almost too much to bear, charity or no.

It was as much as Norma could do to look Kenneth in the eye while she said goodbye to him.

Joanne was waiting by the steps, looking as innocent as a little child; but she couldn't fool Norma. She knew the brazen hussy was just waiting to get Kenneth alone.

There was nothing she could do about it now, but as she crossed the courtyard to her car, Norma couldn't get the image of the two of them in the woods out of her mind. She didn't know how Joanne had done it, but somehow she'd corrupted Kenneth.

That was it, Norma thought as she fumbled open the car door. Joanne had led him on, twisted his proper, pastoral caring into something nasty and sordid. She slid into the driver's seat, intending to go home. But across the way, Kenneth was motioning Joanne to get into his car. She smiled at him and did so. Then he got in too.

The car slid smoothly away. Norma's knuckles were white on the steering wheel as she followed them.

THREE

Schooldays. Best days of your life so they say, Fitz thought, as he waited outside Markham Road Primary. Well, not *his* schooldays. The Jesuit brothers had been too bloody quick with the tawse for that. But somebody's schooldays, anyway.

Now all he had to worry about was a failed marriage, a daughter he might never see again, and a body that was doing its best to fold up on him after a mere four decades of serious abuse.

The Jesuit brothers had nothing on that. Maybe *they* were right. Whoever *they* were.

He lounged against the railings, soaking up the hot sun and watching the kids run out of the playground. The younger ones were met, mostly by their mothers. The older ones got on the school bus.

Despairing of seeing anyone he knew, Fitz shouted to one of the boys as he ran past, 'Excuse me . . . excuse –'

The kid shot him a half contemptuous, half anxious glance. 'Little swine,' Fitz muttered under his breath. Almost before the words were out of his mouth, he saw one of Katie's friends.

It was a wonder he'd recognised her, he thought. All these kids looked the same to him.

'Rosie,' he called out. 'Rosie wait –' The girl turned round. She was scrubbed and smart in her school uniform, and pretty enough in the unfinished way of schoolgirls. Not a patch on his Katie, though. Not a bit of it. 'Have you seen our Katie?' Fitz asked. 'Is she staying behind? It's not her soccer night –'

16

'She's not here any more,' Rosie said. She seemed surprised at the question.

'What? Is she sick?' That had to be it. A tummy bug, or the flu –

'She's gone –'

Now that, Fitz thought, was ridiculous. He took a deep breath and reminded himself not to shoot the messenger. Especially not when she was a ten year old. Even so, his voice was sharper than he'd intended. 'What kind of gone?'

'To a different school,' Rosie said, starting away from him.

'What!' The word exploded out of him. Rosie glanced back uncertainly, but kept walking towards the bus.

Fitz followed her. 'Rosie don't –' She'd know something – Judith surely wouldn't have cut Katie off from all her friends. Again, the girl looked back. Her eyes were huge and startled. She climbed the step into the bus. Fitz started to get on after her, but thought better of it. 'Don't be frightened,' he said, trying to sound soothing. It wasn't his strongest suit. 'It's me. It's me.'

He might as well have said, It's me, Old Nick, the Devil in human form. Which might very well be what Judith had told the girl.

Whatever, she didn't come back. The driver glared at him, and pressed the button for the automatic door. It whapped shut, forcing Fitz to step back.

He walked away, squinting into the sun. 'Well, it was a shite school, anyway,' he said aloud, to anyone who was listening.

No-one was.

Virginia Trant teased her hair with her fingers, watching herself in the mirror as she did so, to make sure each strand achieved the optimum, casual-yet-tidy, effect. Norma stood next to her, with her hands clenched round her comb. Yet she didn't use it. Her face, seen in the mirror, was pinched. There was something wrong. It had been obvious from the

17

moment Norma arrived at the house. Virginia knew it. Norma knew it. Yet neither of them had said anything about it.

'They got away all right?' Virginia said, trying to keep her voice light, and failing.

'Yes!'

'Kenneth is so fussy about punctuality,' Virginia went on, as if she hadn't heard the ice in Norma's voice. When they had both been younger, Norma had had quite a crush on Kenneth. Once, it had worried her, but that was long in the past – she was far too secure in Kenneth's love for her to be worried by something that had only been a dream in the first place. Nevertheless, whenever Norma felt miserable Virginia started to put Kenneth down in subtle ways. It was as if she were telling her friend she hadn't missed out on anything so terribly wonderful after all – which was a lie, but not such a very large one. 'He –'

Norma cut in. 'Michael was ready by seven, sitting waiting –'

She sounded so angry and defensive that Virginia knew she had to do something to help her. She turned round slowly, trying to think of a gentle way of putting it. 'Norma?' she said. 'Is everything –'

'Ginny,' Norma said, without looking at her.

Michael, Virginia thought: it had to be Michael. He was a prime candidate for an affair: always in his brother's shadow, never quite confident of himself. Poor Norma, Virginia thought. She had to help her friend, but to do that, she had to get her talking; and there wasn't a gentle way to ask the question.

After a moment, she said, 'Is everything all right – with you and Michael?'

Norma seemed surprised. 'Michael? Yes. Yes –' Poor thing, Virginia thought. She probably hadn't realised anyone had noticed. It would be up to her to make sure Norma realised that she had Virginia's sympathy, not her pity. Norma took a breath. 'No. It's – it's –' She broke away.

18

Virginia caught her arm. 'Norma, what's wrong?'

The other woman didn't reply. She continued across the room to the French doors, which stood open, letting the early evening sun into the room. She slumped against the door jamb. Virginia thought she might be crying.

Virginia followed her. 'Norma, what is it?' she asked, knowing that she had to get her friend to talk.

Norma turned round. Her eyes were dry, her mouth pursed. She didn't say anything, just swung her bag off her shoulder and fumbled in it. Sunlight glinted on her wedding ring as she took out a packet of photographs. For a moment, Virginia didn't understand. Then she realised that they must be of Michael and some woman. As she took the first one from Norma, she wondered who had taken them.

So for a moment she didn't understand what she was looking at.

Kenneth.

That girl, Joanne, from the Fellowship.

Doing something unspeakable, in the daylight. In the daylight.

Virginia felt herself start to shake. She managed to lower herself into one of the garden chairs. Norma was staring at her, not with pity, but with sympathy.

It was all the same.

Norma placed another photograph on the table, and then another. Virginia felt the world turn dark and begin to close in on her. 'If it had been anything else,' she said. 'If somebody had just told me –'

'I'm sorry –' Norma said. Her voice was gentle.

'How long have you known?' Virginia could hardly get the words out.

'I didn't know. But I was suspicious.'

'How long have you been suspicious?' It was inane, but it was a way to get through another few seconds, while her throat closed up and her mouth was dry, and something inside her that wanted to scream had to be kept quiet.

'Ever since she came to the church.'

'I feel so stupid —' It was a ridiculous, inadequate thing to say. Norma didn't respond, just sat looking at her with all her *bloody* sympathy. 'If you were suspicious — who else was? Who else knows? Michael?'

'He said he didn't —'

For a moment it seemed a worse betrayal than what Kenneth had done. 'You told him?' Virginia couldn't keep the hurt out of her voice. 'You showed him those —'

Norma didn't say anything. She didn't need to. The embarrassment on her face said it all for her.

'He knows. And who else?' It was beyond bearing. 'Filthy little tart,' she yelled, and slammed her hands down on the pile of photographs. Her wedding ring glinted dully in the sunlight.

FOUR

Joanne hated her school uniform. She shifted her bag on her shoulder and tried to enjoy the warmth of the sun on her face; but she couldn't ignore her skirt flapping around her bare legs, or its band rubbing at her waist.

It wouldn't be long now, she thought. Not long at all before she could leave school and be with him all the time. Then everyone would realise how much he loved her, and how much more than a mere schoolgirl she was. Hadn't he said so? Hadn't he said God had sent her to him? Soon, everyone would know –

A car pulled up beside her. She hadn't even heard it approach. She bent down and peered in at the window, expecting the driver to ask for directions.

Kenneth's wife stared back at her. 'Hop in, then,' Virginia said. 'Better than the school bus.' She was smiling, but there was something odd in her tone: it took Joanne an instant to realise that the woman was being too nice, and by that time her hand was on the car door. She searched around for a good reason to refuse the lift, but she couldn't think of one. She smiled back at Virginia, and slid into the passenger seat.

When they had gone a little way down the road, Virginia said, 'Charity beareth all things, believeth all things, hopeth all things, endureth all things –' Her voice had a breathy, sing-song quality to it. Joanne thought she made the verse sound terrible, but she smiled slightly at the older woman anyway. The bright sunlight picked out the tiny lines round Virginia's eyes. Somebody ought to tell her she wears too much eyeshadow, Joanne thought, especially with her eyebrows plucked out like that. She squashed the thought immediately: it was petty, and unworthy of her. 'You read those words so beautifully the other day,' Virginia said.

'Thank you.'

Virginia turned left. Joanne frowned, wondering if Virginia knew of a short-cut, or something. She shifted slightly in her seat, but before she could speak, Virginia said, 'And they are such beautiful words, aren't they?'

'Yes . . .' A short-cut, that was all. Virginia turned to her, and smiled. 'Yes, they are such beautiful words,' she finished, trying not to sound too concerned.

She knew where they were now.

Sure enough, Virginia took another right, and then a left, then swung into the wide gravel drive in front of the house she shared with Kenneth.

Joanne had never thought of it like that before. Her Kenneth shared this house with *this* woman.

She wondered if he'd told her yet. Perhaps, she thought, he was at home. He might even have instructed Virginia to come and get her. He would want Joanne there when he explained things to his wife, after all.

She was almost certain that was it, but it would be better to know what was going on before she saw him. 'Is Mr Trant home?'

'Mr Trant is not at home,' Virginia said. She didn't look at Joanne. She spat her words out rapidly, like machine gun bullets. 'Mr Trant is in Bristol with his brother, moving his mother to their sister's home. Mr Trant will not be back until tomorrow.' At last she turned to face Joanne. 'As I'm sure he must have told you,' she finished. She looked at Joanne out of the corner of her eye and smiled slyly, like a cat. She got out of the car, then turned and leaned in towards Joanne. 'You'd better come in,' she said.

Dean liked to please Mr Michael. Before he left that morning, Mr Michael had told him to make sure all the old boxes were put in the crushing machine.

You put the boxes onto the conveyor belt and pulled the handle. The conveyor belt went rumbling along, taking the boxes with it. Then it went under the crushers, so you pushed the button and the crushers went chomp chomp chomp, like a great big animal eating its dinner.

When Dean had first come to work at the yard, he'd been scared of the noise of the crushing machine, and he'd had to make his special sign at it so it couldn't hurt him. Mr Michael didn't like Dean to do that, and anyway, Dean knew now that the machine couldn't hurt him, just as long as he did what Mr Michael told him.

So he had put all the waste boxes in the crusher, and then he had started to sweep up, just like Mr Michael told him to. Nearly finished, he thought. Nearly, nearly, nearly finished. Swoosh went the brush as he pushed it along. Swoosh, swoosh, swoosh, and then he was done.

He was finished, but it was too early to go home yet. He went up the stairs to the office, and got some paper out of the scrap paper box. He had his own felt-tip pens. Mr Kenneth had given them to Dean for his birthday. Dean didn't like Mr Kenneth much. He was scared of him. But he did like the pens. They were fat, and nice bright colours. He got a comic out of his locker, and started to copy from it.

He liked copying things, Dean did.

Virginia could hardly stop herself from shaking. She stared for a second at Joanne, who stood in the middle of the living room and at least had the good grace not to try and meet her eyes.

Her living room. Hers and Kenneth's. What could this slut of a brat know about twenty years spent together, building something as fine as she and Kenneth had?

She went over to the bureau, feeling the heels of her stilettoes sink into the shag-pile carpet she and Kenneth had chosen together. She dragged open the drawer and took out the folder of photographs.

She had to brush past Joanne to get to the coffee table.

'I've got something to show you,' she said, making a point of turning to look at the girl. Joanne only glowered, then followed her over to the table.

Virginia laid the pictures out as quickly as she could, considering how badly she was shaking. She could see herself reflected in the highly polished veneer. Surely, she didn't look too bad? She was glad she'd taken the time to repair her make-up before she had gone to get the girl.

She could feel the little tart's breath on her, almost feel the heat of her eyes. 'Look at them!' Virginia said. But Joanne wouldn't look. She gasped and screwed her eyes shut. Virginia couldn't bear the sight of her, all that wide-eyed fake innocence – it scarcely masked the gloating arrogance that would ruin all Virginia's happiness, take it away, leave her nothing. She grabbed Joanne by the collar and tried to haul her round. 'Look at them!'

Joanne struggled against her, trying to turn her face away from the evidence of the awful thing that she had done.

'What's the matter?' Virginia demanded. 'Can't you even look at them? You find them disgusting?' She was holding the girl far too tight. She could feel the thin flesh of her through her school jumper. She didn't care though. She was beyond caring. She shoved her face right up close to Joanne's. 'They make you feel sick? Because I tell you, I tell you, they make me feel sick, utterly sick.' She shoved Joanne, harder than she had intended but not nearly as hard as she wanted to.

Then she sat down on the sofa and wept. It wasn't anything she wanted, but she couldn't control the absolute despair that swept over her. She covered her face with her hands and let the tears come, not caring what Joanne thought at all.

After a moment, Joanne said softly, 'It's not,' just as if the words were meant to be a comfort. Virginia felt her sit down on the far end of the sofa. She took her hands away from her face. Now it was she who could not face the girl.

'It's not sickening. It's not disgusting. Only the photos

make it look like that.' Joanne's voice was still soft and reasonable.

Manipulative little so and so, Virginia thought. 'How can you say that –' she began, but then the tears came again and she couldn't speak.

'We love each other.'

'He said he loved you, did he?' Virginia knew she should have expected it, but still it seemed to bring the darkness that threatened to smother her a little closer.

'He does love me. And I love him,' Joanne said. She leaned forward a little. For one awful moment, Virginia thought the girl might be about to take her hand. It occurred to her then that Joanne believed what she said.

'You believe that, do you?' She couldn't keep the pain out of her voice. She took a long, ragged breath, then looked away while she wiped her nose.

The lack of dignity was almost as bad as having to listen to Joanne's earnest young voice tearing apart everything in her world. Not that there was anything in it – this talk of love – but it was the betrayal that hurt; and knowing that what she had with Kenneth could never be the same again. She stared through the French doors at the unreasonably brilliant sunshine in the garden. It should be raining, she thought.

She tried not to listen to Joanne's voice, but there was no avoiding it. 'It's true. We do love each other,' she said, getting more and more excited as she spoke. There was a tiny fragment of Virginia that was beginning to feel sorry for Joanne, with her hopeless, helpless love. 'We want to live together. We want to get married.'

'Married!' She turned to face Joanne, not caring that her face was smeared with tears.

'Yes. Because –'

'He's already married,' Virginia said harshly. Pity was one thing, but this was simply ridiculous.

'He'll get a divorce.'

'Divorce!' Virginia couldn't keep her voice steady. For a

second she stared at this ... this child, who had read so beautifully at the Fellowship, and who now stared calmly back at her, denying everything their faith stood for. 'Marriage is a holy sacrament,' she said at last. 'You can't believe that Kenneth would –' But the look on Joanne's face told Virginia that the girl did, indeed, believe that Kenneth would do it. Once again she felt the first faint stirrings of pity for the girl; but Joanne just watched her quietly, until Virginia could not bear to look at her any more. Anger and pity rose up together in her, until she knew that if she didn't do something she would end up hurting the girl. She turned away. 'God help you.' She turned back. Joanne was sitting as calmly as ever. 'Surely you can see that he will never, never –'

'He will,' Joanne cut in. She licked her lips. There was silence for the space of a heartbeat. Then she said, 'For the baby.'

FIVE

Virginia served tea in her best china. Ham sandwiches. Earl Grey. Fairy cakes. There was comfort to be found in familiar things; besides, no matter if the world were falling apart around her, she could still observe the niceties. She poured the tea. Joanne smiled at her, and sipped her tea. Neither of them spoke. What was there to say?

Joanne took a ham sandwich and nibbled at it. The silence stretched out between them. Virginia took a sip of tea; when she put the cup down, her hand shook so much that the cup rattled against the saucer.

She stared at Joanne, trying to see the girl with Kenneth's eyes: that smooth, creamy-gold skin, huge eyes; willow slim with just a suggestion of hip and bust. But young. That was it, of course. The one argument Virginia could not answer.

Joanne took another sandwich. Well, Virginia thought, she *is* eating for two.

The very thought made her want to scream.

Joanne. Kenneth. Up against a tree. In the daylight.

The girl looked at the fairy cakes. Virginia had made them for the Cancer Research jumble sale.

'May I?'

'By my guest,' Virginia said. Again, there was silence. 'Excuse me,' she said at last, as if she needed Joanne's permission in her own house.

She stumbled outside, then paused. What to do? What to *do*? She grabbed the phone and punched the number from memory. 'Come on. Come on,' she hissed down the mouthpiece.

Norma answered.

'She's here,' Virginia said. 'She's –' she wanted to say, *she's pregnant*, but she couldn't get the words out. 'She's just sitting here. I don't know what to do –' She was almost crying again; she didn't want to cry in front of Norma. Once was enough. Then Norma said she would come over, and Virginia knew everything would be all right.

It took Fitz half an hour and three wrecked phone boxes before he found one that was working. Even then, it was set in a concrete wasteland beneath an overpass. It was right next to a main road, and the local kids were using it for a skateboard run. It stank of that mixture of unwashed bodies, stale lager and urine that is peculiar to phone boxes, and the floor was slick with something Fitz didn't even want to think about.

He pushed his bulk into the box, trying hard to find a dry spot for his feet. 'Outsize phone boxes for all, I say,' he muttered. 'A TARDIS on every street corner –'

The box had recently been decorated by the local pimps. Fitz pulled one of the cards off the wall while he punched Judith's parents' number. 'Safe sex is breast worship,' he read out. Boring. The picture was so small and badly drawn you could hardly make anything out. He took down another card. 'Fantasy foot massages –' Better, though the foot as shown looked like it belonged more to one of the Ugly Sisters than to Cinderella. The phone was still ringing. 'Come play in my wardrobe, open late –' It was the worst yet. Maybe if he ever got bored with psychology, he'd get a job as a copywriter for the local brothel. 'What's wrong with good old French lessons?' he mused. 'I'll tie and tease till you say please –' he read out, in his best seductive tones.

Someone spoke to him. How long –? 'Oh my God, don't you say hello when you pick up the phone?' he demanded.

'If this is a dirty phone call, you –' Belatedly, Fitz recognised the voice of Judith's father.

'No, this is not a mucky phone call,' he said, thinking, You should be so lucky.

'Oh, it's you, is it,' said the voice. If it was cold before, now it turned positively Arctic.

'Yes, it's me, your daughter's erstwhile husband,' Fitz said. The phone went dead.

Fitz glared at the handset. 'Charming. You didn't hang up when you thought you were on to a good thing, did you, you old fart?' He punched the number again.

'Yes?' said Judith's father almost immediately.

'Hello, Vlad the Impaler again,' Fitz said. There was a hissing sound that might have been line-noise; but Fitz knew it was actually Judith's father expressing his disapproval. Damn, he thought. Might have known the old bastard wouldn't recognise irony when he heard it. I might as well have married an American. He sucked his lower lip. 'Is she there? If she's there I'd like to –'

'She's not here –'

'Then where is she?'

'Seeing some friends –' said the voice, rapidly approaching absolute zero.

'She hasn't got any friends –' Fitz said.

'Charming.'

'Not on her own.' Fitz struggled to keep his temper. 'They're our friends.' He could just picture the old so and so, sitting in his neat little house with his neat little retirement pension from his neat little teaching job, tapping his pen against his address book as he thought up yet another excuse why Fitz shouldn't be allowed to speak to Judith. It was about time something punctured that suburban complacency, Fitz decided. 'Just give me her number,' he said, feeling the rage begin to build in him. There was no holding it back now. 'I want my wife; I want my daughter, you old bastard –'

'That will do, thank you,' said Judith's father, in the tones of a schoolmaster dealing with an unruly fourth form on a wet Wednesday afternoon when games have been cancelled.

Fitz was damned lucky he hadn't put the phone down,

and knew it. 'I'm sorry,' he said, but he couldn't keep the sarcasm out of his voice. Who did the jumped-up little pipsqueak think he was, anyway? 'My fault. Lost my temper. Language, Fitz!' He put one wrist close to the mouthpiece and awkwardly, but loudly, slapped it with the hand holding the hand set. 'There I've slapped my wrist –'

'Are you making fun of me, young man? Because if so –'

'No no,' Fitz said, thinking, Yes, of course I am, you old codger; though now you come to mention it, maybe it wasn't the smartest move in the world. 'No. I want to talk to Katie at least.'

'She's out at the park. And before you ask, I'm not going to tell you which one.'

One last chance, Fitz thought. 'Then will you convey a message? Ask her to phone me at home, do you think you might manage that?' It was no use. The anger just kept bubbling through.

'I'll see what I can do.' There was a definite edge to the old man's voice.

'Please.' There was a click as the line cleared. 'Thank you. Too kind,' Fitz said to dead air. 'The argument for patricide,' he said as he slammed out of the phone box. 'I rest my case.'

The girl was quite unrepentant. She sat slowly picking the case off one of Virginia's fairy cakes. Norma could understand that she would have driven Virginia to distraction. She had been trying to get Joanne to speak for ten minutes. In all that time, the girl had said nothing.

Norma was quite out of patience with her. 'Have you told your parents?' Nothing. 'What are they going to think about it?' Still nothing. I should give up, Norma thought. But one glance at Virginia's tense face told her that she couldn't. 'What are they going to say?' she said fiercely.

Joanne simply looked at her fingers as they turned the cake into crumbs on her lap.

'Have you?' Virginia asked. Her voice was soft, almost pleading. 'Told them?'

At last Joanne turned to her. Her face was set like stone. 'No,' she said.

'But you can't just carry on –' Virginia said. She almost sounded concerned about the girl's welfare. Irritation flickered in Norma. Sometimes Virginia took charity too far.

'Kenneth will.'

'Kenneth!' Virginia turned to Norma, plainly shocked.

'He'll talk to them first.' Joane's voice drifted on the early evening air like thistledown. She seemed completely unaware of the ridiculousness of what she was saying, or the terrible effect it was having on Virginia. It was in that moment that Norma understood that she hated the girl. 'Do you mind if I use the loo,' she went on, as if they had been discussing the church flower arrangements.

Virginia was staring into space. With her right hand, she was twisting her wedding ring round and round.

'No,' Norma said. 'It's upstairs, to the –'

'I know where it is,' the girl said.

She's doing it deliberately, Norma thought. Doing everything she can to hurt us.

As the girl walked across the room, Virginia stared numbly at Norma. Before either of them could speak, the girl stopped and turned. 'Maybe you're right. Maybe I ought to talk to my parents first,' she said. For a moment Norma thought she had come to her senses. 'Kenneth will speak to them later.' Then she turned and left.

'She knows where it is,' Virginia said. Her voice was a monotone.

Norma went over and sat on the sofa next to her. 'Ginny . . .'

'She knows. She knows where it is.' Virginia's words were getting faster and faster. 'She's been here before. He's brought her here. Here.' She twisted her wedding ring harder and harder. 'I suppose he took her upstairs. Upstairs to our bedroom – I suppose they –'

31

She was nearly hysterical. 'Ginny,' Norma said sharply. 'Shut up. Now listen –'

It didn't work. Virginia took a huge, gulping breath. 'I have always tried to be a good Christian woman, but . . . Oh God help us. Help us –' She turned and stared at Norma. 'Help me,' she said again.

Joanne liked the Trants' bathroom. It was warm, and it had a wonderfully thick carpet. The towels were big and soft, big enough to go round her twice, as Kenneth had said when he'd wrapped her in one. Then he'd picked her up and carried her to his room, where he had just as carefully unwrapped her. Like a gift, he'd said, as he'd run his tongue over her breasts. Like a gift from God.

She smiled, remembering, and finished drying her hands. Then she realised she would have to go back downstairs and face Virginia and Norma, and the smile faded. They were so angry with her. She would have to make them see that everything would work out for the best in the end.

Still, her mouth was dry with nerves as she started down the stairs, and she clutched the banister so hard her knuckles went white. She paused at the turn in the staircase. The murmur of voices drifted up from the living room. They were talking about her. She was sure of it. She strained to hear what they were saying, but it was no use.

She carried on down. By the time she got to the bottom, Virginia Trant was waiting for her. She was standing at the far end of the hallway, between the front door and the closet. The woman's eyes were huge and red-rimmed in the fading sunlight.

She glared at Joanne, who had to force herself to stare back. She wanted to bolt through the front door, to go home: better yet, to find Kenneth and be safe within the circle of his embrace, away from these furious, meddling women. But Virginia had said that Kenneth had gone to Bristol, and anyway Joanne would not let him down by showing weakness in front of this woman who – Kenneth had told her

32

time after time – was his wife in name only. So she met Virginia's stare, even though her heart was hammering in her chest, and there was a horrible, metallic taste in her mouth.

'Do you realise what you're doing to him? You'll ruin him,' Virginia demanded. I won't, Joanne thought. I'll make him happy. Happier than you have. But before she could get a word in, Virginia continued, 'All you care about is the baby. You don't give a damn what this will do to –' Joanne opened her mouth to try and speak, but Virginia just went straight on. 'You'll ruin his career, he'll have to leave, he'll never get another position. And his family –' She rushed over. For a moment Joanne thought Virginia would hit her, but the woman just thrust her face close to hers. Her mouth opened and closed like a puppet's, so that the words didn't really seem to be coming from her at all. 'You selfish little bitch! You did it deliberately, didn't you? You knew what you were doing, you led him on. You came to the Fellowship and then . . .' Her voice trailed off. Joanne thought, Now: I should say something to her now, try to make her understand. But the woman had things so wrong that Joanne knew she could never get through to her. 'Oh God, the Fellowship!' Virginia said. She turned away, and covered her face with her hand.

Somehow, the older woman's tears frightened Joanne more than her anger had. She had to get away. She licked her lips. 'Do you mind if I phone my dad and ask him to collect me?' she asked. She didn't sound scared. That pleased her.

'That won't be necessary.' Norma's voice came from behind Joanne.

She turned. Norma was standing in the living-room doorway with her arms spread out, so that she was filling the space completely.

She was staring at Virginia. Joanne looked from one woman to the other, and back again. They're planning something, she thought. She felt herself starting to panic. What are they planning?

'No,' Virginia said. She sounded nervous. 'No, you can stay the night here.'

It was a ridiculous, impossible suggestion. Virginia had to know that. But the only word Joanne could get out was, 'Here?'

She sounded scared. She despised herself for that. God was on her side. Kenneth was. She should be stronger than her fear.

She felt Norma push her from behind.

As she stumbled forward, Virginia said, 'Talk to Kenneth tomorrow.'

Norma propelled Joanne forward, first one step, then another.

'I can't stay here,' Joanne said. The front door was only a step or two away. She made a break for it. One step. If she could get the latch open –

Norma grabbed her arms. Joanne struggled, but Norma was bigger and heavier and her fingers bit straight through Joanne's cardigan into her arms.

'I can't,' Joanne said, as she tried to yank herself free. 'Please –'

Virginia had moved to stand nearer the closet. Norma hustled Joanne forward, still holding her tightly. Joanne tried to fight back, but she could barely believe what was happening. Virginia opened the closet door, and Joanne saw that it wasn't a closet after all. It was a cellar.

Norma shoved her hard in the back. She stumbled forward into the dark. 'Don't –' she screamed.

Her foot caught on something, and then she slipped. She tried to grab the banister, but it was too far away. She overbalanced. The world turned over in front of her eyes. She pulled her hands up to protect her face, just as she slammed into the floor.

And then there was only the quiet and the dark.

SIX

Joanne woke to darkness. Everything hurt. For a moment she lay without moving, not quite able to remember what had happened. She listened to the sound of her heartbeat, and the slow rush of her blood in her ears.

Her hip was sore, and so was her wrist. She had fallen. Norma Trant had pushed her. She remembered now. Her hand moved to her belly, to where Kenneth's child grew inside her. Virginia had called her a bitch, had said she cared more for the baby than for Kenneth. Perhaps they hoped that the fall would make her lose the child.

She didn't understand why they hated her so much.

In a moment, she would sit up and try and think of what to do, what to say. In a moment, she would be strong.

But for now, all she could do was cry.

Katie hadn't phoned. Neither had Judith. Fitz was sure of it, because he'd fallen asleep on the sofa, right next to the phone.

Light streaming in through the window woke him. He squinted up at the sun. 'Sodding thing ought to have more respect,' he muttered.

His mouth tasted like a gorilla's armpit, and he was pretty sure he smelled. It was either that or the ashtray he'd left on the arm of the sofa.

Shower, he thought. First thing. Right after a hair of the dog . . . beat Worcester sauce and a raw egg any day. He was pretty certain there was an open bottle of whisky somewhere in all the rubbish. There'd better be, he thought. There certainly wasn't a full one.

• • •

Dean watched the cardboard rumble up the ramp towards the whirring blades of the rubbish machine. He was sitting on top of one of the waste bales it had made, making sure it was tied up properly. He was working so hard that he didn't hear Mr Michael and Mr Kenneth arrive.

They were in Mr Kenneth's car, but only Mr Michael got out. Dean was glad about that. He was a bit scared of Mr Kenneth. He had to make his sign at him a lot, and that made Mr Michael angry. Then Dean was scared of Mr Michael as well as Mr Kenneth.

But it was all right today. Mr Kenneth drove away. Mr Michael stared at the car as it left the yard. Dean thought he had a funny kind of look on his face. He didn't ask about it though. Mr Michael always told him that if he looked after his own business, and didn't pry into other people's, then God would be his friend and look after him.

Dean liked God. At least, he liked going to the prayer meetings, and seeing all the people and Joanne and joining in the singing. Having a God for a friend seemed like a good idea to Dean.

Mr Michael came over. 'Any problems, Dean?' he asked.

'No problems, Mr Michael,' Dean said. He hoped Mr Michael would notice what a good job he had made of sweeping up, and how well the bales were packed; but Mr Michael just said, 'Good boy. I'll put the kettle on.'

Kenneth Trant's car purred along the almost empty roads that led from the yard to his house.

The sunlight had banished his gloom of the night before. On a morning such as this, with the perfect blue of the summer sky above him and the world fresh and green all around him, it was impossible not to believe that he was part of God's perfect plan.

He started to run through what he had to do. Sheila Jackson, his deputy, was very reliable, but he liked to keep his finger on the pulse, as he often told her. There were the arrangements for the Year Nine testing to go through; then he'd promised to check through the Journey Fund's planning; he'd hoped to have a chance to work on his lesson for the next Fellowship meeting, but he'd probably have to leave it till later in the week . . .

He swung into the driveway of his house. The garden, he thought, was looking splendid. He made a mental note to compliment Virginia on all her hard work. He glanced at the clock on the dashboard. Seven-thirty. Just enough time to grab some toast and coffee before he went to work.

He parked up under the leaded kitchen windows and got out of the car.

Norma opened the front door just as he reached it. There was something wrong. He could see it in her expression, and in any case he got the impression that she had been looking out for him. He started to go past her into the hall.

'Norma.' He tried to keep his voice light. 'Just dropped Michael at the yard.' She scowled at him. So he was right. 'Everything all right? Is there anything –'

'Virginia's in the dining room,' she said, as if it were a perfectly sensible reply to his question. She gave him an odd smile.

He was inside before he managed to place what was odd in it. Triumph, he thought: triumph and bitterness.

He frowned and went into the dining room.

Virginia was sitting at the table by the French windows. She looked awful. Her eyes were red and sore, and she was even paler than usual.

'Darling,' he said. 'What's the matter?' He crossed the room to her, and reached out to her.

She twitched her hand away from him. She whispered something so quietly that he only heard the last word: 'Affair.'

'Affair?' he said. For a moment, he couldn't believe that she had said the word. Then he looked at her – at her red-ringed eyes – and knew that she knew.

It was over then. The knowledge knifed through him. In the space of a single heartbeat, he saw himself living alone in some ratty little bachelor flat, the headlines in the tabloids – *Schoolgirl Frolics* – the Fellowship turning their backs on him, on the word of God that only he could bring them. He couldn't let that happen. Besides, he owed it to Virginia. He couldn't let her suffer all that shame, all the hurt and betrayal. And in any case, she probably didn't know. She had probably been listening to rumours and gossip, spread by some foul-mouthed baggage with malice in mind.

She looked up at him. 'Yes. With that girl. Joanne. *You know –*'

Oh yes, he thought, I know. Perhaps he should try to explain the deep terror that came upon him sometimes; the terror that made him feel as if he were staring out across a darkling plain on a starless night, when the universe had ended in that final cataclysm the scientists promised.

In all that darkness, there could be no light, and no God to move upon the face of the waters and to say 'Let there be light'. It would not even be damnation, because damnation admitted the possibility of redemption.

That was what was waiting for them at the end of time: at the end of time, when they died, it was all the same.

He had tried to explain it to her before, but each time she had refused to listen. So how could he explain that he could only hide from what he knew by burying his face between the breasts of someone like Joanne? By giving himself over to the first and final act of redemption and oblivion that came when he drove into her? And then by telling himself that God had sent her, so that he could know that he was wrong to fear the darkling plain.

It was impossible. She would never understand. Denial was all that was left to him, or else there was nothing at all.

God knew what was in his heart. God would help him convince her. 'I don't know what tales you've been listening to, but –'

'You and her. Doing things together. For months now, behind my back. She told me.' She was going to cry. He schooled himself not to lose his temper. That would be a mistake.

'But Virginia – this – this is monstrous. You surely can't believe it, any of it –'

'You have to tell me the truth, Kenneth. The truth.' Her voice was quiet but implacable. She didn't seem to see the irony of the situation: that she was accusing him of betraying her, while at the same time refusing to trust him; and in that refusal, betraying him in turn. That understanding bolstered him. 'Fantasies,' he said firmly. All she needed was proper guidance, and she would see the truth of her situation: that her place was with him, maintaining her marriage vows – 'For better, for worse' – no matter what. 'Fantasies,' he repeated. 'That's all they are.'

'They are not fantasies,' Virginia shouted. She was close to tears. Kenneth could hear it in her voice. That was good. She would cry, he would forgive her gullibility, and then they would put this whole thing behind them.

No more Joanne. A moment's regret flickered through him. The loss of her was obviously the punishment God had chosen for Kenneth's weakness in fearing the darkness.

'Look,' he said. 'She's seventeen years old. She's thirty years younger than I am. You know what girls of that age are like. Their imaginations just run riot –' He thought, I should tell her that no seventeen year old could be more attractive to me than you are; that no child could shake the love I feel for you. He would have meant it, too. Part of him would. But looking at her sitting there, with her dishevelled hair and her make-up in ruins, he couldn't bring himself to say the words. She started to say something, but he carried on. 'I wasn't aware of it, but maybe she did have a crush on me.' He leaned his weight on the back of the dining chair across from Virginia, so that he could look her straight in the eyes. 'Girls that age often do get a crush on an older man.' Surely she could see the simple truth of that. 'She's just fantasising about –'

'Is she fantasising about being pregnant?' He had

39

overplayed his hand. There was no trace of tearfulness in Virginia now, only anger.

'Pregnant?' Kenneth murmured. His heart slammed inside his chest. The darkness was all around him despite the bright sunlight. 'She told you that?' Ludicrously, all he could think was, She didn't tell me. Why didn't she tell me first?

'Yes,' Virginia said, so softly that the word hardly disturbed the silence in the room at all.

For a moment Kenneth didn't move, couldn't speak. Then he went slowly round to sit at the table next to Virginia. He sat, as she was sitting, with his hands clasped in front of him on the polished table; mirroring the other person's posture to put them at their ease was a trick he had learned long ago.

'Would you take that girl's word against mine?' he said quietly, forcing Virginia to meet his gaze.

'It's not just her word.' The panic was back in Virginia's voice.

'What then?' If she didn't have proof, he might still be able to convince her of his innocence. 'Has somebody been slandering me? Even I have enemies –' It sounded a little more arrogant than he had intended, so he hurried on, 'You mean malicious gossip?'

He reached out to her. She moved her hand away, but he clasped it quickly, and folded it in his own larger one. If he could only help her to feel secure in his love, she might not pursue this. 'Virginia, we've always trusted each other. I can only ask that you trust me now . . .'

The door clattered open behind him. Virginia's eyes went wide. He turned in his chair.

Norma stood in the doorway. Joanne was beside her.

Kenneth stumbled to his feet. Joanne flung herself at him so hard that he almost went flying. She clung desperately to him. His arms went round her just for a second. He threw a desperate glance at Virginia, and tried to push Joanne away.

'Kenneth,' she said, clinging to him. 'Thank God you're here.' Her fingers dug into his back. She pressed herself against his chest.

Virginia and Norma were watching him. He could feel their disgust as if it were acid rain. He tried to push Joanne away, but she held on even tighter. Then she looked up at him and said, 'Tell her, Kenneth, please tell her –'

He stared down at her. She was wearing her school uniform, and without make-up her face looked as round and bland as a baby's.

He'd risked his marriage, his career and his leadership of the Fellowship for this. For a moment, she disgusted him. He disgusted himself, for his stupidity.

'What are you doing –' he said.

The wretched girl was beginning to cry. 'Tell her you love me,' she said.

Kenneth understood then. He murmured a silent prayer of thanks to God. It was obvious: she had panicked when he had been away, yesterday; she had come here, to see if he were all right; and Virginia had got her talking. Foolishly, she had admitted their involvement. But that was all right. As long as Virginia could be persuaded it was just schoolgirl prattle, everything would be all right.

He shoved Joanne away from him, hard. She stumbled back into the fireplace.

'Love you?' he demanded. 'You're out of your mind.' She stared at him like a kicked puppy. Norma glared at him. He didn't have to see Virginia's face to imagine her expression. 'The girl's fantasising,' he said. He turned to Virginia. Her face was an expressionless mask, not at all what he'd been expecting. 'I told you,' he said, trying not to sound desperate. 'She's sick –'

'Sick?' That was Joanne.

'Sick,' he said firmly. He glanced again at Virginia. Her eyes were closed, as if she were fighting to block out pain. 'A sick child –'

'I'm not a child,' Joanne protested before he could finish the sentence. 'I'm pregnant.'

No, thought Kenneth. It couldn't be, mustn't be. Though it changed nothing. Later, it would be a problem, but he could deal with it then, in private.

For now – 'You're lying,' he said to her, and then again, to Virginia: 'She's lying –'

Virginia just stared at him.

'Ginny?' Norma said. She stepped towards the table, holding out some photographs.

Virginia turned her face away. Tears glinted on her cheeks.

Dear God, Kenneth thought. What now?

Norma paced slowly towards him. There was no mistaking the look of triumph on her face. She held out one of the photos.

Kenneth looked at Virginia. She was still facing away from him, but he could hear her whimpering softly as she chewed her fingernail.

He looked at Joanne. She seemed terrified. He could see her chest rising and falling beneath her school jumper as she snatched at breath.

And then, when he had no other choice, he looked at the photograph. Joanne's face, contorted in the moment of orgasm, stared up at him. And there he was in the photo, ramming into her.

Norma was relentless. She laid the photos out on the table: close-ups and middle-distance shots, before and during and after, and in all of them there he was pleasuring himself on Joanne, seduced by her youth, her beauty, her brightness –

There was no mercy in Norma's eyes. But if God was merciful, he might hope for better from Virginia.

He fell into the chair. 'Oh God,' he moaned. 'Oh God, forgive me, I was tempted and I fell.' He was surprised to find that the tears, as they began to flow, were genuine. 'I have sinned, I have sinned most grievously.' He could hardly speak, but even through his tears he murmured, 'Virginia, forgive me – oh Virginia . . .'

Virginia's hand touched his, just for an instant. Then it was gone again: but it was the sign he had hoped for.

42

SEVEN

Jane Penhaligon had known what was going to happen the moment DCI Wise called her to his office. It was the same old story – 'Get down there, talk to the parents' – that she would have got from Bilborough.

But Bilborough was dead, had been dead before she'd got to him as he lay dying in the road, bleeding out his life from a wound made by Albie Kinsella's bayonet.

It had taken a long time, but she was all right with it. She hadn't had a nightmare in weeks.

As for Wise, he treated her much the same as Bilborough had. He just didn't disguise it with any of that New Man crap Bilborough had tried on.

So, here she was, sitting with yet another pair of worried parents, drinking yet another cup of tea. She took the opportunity to have a good look round the room while she waited for Mrs Barnes to fetch the photograph album.

It was a pleasant enough place, she supposed, if you liked over-stuffed furniture and plenty of knick-knacks. Plenty of *religious* knick-knacks, she realised suddenly: she counted at least three Madonna statues, and two pictures of the Sacred Heart, plus a couple of crucifixes.

Roman Catholic, then.

The television blared out a commentary on some boxing match or other. The girl's father stared at it intently. DC Harriman sat next to him. He wasn't attempting to talk to the man. He should have known better, but he couldn't keep his attention off the two men pounding each other into hamburger in the ring.

How can he do that? Penhaligon wondered, looking at Mr

Barnes. His daughter's been missing for over a day, and all he can do is watch the telly –

Mrs Barnes came in with the photograph album under her arm. She was a homely woman, plainly dressed to the point of drabness. A crucifix on a fine gold chain swung against her chest as she walked. Her husband scowled at her as she got in the way of the television.

She settled herself next to Penhaligon, and they started to go through the photos. 'Has Joanne stayed away before, Mrs Barnes?' she asked.

'No. Oh –' she glanced at Penhaligon and managed a brief grin. It turned her plain face pretty. 'Mary.'

'Jane.' It wasn't just politeness, or even friendliness. The more at ease the woman felt, the more co-operative she would be. Penhaligon smiled, noticing out of the corner of her eye that Harriman was at last paying attention.

'No, never,' Mary went on. 'I mean, never without letting us know.' She shot a glance towards the hallway. 'I've sat by that phone all night. I couldn't think what else to do.' Her voice was suddenly hoarse. She turned her attention to the photograph album.

'How old is she?' Penhaligon asked quietly.

'She's seventeen,' Mr Barnes said loudly. He didn't stop watching the television.

'Yes. She had her birthday last month,' Mary agreed.

'Did she have a party?' Penhaligon asked. She leaned forward slightly, and to make it even clearer that the question was aimed at Joanne's father, added, 'I'm sorry, I don't know your name.'

'Mr Barnes.' His attention never wavered from the television screen.

Penhaligon grinned. The look Mary gave her clearly said, 'Never mind him. He's always like that'; but aloud all she said was, 'She's not the party type, our Joanne.'

She flipped over the pages: Joanne as a baby, Joanne at the beach, Joanne in a party dress.

Penhaligon realised that Harriman was losing interest

again. His loss.

Mary turned another page, to reveal a black and white picture of Joanne in a white dress, almost like a bridal gown. Penhaligon groped for the right expression. 'Is that her First Holy Communion?' she asked.

'Oh yes,' Mary said. 'She loved that day; her favourite ever, she says.'

Penhaligon smiled. She couldn't help it. The affection in Mary's voice was almost infectious.

The boxing match picked up the pace. Penhaligon could hear but not see it from where she sat.

'Yes! Yes! Yes!' shouted Mr Barnes. The referee began to count someone out.

'Ahh that's a brilliant right hook,' Harriman said. He glanced guiltily at Penhaligon. She grinned at him sourly, thinking, oh for Christ's sake.

She forced herself to concentrate on the photos. One of them had to do the job right, and she knew from experience it wouldn't be Harriman.

There was a large head-and-shoulders shot of Joanne in her school uniform. She was a pretty girl, with blonde hair in a neat bob, and huge blue eyes.

'Can I take that?' Penhaligon asked.

Mary lifted the transparent film that covered the photograph. 'I would like it back,' she said as she handed it over.

'Of course.'

'I hate to lose any bit of her.' She tried to smile, but she was closer to tears.

In the background, leather gloves smashed against flesh as a replay of the boxing match started.

Kenneth didn't love her.

Kenneth had lied to her.

Joanne watched his face intently as he sat at the end of the big formal dining table. He was struggling with himself. She could see that. Perhaps he was trying to find a way to tell his family – they were all here, Norma and her husband

45

Michael as well as Virginia – that he had been wrong. That now that he had had time to think about it, he realised he loved her.

Please God, let that be true. Her throat was raw from all the crying she had done; and her face was coated with tears, but she refused to wipe them away. Perhaps, she thought, perhaps he was testing her: trying to discover if she were a fit mate for him, or, like Virginia, a broken reed. I am strong, she thought. I am strong, and that means you can tell them.

But he didn't speak.

She stared around at their stony faces: Virginia, who would not look in Joanne's direction, much less meet her gaze; Norma, with that constant eating-lemons grin playing around her lips; and Michael, like a weaker version of Kenneth.

They hated her. She knew it. Only Kenneth could save her from them. She stared at him, willing him to look at her, to acknowledge her love, to let her know that she was still alive.

In the end, it was Norma who spoke. 'It's the only solution –'

'What is?' Michael Trant said, smiling nervously.

'Abortion.' The dreadful word hung in the silence.

She can't mean it, Joanne thought. It's a sin. It's –

'I don't know,' Kenneth said. Joanne found that she had started to breathe again. 'It's –' he started, and Joanne thought, don't Kenneth. Don't give in to them. He stopped speaking and rubbed his mouth with his hand. 'Of course in normal circumstances we'd never countenance such a thing, but –'

'Quick,' Norma said, staring round at each of her relatives. 'Painless. And Joanne's parents need never know. Nobody need ever know, except us –'

Virginia looked hesitant.

'I think Norma's right,' Michael said, and then added defensively, 'It's one solution.'

They would do it. She could see it in their faces: the

46

gathering determination to kill her baby. The child that Kenneth had given her, out of his love for her, because she was the gift God had sent to him.

He had forgotten, that was it. He had seen how badly hurt Virginia was, and he had taken pity on her. That was kind of him, but it was still wrong. All Joanne had to do was remind him, surely?

'No,' she said to him. She put out her hand to Kenneth. He moved away from her. 'It was God's will that I became pregnant,' she said. He wasn't listening to her. She could see from his face that nothing she said, however righteous, would change his mind. Yet she had to try. 'I'm not having an abortion. I'm having your baby.'

That was it, she thought. She would have the baby, and then he would remember that he loved her. How could he look on her and his child, and not remember that they were God's gift to him?

She stood up. 'I'm going home now.' She tried to keep the tears out of her voice, but it was useless. 'I'm going home and I'm going to tell my parents that I'm pregnant.'

There was a long, dreadful silence. Kenneth wouldn't look at her, but she felt the hot eyes of the others on her.

'Kenneth?' Joanne said at last. He looked up at her. That was something. 'I want you to come with me.'

'With you?' That was Virginia, once again on the verge of tears.

Joanne stared at her. Though she felt sorry for herself, she still had some pity left over for the poor woman. After all, Joanne was sure that though she was going to have to fight for what was right, in the end she would win: she would be like Job, tested by God but not despairing. Virginia though – Virginia would lose everything, because she had been found wanting, by God and by Kenneth. How could Joanne not feel sorry for her?

'You don't have to tell your parents that Kenneth is the father.' Norma's harsh voice cut into Joanne's thoughts.

Joanne understood then. They wanted to keep the whole

thing secret. Anything to keep Kenneth with them. Well, they weren't going to succeed. She wasn't going to go against God's will and have an abortion. She wasn't going to lose Kenneth.

'Oh, but I do. I do,' she said. She couldn't stop the tears from coming, but she said what she had to. 'I'm going to tell my parents. I'm going to tell the whole school –'

That got Kenneth's attention.

'Joanne . . .' he said. Smile at me, she thought. Let me know you're on my side. And he did: a small tense smile meant only for her. She knew it was as much as she could expect, with all his family watching. 'Wait,' he said, standing up. He put his hand on her shoulder.

Joanne swallowed. The anger had gone from her. Her throat felt tight, and she wanted to lean into him and cry and cry. She wanted her old Kenneth back, the Kenneth that loved her and made her feel special. And suddenly, she had him. 'Look at you!' he said, teasingly. 'You look a sight.' He took out his handkerchief and dabbed at her eyes. It smelled of him, of his aftershave. 'You don't want to go home and face your parents looking like that, do you? You'd frighten the life out of them!'

I have to be strong, Joanne thought. We'll find a way out of this. Me and Kenneth. Together. She looked up at him, trying to read some sign of what he had planned in his face.

'Cheer up, Joanne. Don't look so tragic.' He bent slightly, so that he could look her in the yes. 'It doesn't suit you,' he said. He does think I'm beautiful, Joanne thought. It wasn't arrogance. He had told her so often enough. He pulled her chin up, so that she had to look up at him. 'Think you could find a smile? Just a little smile?'

This was better. This was much more like the Kenneth Joanne loved. She took a deep breath, and forced herself to smile. To please him.

'That's better,' Kenneth murmured gently, as if Joanne were the only person in the room. 'Isn't that much better?' For a moment, she was sure he would kiss her. But he turned to the others. 'Doesn't she look better now?'

'Yes,' Norma said, and the others all added their agreement.

Kenneth put his arm around Joanne. She took comfort from the warmth and the weight of it, but when he spoke he turned first to Virginia. 'No more conflict,' he said. Virginia nodded. Kenneth turned to address the others. 'No more division. We are all united as humble servants of the Lord. Let us pray for his guidance.' His hand slid from her shoulder. He touched the back of a dining-room chair. 'Joanne. Let us pray –'

I have to go, Joanne thought. I have to tell Mum and Dad. They'll understand. They'd never make me have an abortion. But Kenneth was watching her. She had never refused him before. She couldn't refuse him now. Besides, she thought, if we pray, God will remind him that He sent me to him.

God will tell Kenneth that I am His gift – that the child is His gift to us both. She sat down.

Kenneth sat down too. 'Let us pray,' he said, and held out his hands. Virginia took one of them. Slowly, Joanne took the other. Michael and Norma completed the circle.

Joanne closed her eyes. 'Let us pray,' she whispered.

EIGHT

Jimmy Beck roamed aimlessly around DCI Wise's office, staring at the mug shots and Police Federation information pinned to the walls. He was listening to Wise. Of course he was. But he was a damn sight more interested in the fact that Penhaligon was at it again: riding her own private hobby-horse while ignoring every principle of good detective work anyone had ever tried to teach her.

'There's something about the family –' she said to Wise, though she must have seen that he was trying to get on.

Wise ignored her, and pulled some papers out of the filing cabinet. 'Door-to-doors, local search, radio, local TV,' he said, speaking to both her and Beck as he walked across the room. Penhaligon pursued him, trying to interrupt. Wise ignored her. 'But we know this already, don't we?' he finished.

He lowered his bulk into his chair. Light glinted on the lenses of his glasses.

'He watched a boxing match, sir,' Penhaligon said.

'Come again?'

'Joanne's dad. He didn't seem bothered. Just watched the fight.'

Oh for pity's sake, Beck thought. He turned and stared out the window. In the street below, a woman pushed a baby-buggy along. If Bilborough had had one fault, he thought, it was that he'd let Penhaligon get away with crap like that. Let her develop bad habits. Wise, now, Wise was a Scouser. Salt of the earth, Scousers. He'd set the little cow straight.

'Is that a crime?' Wise demanded.

Good for you, Beck thought. The woman in the street was

50

a lot closer now. Her kid was about the same age as Ryan, Bilborough's lad –

'I have an instinct about this, sir,' Penhaligon said.

'What d'you want to do?' Wise asked.

Oh for Christ's sake, Beck thought. And then, from out of nowhere: Bilborough's dead. David Bilborough is dead, and that cow is still playing mind games with the rest of us.

'I want Fitz to talk to him –'

Jesus wept, Beck thought; but he didn't say anything, only sighed heavily.

Penhaligon whirled round and glared at him.

'You got something to say?' It took Beck a second to realise that Wise was talking to him.

'No, sir.'

'Nothing at all?'

'No, sir.' Bloody head games, Beck thought.

'Then you may as well piss off, mightn't you?'

If that's the way you want it. 'Sir,' Beck said.

He left the room, being very careful not to let the door slam behind him. Harriman was lounging around outside, carefully Tippexing out a mistake he'd made on some poster or other.

He'd made a lot of mistakes, Harriman had. In Jimmy Beck's opinion, if Harriman had made a couple less mistakes, David Bilborough might still be alive.

Beck steamed past him. 'Reaching for the bat-phone ,' he said over his shoulder, and was gone. Harriman grinned uncertainly. Tough. The stupid long streak of nothing at all would have to work it out for himself.

Joanne felt Kenneth withdraw his hands from hers. She opened her eyes, and blinked against the light. The others were staring at her.

Kenneth steepled his hands in front of him. 'Joanne,' he said. 'I have prayed, and God has shown me the error of my ways.'

Now, she thought. Now he will tell them that God gave

51

me to him – that it is Virginia who must leave, not me. That I must bear his child. Denying that was his error. She smiled at Kenneth, marvelling at the depths of his dark eyes.

He stared back at her, with those eyes that seemed to see into her soul. 'And you, Joanne,' he said. 'Have you seen the error of your ways?'

'Me?' She looked round at the others. Michael smiled weakly at her. Norma glared. As for Virginia, she seemed to be sitting a little straighter. There was almost a hint of a smile playing across her lips. She thinks she's won, Joanne thought. She thinks she's blinded Kenneth to God's holy truth. 'I haven't sinned,' she said. No-one moved. No-one spoke. 'You've sinned.' She leaned across the table and jabbed her finger at Virginia. 'You've tried to take him from me, even though you know that God has decreed that I am to be his wife. The mother of his child –' Still no-one spoke. Kenneth was frowning. Slowly, Joanne sank back down into her chair.

'Joanne,' Kenneth said. 'I can see that you need more time to think about what has happened, and to pray for God's guidance.' He stood up and moved round the table to her. 'Come with me, now. You must be apart from us, to pray – as Jesus went apart from his disciples to pray in the Garden of Gethsemane.' He touched her on the elbow. Almost without thinking about what she was doing, Joanne stood up.

'If you want,' she said.

'Good girl.' He smiled, lighting up the world. 'And you know that we will be here, praying for you.'

He led her into the hall, and opened the door to the cellar. The front door was tantalisingly close. She could still leave, find a phone, get her father to come for her. But Kenneth was gesturing for her to go down into the darkness, alone. She could not deny him.

The Barneses were pretty much the way Panhandle had described them, Fitz thought. Good working-class stock, dealing any way they could with the chaos that had suddenly risen up out of the dark to grab them.

Catholic, too: and judging by the number of crucifixes and Madonnas and other icons they had littering the walls and every flat surface, Catholic of the old school.

None of this listening to Mass on the Sunday radio service and eating meat on a Friday. No, they probably fasted the full twenty-four hours before they made Communion and went to confession every single Saturday evening to confess whatever timid sins of the mind and the flesh they had managed to commit. Mass in Latin of course, if they could find a priest who still said it that way: none of Pope Paul's revisionism for them.

They'd know about the dark, Fitz thought: being Catholic, they'd never admit it, but they'd know far more than anyone needed to about guilt and repression, and that hard place in the heart that hangs its head in shame and averts its eyes from good hot human passion.

He perched himself on one of their spindly, too-small dining chairs, in front on their spindly too-small dining table and flipped open the photograph album Mrs Barnes had laid carefully in front of him.

'Lot of school – sports day, school trips,' he said, keeping an eye on Mr Barnes as he did so. Penhaligon was right. The man was still watching the sport – a boxing video. He had the remote control in one hand, and he leaned forward in his chair as if willing his favourite on. Fitz wondered briefly if he had had a bet, then dismissed the idea. Not that the Church forbade gambling – where would church fund-raising be without the odd charity bingo game? – but he was pretty certain Mr Barnes would see it as a waste of money.

He wished to hell that the man would turn over, so he could hear the racing results. It was the first time he'd thought about betting since he'd got Panhandle's call.

Damn job would make a saint of him yet.

'Joanne's very involved at school,' Mrs Barnes said. She

flashed a proud smile at Fitz. 'And not just on the work side. Socially, too.'

Joanne smiled up at him out of the photographs: Joanne in school uniform; Joanne in the park; at the beach, in a demure one-piece swimsuit; at a church fete; with her friends – girls only, no boys.

Joanne: teenager, schoolgirl, daughter, saint. You could see it in Mary Barnes's eyes, Fitz thought. Joanne was perfect, unsullied, incapable of misdemeanour, never mind sin. He wondered if they felt unworthy of her. If they had any pictures of themselves with her, they weren't in this album. No uncles or aunts, either. That might explain it: if Joanne was all the kin Mr and Mrs Barnes had, she would naturally have become the focus of their lives.

'Any of the family?' he asked.

'We are the family,' Mr Barnes said sourly. He punched a button on the video remote. The commentary stopped as the machine clicked and whirred into rewind.

You can't think about it, can you Mr Not-Good-Enough-to-Wash-Your-Daughter's-Feet Barnes. Think about it and you make it real. Think about it and chaos is let loose in the world. Think about it, and anything at all can have happened.

'What do you do with yourself – ah, Peter, isn't it?' Fitz asked.

The boxing commentary started again, punctuated by the whap, whap, whap of leather on flesh.

The father held the key. He was pretty certain of that: maybe not to where Joanne had gone, but certainly to why she had gone. Once he knew that, he'd be able to work out where they should look to find her.

'Do?' Mr Barnes said, as if it were an alien concept.

'Prefer Pete?' Fitz asked. He was suddenly aware that he wasn't making any headway, and that Panhandle was watching him.

'I mind my own business is what I do.' He punched the video remote. The tape went into replay.

Bastard, Fitz thought. 'Nice work if you can get it,' he said, and turned back to Mrs Barnes. 'Any boyfriends? I mean, Joanne.'

'Joanne's a good girl.' Mrs Barnes sounded shocked, as if he'd asked whether her daughter used crack or heroin as her recreational drug of choice.

Yeah right, Fitz thought. He had a pretty strong idea what they meant by *good*, too – Yes Dad, no Dad, three bags full Dad, done my homework Dad, won't say boo to a goose, let alone a boy, Dad.

Well, it might be true, but coming on like a rabid rottweiler over it wasn't going to get the Barnes talking. He thought it over for a second, unwilling to talk about his own family in front of Panhandle.

Well to hell with it. She was a grown woman. She'd have to live with it. He reached into his jacket and pulled his wallet out. He fumbled through it, not wanting to bring out the picture of his son Mark, who had more in common with a toxic waste dump than one of God's little angels, or so Fitz thought most of the time.

He found the photo and laid it on the table. 'My Katie,' he said. Katie smiled brightly up at him stirring memories of a summer's day before he and Judith had started having problems: a time when the world was golden and ripe with infinite possibilities. A load of bullshit, that was, he reminded himself. It had been earlier that year, just before Bilborough had died. They'd gone to Calais on a shopping trip. He'd got drunk on cheap French plonk, insulted a waiter and they'd been thrown out of the brasserie. But that was in the evening. There'd been several good hours together before that. He sighed heavily. Better get on with it. 'Course, she's not got those hormones pumping through her yet, and I know I'm not ready for when she does.' Mrs Barnes gazed at him levelly. So did Panhandle. 'A good girl?' Fitz continued. 'Katie's the goodest, most intelligent, most funny, most attractive girl there ever was in the universe.' Mrs Barnes expression said quite clearly that he was wrong: obviously he was wrong, because how could all those things apply to Katie, when she knew they applied to Joanne? 'And one day she's going to be on the doorstep snogging with some spotty string of slime not good enough to clean her shoes,' he concluded. Suddenly he wanted to get this over with, to finish finding out where Katie's new school was and visit her there. 'I know it; but I'll never be ready for it.' God no, he thought. The good old male imperative would see to that: it didn't matter whether it was his wife or his daughter, if one of his women was involved he'd kill any man who made a move on her.

Mrs Barnes stared at her fingernails. For a second he thought she had something to tell him, but all she said was, 'No.'

Panhandle seemed uncomfortable. She stared at Mr Barnes for a moment. She thinks I ought to be talking to him, not the wife, Fitz thought. She was right. But the only way to get to him was to chip chip chip away at Mrs Barnes where he could hear. Sooner or later, he'd crack.

'It doesn't reflect on us, or on our kids, if they start exploring their sexuality,' he said just loud enough so he could be certain Mr Barnes would hear it.

'Perhaps,' Mrs Barnes murmured.

'Joanne is not that kind of girl,' Mr Barnes cut in. His voice was flat, brooking no opposition. He punched the rewind button yet again.

Before Fitz could push him any further, Panhandle said, 'If you have any idea, however strange . . .'

Abruptly, the telephone rang. Mrs Barnes was out of her chair before it had rung twice. 'Excuse me,' she said, already halfway to the hall.

Panhandle turned to watch her. Fitz kept his attention on Mr Barnes, all the while listening to the rise and fall of Mrs Barnes voice: first excited and hopeful, then disappointed, and finally apologetic.

If this turned out badly it wouldn't go easy with her; but it was Mr Barnes that really worried Fitz. The man couldn't bend, so when the storm hit him – and all Fitz's instincts told him to expect the worst – all that would be left would be for him to break.

Mrs Barnes came back in. 'Father O'Ryan,' she said, to her husband. He didn't react. She turned to Fitz and leaned on the back of the dining-room chair she had been sitting in. 'Wanting to know if there's any news on Joanne.' She paused. Her knuckles tightened on the chair back. 'Well, he wants to help.'

'The parish priest, is he?'

'Yes,' Mrs Barnes said, and pulled the chair out so she could sit down.

Mr Barnes hit the replay button again.

'Joanne used to be very devout,' Mrs Barnes said. 'But – well, she hasn't been going for a few months now.' She sounded embarrassed. Defensive, even. 'You know what they're like, at that age, the young ones.'

Panhandle smiled, almost conspiratorially. Fitz wondered exactly what she'd been like at that age. Panhandle at seventeen. It was quite a thought.

Penhaligon followed Fitz upstairs as Mrs Barnes led them to Joanne's bedroom. She was glad she'd pushed for him to be involved in the case.

Maybe she still ought to be angry with him. God knew, he deserved it after the way he'd led her along and then stood her up at the airport, when she'd paid out hundreds for him to go on holiday with her. But that had been almost a year ago, before Bilborough had been murdered, and it seemed like another life. It was as if the tears she had cried for the boss – it was going to be a long time before she thought of DCI Wise as the boss in the same way – had washed away her anger; at the very least, his death had made her realise that you had to take what comfort you could, when you could.

Or maybe it was simply that she liked Fitz too much to stay angry at him for long.

Whatever it was, she was glad he was here. At least she knew he would take her ideas seriously.

Mrs Barnes ushered them into Joanne's room. It was painted and accessorised in white, and it was almost clinically neat. There were no posters on the walls, only a couple of nice prints – landscapes, not film stars – and, of course, a crucifix over the bed. The desk was laid out with military precision, and the few cosmetics – cleanser, toner, no make-up as far as Penhaligon could see – were grouped tidily on the dressing table. Only the bed was less than perfect. It looked as if someone had sat on it.

Penhaligon could tell Fitz was startled, though he looked around cataloguing everything as he always did. 'I take it you've tidied up,' he said after a minute.

'No,' said Mrs Barnes. 'This is just as she had it.' She began to cry.

In the darkness of the Trants' cellar, Joanne knelt and prayed.

NINE

Kenneth Trant stood behind a stack of old boxes in the cellar, and listened to Joanne's voice as she whispered her way through the Hail Mary.

'Blessed is the fruit of thy womb, Jesus –' she murmured. Her hair shimmered in the half-light, like a halo.

Idolatry, he thought: the Mary-worshippers of the Church of Rome were no better than pagans, with their painted figurines and their saints making intercessions to God on their behalf.

Only he knew the truth: that God existed in the dark heart of the universe, that place of darkness and light that existed before time and matter became themselves; and that God was waiting for them at the end of time, beyond that compacted moment of being and nothingness which the universe would become when the stars ran down.

Oh yes. How could God exist in a clockwork universe, a universe ruled by the equations of the cold-hearted scientists?

Let Hawking and the rest keep their equations: his God existed outside of all of them, and when He had said, 'Let there be light' the universe had unfolded itself and time had begun.

There was no paradox of faith versus rationality.

That was what Kenneth Trant believed.

He did. He did.

Or else he believed nothing at all.

'Pray for us now –' Joanne said.

He stepped out from behind the boxes. His foot scrunched on the concrete floor. Her voice faltered to a halt, then began again.

He stepped out in front of her. She stared up at him from where she knelt. She was still wearing her school uniform, and she had her hands pressed together in front of her, like a little child.

He felt himself drawn to her. How could he not be attracted to that innocence? She believed in God simply, without any understanding of the darkness inherent in the light. He longed to plunge himself into her brightness, to have the darkness in his soul burned away, to be free to worship God innocently.

No! he thought. She is the temptress. There is only God: and the only darkness is the darkness I allow to overtake me. It will eat me if I let it.

And yet he still wanted to reach out to her, to feel the heaviness of her breasts and the hardness of her nipples beneath his hands, to bury himself into the hot haven between her thighs.

And if he did – if he did taste that darkness, that sanctuary – would he not be partaking of that same darkness that lay beyond everything, that darkness where God dwelled? And if he did – would not God, who forgave all things, forgive him?

He reached down and pulled Joanne to him.

Penhaligon sipped her lager, watching Fitz carefully as he finished his pint of bitter. The pub was almost empty, but the juke box was blaring out something she didn't recognise.

She was beginning to regret having asked for Fitz to be brought into the case. What had it got her? Wise's clever little girl routine, and another one of Jimmy Beck's glowering silences.

And Fitz didn't seem too happy about it, either. He'd been odd on the way to the Barneses' house; they'd hardly spoken, and even their silences had been strained.

The worst of it was that she was pretty certain she'd wasted Fitz's time. He hadn't tried to force anything at all out of the Barneses. She had been sure they were hiding something: or at least, that the husband was – not necessarily anything terrible, like sexual abuse, but a row maybe; or just emotional neglect.

Fitz swilled the dregs of his beer round in his glass. 'Joanne's room . . . very bare, isn't it?' he said. He gave her an odd look. She wondered if he expected her to admit her own room had been exactly the same when she was that age. He'd be lucky. She'd had a real crush on Adam Ant then. 'Monastic, like a cell,' he said, and drained his glass.

'Well, her mother said she used to be very devout,' Penhaligon said. Maybe she'd been right to bring Fitz in, after all. From the sound of this, he thought something was odd at home after all.

'Well but . . . you'd still expect a few pop stars on the walls. Cliff Richard, maybe –' *Cliff Richard*, Penhaligon thought. Give me strength. She must have let it show in her face, because Fitz continued, 'or the Pope.' She grinned. Before she could say anything, he said, 'Are you buying me another beer?'

Bloody hell. 'It's your round.'

'I'm temporarily embarrassed.' Broke, you mean, she thought. She'd never known Fitz to be embarrassed about anything, let alone lack of money.

Typical. It was just typical. Yet she found herself leading the way to the bar. She put her bag down in front of her and leaned against the bar while she waited for the barman.

'Perhaps a chaser too?' Fitz settled himself beside her. The barman appeared in front of them. He raised his eyebrows at Fitz. Penhaligon said, 'Two halves please. And a whisky.'

'Look, his daughter is missing,' Fitz said, as if it were a natural continuation of the conversation. Penhaligon fumbled in her purse until she found a fiver. 'The one thing he cannot admit to his wife or himself is that dank gutter smell coming up from his guts that tells him she's in trouble.'

The barman put the drinks down in front of them, and

Penhaligon paid for them. Before she'd even got the change, Fitz had downed the whisky. She sipped her drink.

'Just like the doctor, just like the dentist,' he said. 'The last person you want to see when there's trouble is a detective whose existence confirms your worst fears.' He held his bitter up to the light. 'Face it, Panhandle, the last person anyone ever wants to see is you.'

Cheers, Fitz, Penhaligon thought. Before she could say anything, he leaned back slightly, and said. 'Judith's pretending to leave me again.'

Oh now we're getting to it, Penhaligon thought. She slammed her glass down on the bar even though she'd hardly touched her drink, grabbed her bag and headed for the door.

'What?' Fitz said. 'What did I say?'

Penhaligon spun round. 'You can spot a guilty cough in a football crowd, and not notice World War Three in your living room.' She turned to go before he could persuade her to stay.

'You've seen our living room,' he said in that fake American accent that had once amused her so much. Just for a second, she was tempted. Like drugs, she thought: just say no.

'Have a nice evening on your own, Fitz,' she said over her shoulder.

Fitz watched Panhandle leave. *Have a nice evening on your own, Fitz*, he mimicked.

All right then, he bloody well would. First off, another drink. He reached into his pocket and pulled out the only coin he found there: a fifty pence piece.

It was enough to make you spit.

He walked over to the nearest fruit machine and shoved it in. Just a stupid fifty pence piece, but the old heart was surging with the adrenaline rush as if it were a grand. All right then, play it like it was a grand. Play for keeps. He punched the start button.

Lemons. He should have known. These days it was lemons all the way.

Joanne could hardly breathe. Kenneth's weight was crushing her. I can bear it, though, she thought. I can bear anything now that I know we will be together, no matter how hard Virginia tries to part us.

She stretched her head up to kiss him. He moved his head away.

'Kenneth,' she whispered. 'What is it? What's wrong?'

He scrambled to his feet. Joanne suddenly felt cold. Her skirt was up round her waist, and he had ripped open her blouse in his excitement.

'Wrong?' he said. 'You're what's wrong. Look at you!'

This couldn't be right, he couldn't be talking to her, he couldn't . . . she could hardly bear to look at the anger in his face. She turned her head away.

'I came down here hoping to make you see – hoping to get you to repent, and what did you do?'

What did I do? Joanne wondered. I love you Kenneth. I thought you wanted me to love you. But all I've done is hurt you.

'You seduced me, that's what you did.' His words were like hammer blows. 'Temptress! Jezebel!'

She turned to look at him, though her sight was blurred by tears. He had finished doing up his trousers, and was straightening his shirt. She supposed he wouldn't want Virginia to know what had happened. I've caused them enough hurt, she thought.

'You had better pray that God will forgive you,' Kenneth said. 'I don't know if I can.'

He turned and left. For a moment there was light as Kenneth opened the cellar door. Then it was dark again.

Joanne prayed.

63

TEN

Panhandle was late. That wasn't like her, Fitz thought as he lounged against the fence outside William Street High School. He glanced at his watch. Eight forty-five, and the school was filling up. Not that he minded. Gave him a chance to have one last fag before he assaulted the bastions of educational excellence.

The driver of the school bus was watching him. Fitz thought he might have seen the bloke somewhere before, but he couldn't place him.

Pervert, he thought at him as the bus drew away.

A moment later, a car took its place and Panhandle got out. She slammed the door dramatically, and sent the driver on his way, so she obviously wasn't going to offer Fitz a lift anywhere today. So now I know where I stand, he thought.

'I was beginning to think you'd ditched me,' he said as she approached. She walked straight past, wearing that sucking-lemons expression he knew and hated. He hurried after her.

The old biddy on the reception desk scowled when Panhandle showed her badge. Probably thinks I'm going to leap over the desk, throw her neatly arranged files and books and records all over the place, nick the school dinner money and then ravish her on the floor, Fitz thought. She should be so lucky.

'The headmaster *is* expecting us,' Panhandle said. The old bat did the impossible, and scowled even harder; but she did pick up the phone.

It was too good an opportunity to waste. Fitz pulled out a cigarette and lit up.

'Excuse me, young man,' the receptionist said. Young man? Coming from her, it was almost an insult. 'This *is* a school.'

Fitz took a long slow drag and puffed smoke in her direction. She looked scandalised. 'That's where I started.'

Panhandle merely looked exasperated. He chucked the fag-end on the floor and ground it out with his heel.

Just at that moment, the headmaster came into the room. He was a tall man, booming and jovial. He seemed to fill the place up with his good humour – at first glance, a far cry from the hatchet-faced, heavy-handed priests Fitz had been taught by.

'Good morning,' he said. 'I'm Kenneth Trant. How can I help you?'

You wouldn't want to get on the wrong side of him, though, Fitz mused. He'd make you want to please him, but if you crossed the line he drew, he'd make you feel as if your very soul was withering inside you.

It was the emotion he would crave: adoration or fear, it wouldn't matter, just as long as he could feel you responding to him.

Charismatic leaders. They were all the same. Manipulative bastards. Machiavelli would have been plainer dealing.

Seemed to work though, he thought as Trant led him and Panhandle down the corridor. He had to give the man that. The place was alive with children. They seemed unafraid of him – there were no sudden silences when he approached – and he greeted several of them by name as he passed them.

He opened a door and ushered them inside. 'You won't be disturbed in here,' he said. 'I'll ask her form teacher to send some of her friends along to speak to you.'

Fitz and Panhandle went in. It was an art studio. Talented lot, Fitz thought, glancing around at the walls, which were covered in prints and paintings.

Then again, they might not be. How the hell would he know?

● ● ●

Fitz was revelling in it, Penhaligon thought, as she watched him light up yet another cigarette. It was the chance to shock that he liked. The only thing that really surprised her was that he hadn't lit up in front of the headmaster.

Still, at least she'd persuaded him to stand by the window. She didn't want anyone phoning Anson Road to complain about the smell of cigarettes after they'd gone.

Unfortunately, the lower, easily accessible part of the window was a solid pane of glass. Anyone else would have given up and gone without. Not Fitz. He'd given her one of his despairing-at-the-pettiness-of-humanity grins, grabbed a stool and balanced precariously on it while puffing smoke out the window.

She tried not to look at him. Tried to keep her attention on the case, to keep reminding herself of the questions she needed to ask, the kinds of information it would be useful to have, the law relating to dealing with juveniles. Anything but look at him.

But there he was, in his trademark baggy suit, a great big magnificent lump of a man, and she couldn't keep her eyes off him. If he'd only finish things with Judith once and for all: or even just stop bringing her into the conversation all the time –

Dammit, she thought. I'm not a kid. He's not a packet of sweeties. Just because I want him doesn't mean I can have him.

He was trouble. She knew it.

She still looked at him.

He knows, she thought. He knows I'm looking, and he likes it. Damn you, Fitz.

She turned away and went into the corridor. It was almost empty, but a teenage girl was walking slowly towards the art room. She looked maybe fifteen.

Here we go, Penhaligon thought. She turned back to Fitz. 'Put it out,' she said.

He grinned at her and chucked the butt through the window.

Bastard, she thought, but inside part of her was laughing with him.

So it was the Fitz and Panhandle show, on yet another whistle-stop tour of the witness's psyche, Fitz thought. He only hoped to God he did a better job than last time. That had been a good 'un, that had: Bilborough lying dead in the street and that woman journalist blown to buggery. And the one before that: the school teacher Cassidy banged up for so long that when he was getting out didn't matter, and all for a murder he didn't (probably didn't, said a little voice) all right then, probably didn't commit. And then there had been Sean. Oh yes: blew himself to smithereens, and damn near took some poor blind girl with him. Well at least *he* was as guilty as sin.

And what's brought this on, Fitz? he asked himself. And replied: Well, Doctor Fitzgerald, here I am trying to track down Joanne who's missing, and there's another girl just liking her sitting opposite me to remind me what's at stake. Meanwhile my own daughter's been taken away from me and I can't find her. So of course I feel a failure and everything in my life's a failure and if I can only find Joanne then maybe I can get on and find Katie too, but to do that I have to talk to this girl, but if I talk to her I may fail and if I fail I may never find Katie and –

– and meanwhile Panhandle's talking to her anyway. So you may as well get on with it, make sure it's done right, and prove you can do it.

And then I can go and look for Katie? Yeah, right.

'So, you're her only friend?' Panhandle was saying.

The girl was called Sarah. He'd caught that much before his moment of indecision had grabbed him. She was pretty, in a big-boned way; she had a mass of curly hair that just might have been permed. Her skirt and blouse were neat, her school tie tightly knotted. She perched on the edge of her stool with her knees pressed tightly together and her feet flat on the floor, even though her skirt was far below her knees.

67

Her hands worked at each other.

She was obviously nervous, but you didn't need to be a psychologist to work that one out. There was something else, something she was holding back, but Fitz just couldn't get a handle on it.

'It's all right, Sarah,' Panhandle said. She sat on the edge of one of the desks, and mimicked the girl's posture. It would help to put her at her ease.

'We just want to make sure Joanne is safe and well. You won't get her into any trouble,' Fitz added.

Sarah licked her lips. She obviously wasn't comfortable with Fitz. He decided to let Panhandle lead the interview.

'You're in the year below Joanne, right?' she said.

'Yes.' She sounded almost defensive.

Something odd there, Fitz thought. Maybe she'd been teased about her friendship with the older girl, who was seeming more and more to have been a social outcast in the school.

'Didn't she have any friends in her own year?'

Sarah shrugged uncertainly. Maybe she thought it would look bad if she said Joanne had no other friends. She might be afraid of sounding bitchy, or as if she'd somehow persuaded the older girl away from friends her own age.

When Panhandle didn't say anything else, Fitz said, 'Did Joanne have a boyfriend?'

'No. Her parents thought she was too young for that. . . .'

That seemed a more spontaneous response. It fitted with what he knew of Joanne's parents, too.

'So were you and Joanne pals outside school? I mean, did you go to –' Fitz rolled his eyes for a second, as if searching for today's 'yoof' expression. He knew it made him look ridiculous. He also knew it would get Sarah to relax. '– raves and all that?'

Sarah stifled a giggle. Fitz knew she had him placed now: just another boring old fart – he doubted she'd have used the term – to put up with. She'd stop worrying quite so much now.

'No?' He grinned at her. They were friends now, that grin would tell her. He wasn't an ogre after all.

'Her parents wouldn't let her. They were very strict. They wouldn't even let her wear make-up.'

That fitted with Fitz's picture of the Barneses, though from what Mrs Barnes had said, Joanne had never shown any interest in make-up or boys. Well, it would hardly be the first time parents hadn't noticed what was going on in their children's lives. God no. Look at him and Mark. . . .

Better check to be certain, he thought, but before he could say anything, Penhaligon said, 'And she wanted to . . .'

'Oh yes. Yes, she wanted to.' Sarah was speaking just a little too fast. 'She wanted to be like all the other girls. She said she couldn't wait to get away from home. She said once she wanted to run away to London.' Her hand went to her hair, and she twisted a lock of it round her finger. She was obviously uncomfortable again.

Getting anything out of her had been like pulling teeth, yet she had volunteered the information that Joanne had said she wanted to run away to London. Now why –

Before he could follow the thought through, Panhandle glanced at him, then stood up to indicate the end of the interview. He had one or two more things to ask, but he thought he would get better responses if Sarah was a little off guard, so he didn't protest when the girl stood up.

'Thank you, Sarah,' Panhandle said. She shifted her bag on her shoulder.

Sarah smiled.

Damn, Fitz thought. There had been something he had wanted to ask about . . . maybe it was true. Maybe the booze did rot your brain like the doctors said. Aah well. It would come back to him.

In the meantime he ad libbed. 'You said her parents were strict. How strict? Like – did they ever hit her?'

'Sometimes.' She glanced at Panhandle, then held Fitz's gaze. He was surprised by that: you would have expected her to be embarrassed by it.

There was altogether something not quite right. He knew it, but he couldn't pin it down, and he could hardly badger a schoolgirl into a confession.

'Thank you,' he said, and gave her his very best smile. 'You've been very helpful.'

Sarah turned and left. Panhandle stared at her retreating back. She looked about as unconvinced as Fitz felt.

They swung down the school corridor together. Against her better judgement, Penhaligon liked the sound of that. She liked being able to see him out of the corner of her eye: that massive, comforting bulk, holding a brain big enough not to need to make her feel small.

Yet Fitz was at it again, making his impossible demands, expecting her to find a way to make everything come out the way he needed it.

'Don't tell Wise,' Fitz said. He wasn't asking her, he was giving orders and she didn't like it.

'I have to tell him something.' She knew he wasn't used to office politics, let alone police procedure – though after all this time, you'd have thought with all his brains he'd have started to catch on – but surely even he could see that.

'He'll have her down as a runner,' Fitz said, almost shouting. There were a few more people around now: teenagers in uniform, an overalled caretaker, adults who could have been teachers, social workers or even intruders. At least they wouldn't look too far out of place. Penhaligon scowled at him, hoping he'd have the wit to lower his voice.

'Well, she might be,' Penhaligon said. She knew it would trigger Fitz into giving her an explanation, which she could then relay to Wise.

'Show me a girl who runs away, I'll show you a girl who's tried to make friends and failed,' he said as they continued down the corridor. 'Joanne never even tried. I'll show you a girl who's tried alcohol, tobacco, soft drugs. That's not Joanne.' No argument there, Penhaligon thought.

They turned into the reception area. 'I'll show you a girl who rows with her parents, who sags off school. That's not Joanne either.' He didn't believe Sarah, Penhaligon thought. Not about wanting to run away, and not about Joanne's parents hitting her. She noted that for future use as they walked out across the car park. 'She hasn't run away,' Fitz repeated. Penhaligon couldn't find any reason to disagree. But she would have bet Wise and Beck would.

Kenneth Trant laid a fatherly arm around Sarah's shoulders. That was all right, even in school. Together, they watched the policewoman and the psychologist leave the school.

Sarah looked up at him anxiously. 'Good girl,' he murmured to her. He smiled, and she relaxed a little. He patted her shoulder. She leaned into him. Nothing unseemly; not in school. She was more sensible than Joanne. He could see that now.

He was quite sure that Sarah had said and done no more and no less then he had instructed her.

They would prevail. After all, God had sent her to help him.

ELEVEN

Joanne was too hot. The sun beat down at her through the mullioned windows of the Trants' dining room. The backs of her thighs hurt where they chafed against the brocaded chair seat.

How long had they been sitting here, reading from the Bible? She didn't know. A long time. It had begun when the three of them – Michael, Norma and Virginia – had brought her up from the cellar and told her to pray with them. She was frightened of them, but she knew they were right. It had gone on, and on, and on, until she wasn't hearing the words of the prayers, but feeling them pounding at her. She wanted to tell them to stop, but she knew only an evil person would object to praying.

Kenneth had come in from school. He looked tense, hard-faced. They had gone out of the room together. Kenneth told her to stay where she was, and pray for her immortal soul.

She was evil. She was corrupt. She knew these things. She had heard them in the kitchen, clattering crockery. She would have liked to go and ask them for a drink of water, but she knew she did not deserve one. She had thought of going out of the dining room, out of the front room to –

Where? To her parents?

Once, she had had parents. She had not deserved them. She must not think of them. Kenneth said so. She was not fit to walk in the wider world. Her only hope was to stay here and pray, to offer up her repentance and her soul to God, and hope that she could be made clean by Him.

Kenneth had said that he would show her the way.

Fast, he said. Fast and pray. She had eaten nothing, drunk nothing. There was a slow pounding in her head that she knew was the devil trying to come out of her. She was aching with tiredness, but Kenneth said she must not sleep. If she slept, the devil would gain strength from her weakness.

And so now it was all she could do to follow along as the others read. The words danced on the page.

Kenneth said, ' "And I heard another voice from heaven, saying, Come out of her, my people, that ye be not partakers of her sins, and that ye receive not her plagues." ' He read beautifully, he was beautiful, but that was the sin of lust and so she mustn't think of that, and had said she read beautifully and she agreed but that was the sin of pride and Joanne did not want to be prideful, and all the words were merging in to one in her head.

Virginia was reading, was talking about her, ' "For her sins have reached unto heaven, and God hath remembered her iniquities." ' He will remember me, Joanne thought. All through eternity, remembering my iniquities as I burn as I burn. Her eyes were burning, tears streaming like lava down her face. Yet she made no sound. To make a sound would be prideful, when Kenneth had told her to be not proud. How could the devil be proud?

And now Michael – Michael who had seemed so weak and pitiful before, but who was so much more blessed than Joanne, because he was not wicked and because Kenneth loved him – began to read. ' "Reward her even as she rewarded you, and double unto her double according to her works. In the cup which she hath filled, fill to her double." ' It was fair, it was just, but the thought of it made Joanne want to scream. What had she done? What had her works been? She had loved Kenneth, and she had seduced him. She had forced him to give in to unGodly urges and sinful pleasures. She had made him harm Virginia, poor Virginia. Joanne's heart began to pound. She was going to be sick, but nothing could stop it: she would burn in Hell for all eternity, deprived of God's love, deprived of Kenneth's love, flesh crisping and charring in the furnace heat that she had bought for herself with the fire of her lust. I'm sorry, she thought. I'm sorry I'm sorry I'm sorry. And yet she looked up, and saw Kenneth staring at her, and even in the midst of her repentance she couldn't help being drawn to the intensity of his brown eyes. Her mind flashed on the first time she had drawn her fingers through his thick hair, and that was when she knew that she was certainly damned.

And God knew it too. Why else would the next words she heard be Norma reading ' "How much she hath glorified herself, and lived deliciously, so much torment and sorrow give her; for she saith in her heart, I sit a queen, and am no widow, and shall see no sorrows." '

Glorified myself, Joanne thought. Yes I have. I have thought I could deserve Kenneth's love, and I have glorified myself above Virginia, who is his wife in the eyes of God and the Church.

They were waiting for her to read. She could feel their hot eyes on her. The words blurred on the page. Her tongue felt swollen in her mouth. If she had dared, she would have asked for water. Just a sip. But Kenneth was waiting for her to read. Slowly, she said, ' "Therefore shall her plagues come in one day: death and mourning and famine; and she shall be utterly burned with fire; for strong is the Lord God who judgeth her." '

Judged. Yes.

There were two things you could be sure of, Jimmy Beck knew. You pulled that fat over-rated psycholo-wanker into a case and pretty soon Penhaligon would start saying his lines for him if he wasn't around. That was one thing. The other was that it would be a load of bollocks.

They were in Wise's office. He watched Penhaligon make her pitch. Stuck-up little cow, had to be pushing, pushing, pushing all the time. Couldn't wait in line for promotion, no sir. Had to be coming up with some theory or other all the time to be getting herself noticed.

'This isn't a runaway,' she said.

Crap, Beck thought; but he knew that wouldn't get him very far with Wise. 'Cheesed off at home,' he said, waving his hand for emphasis. 'Sticks out her thumb, down to the smoke and never looks back.'

Penhaligon looked at him as if he were talking shit. Which was rich coming from her, when you thought about it. 'In her school uniform?' she said. She turned to Wise as if Beck wasn't worth convincing. Bitch. 'It's what she was wearing.'

'A sudden impulse,' Beck improvised. 'She runs off with a fella . . .' Wise looked at him. Beck could see he was beginning to get through.

'I don't buy that.' Penhaligon's voice was flat, like it was her shout and she thought he ought to impress her.

No, darlin', Beck thought. Don't suppose you would buy the idea of her running off with a fella – because I don't suppose you'd know what to do with a bloke if you had an instruction manual. Always supposing you could get the fella in the first place.

'She's up the jack and runs off with the fella –' He was getting bored. Come on, he thought. Come on, it's as plain as the nose on your face. Let's close this one up and get on with something a bit more important than a tarty little schoolgirl who's obviously been hot to drop her knickers for the first bloke who'd buy her a vodka and orange.

But Penhaligon just wouldn't let it drop, and Wise wouldn't shut her down. Beck was rapidly losing what little respect he'd ever had for Wise, which wasn't a lot. Beck didn't trust fat men. Too much sitting around. Too much thinking.

'Joanne's never tried alcohol, tobacco, drugs,' Penhaligon said, ticking her points off on her fingers like a regular schoolmarm. 'She's never sagged school. That's not your typical runaway.' She stared earnestly at Wise.

Got you now, you bitch, Beck thought. Wise might not have recognised what was going on earlier, but even he would surely realise that she was simply spouting Fitz's psycho-shit.

Nothing. He just kept watching the pair of them, like a man at a dog fight looking to see which one would win and which would be left with its guts spread on the ground.

'Typical Fitz-speak,' Beck said, just so that Wise would know.

Penhaligon looked ready to spit tacks. Go ahead, darlin', Beck thought. I've got my bulletproof vest on all ready for you.

'That's him talking.' Beck was quite prepared to push it. He sauntered over to the window.

Penhaligon still didn't say anything. She's dead meat and she knows it, Beck thought. About fucking time.

'Is it?' Wise asked. He didn't sound particularly bothered one way or the other.

Penhaligon turned to Beck. She glared at him as if she'd like to bite his balls off. 'Yes,' she admitted.

There was a pause. Wise tapped the end of his biro on the desk. Jesus Christ how much more does he need? Beck wondered.

'OK,' Wise said. 'Carry on, but I want proof – I want proof that a crime's been committed.'

Penhaligon smiled triumphantly at Beck as she left the room. Bloody hell, he thought.

The best day of his life, Fitz mused as he waited outside Katie's new school. Well, maybe that was an exaggeration, but only a tiny little one. Judith had decided to be reasonable – she'd left the name of the school on the answering machine – which meant she was thinking about him, even if the thoughts weren't entirely pleasant. And any minute now, he'd be with Katie. What had he said to the Barneses? That she was the goodest, most intelligent, funniest girl in the world? He'd understated the case woefully.

All he had to do was put up with all these shouting kids and nattering mothers and babies smeared with ice cream and chocolate for a few more minutes until –

And there she was, coming out of the door with a couple of other kids. Being Katie, she was sure to have made masses of new friends already.

She spotted him. 'Dad!' she yelled, and pitched herself at him.

He managed to get his hands out of his pockets in time to grab her as she leapt up for a hug. He swung her round as if she were still a three year old, then set her back on the ground carefully.

Her hair shone in the sunlight, and at the front wispy little curls escaped from her pony tail. Her eyes were bright, her smile lit up her face. Fitz wondered if she'd missed him. She seemed different somehow. More mature, maybe. Trauma could do that to a child, Fitz knew.

It was amazing how fast children grew up, he thought. Clichés got to be clichés because they were true. He made a sudden resolution: he was going to see Katie's growing up, Judith or no.

'Have you got taller or have I got shorter?' he asked. She was almost up to his armpit. 'Been a long time, Katie.'

She giggled. 'It's only been two months, Dad.'

She thought he was joking, but he was deadly serious. It had been the longest two months of his life. At least since the last time Judith left him.

'Your mother's not here yet,' he said to change the subject. 'I thought we could –'

Katie cut in. 'Mum sent you this.' She handed him an envelope.

'I see.' Don't get angry with Katie, he warned himself, though he could feel the slow fuse of his anger beginning to burn. Don't get angry in front of her.

It was hardly Katie's fault if he'd built up a picture in his head of how they would all go out to eat together, and he and Judith would banter until the sharp words turned coy and loving; and how Katie would sit there looking slightly embarrassed as her parents cooed at each other like lovesick

77

teenagers; and then they would all go home together –

'Can I have an ice cream?' Katie asked, nodding towards the van that was parked near the gate.

Oh shit, Fitz thought. He was out of cash again. He patted his trousers dramatically. 'I'm so stupid,' he said. 'I've left my wallet at home. Can you believe that?'

Katie's expression said that she didn't believe it for an instant. 'Mum put some money in with her letter,' she said.

'I never knew your mother was psychic,' he said. Anything but lose face. He fumbled open the envelope. There was a letter inside, wrapped around a ten pound note. More of Judith's carping. It probably said he should spend the money on luxuries like food, not gambling, booze, fags or any of life's other necessities.

Well, he wasn't going to ruin the day thinking about it. Not with Katie smiling up at him the way she had when she was little and he'd made pennies appear from behind her ears.

With the air of a conjurer, he crumpled the letter up and popped it in his mouth. Katie looked unimpressed. For a second, she looked remarkably like her mother.

'I've forgotten my bag,' Katie said. 'Can I go and get it?'

'Ypphh,' Fitz said round a mouthful of damp paper. He stroked Katie on the cheek.

She ran off. As soon as she'd gone, he spat the paper out of his mouth. Ice creams all round, he thought.

He went out of the gate and across the road, smiling at the bus driver – he had *definitely* seen the man somewhere before – in passing. There were a few children waiting at the ice-cream van. Standing behind them, Fitz felt like a giant among pygmies. What'll it be? he wondered. Two large ice creams, with strawberry sauce and a flake. Or he might have a banana – no, a *cider* – ice lolly. He grinned. It had been a long time since he'd done anything as silly as buying ice cream from a van, and –

'That's him!' a male voice shouted. Fitz ignored it. Nothing to do with him, and anyway it was his turn to be served next. 'Bloody pervert!" yelled the voice. Out of the corner of his eye, Fitz saw the bus driver striding towards the van. Towards him. A couple of plods were following him. He turned to face them. 'Menacing our kids!' the man shouted, jabbing his finger in Fitz's direction.

The children scattered out of his way. He whacked Fitz on the arm – not hard, but enough to push him round. 'You've got it all wrong!' Fitz said, struggling to keep his temper. He turned to the policewoman, as the obvious centre of power. 'That is my daughter! I was picking up my daughter and –'

'Can't all be your bloody daughter, can they?' the driver cut in, contempt vying for supremacy with the righteous indignation in his voice.

One or two of the kids giggled. Fitz wondered when a good old-fashioned clip round the ear had gone out of fashion, and whether now would be such a very bad time to reintroduce it.

'Mind your own business,' Fitz said, directing his words to the policewoman.

'Hanging around schools all day –' That was the driver. Scummy little jobsworth poking his nose in where it wasn't wanted, instead of doing something useful, like cataloguing his cockroach collection.

It was too much, too fucking much. 'Piss off,' Fitz yelled, and shoved the heel of his hand into the man's face.

One of the kids cheered. Or possibly jeered.

The man stumbled back into the bushes. 'Go on,' the driver yelled. 'Arrest him.'

The two police officers moved up on either side of him. The kids stood around gawping at them. 'There's a perfectly reasonable explanation, I assure you,' Fitz said loudly, as they marched him away.

Fitz heard Judith's voice before he saw her. He was walking down the corridor from the holding cells to the reception desk ('You can go now,' they'd said, with never a word of apology), and her voice echoed off the dreary walls.

Actually, they looked like they'd just been painted; but Fitz reckoned police stations ought to be a bit squalid.

'Six foot one, nineteen stone, Caucasian,' she said. She sounded bored, and she hadn't even been banged up in a cell for the past two hours. Fitz paused in the corridor outside the reception area to hear what other delights she might add. He soon wished he hadn't bothered. 'Untidy, greasy hair, severe yellowing of fingers on right hand; exhibits tremulousness when deprived of alcohol; permanently wrinkled suit; old appendix scar; large mole on left buttock . . .'

Christ, he thought. Did she have to say that? What did she think they were going to do? Strip search him?

'Thanks love, we've got it,' said the duty sergeant.

Fitz pushed open the door and walked in. Judith turned round. Even furiously angry, even in the unforgiving fluorescent light, she looked more beautiful than he'd ever seen her.

'Yes, that's him,' she said. 'That's my husband.'

She thought it was his fault.

There had been a time when something like this would have been a joke. They would have had a giggle about it on the way home. But that was when Judith had trusted him.

That time had long gone.

'And that's my wife,' Fitz said. He went up to the desk and jerked his thumb at Katie, who was waiting by the wall. 'And that, as I've told you, is my daughter.' Katie dragged herself forward and stood by him. He scrabbled around on the desk for a pen and paper. 'I want the names and divisional numbers of the two arresting officers,' he demanded. The desk sergeant stared blankly at him.

'Fitz.' That was Judith. That bloody well would be Judith, but he was going to bloody well show her who was right and who was wrong this time.

'Because when I'm finished with them they'll wish they stayed on traffic patrol.' He glared at the sergeant.

'Come on, Katie. We're going home.' With a rustle of fabric and a swirl of perfume, she had gone.

Fitz slammed the pen down. Damn thing didn't write anyway. 'Wait a minute,' he said. She didn't stop. 'You think I was drunk.' He pursued her down the corridor. To hell with dignity. 'I was not drunk, Judith.'

TWELVE

Joanne couldn't speak. Tears clogged her throat, but she knew the real reason was that her sin prevented her. The devil had his hand around her throat and she could not say the words that would save her soul.

She was evil. Evil.

She knelt in between them. Staring up, she saw a ring of mouths, moving; of eyes, glaring. She felt dizzy, and had to look away, but she could not shut out the voices that pounded at her. Yet she could not understand the words, either. They were good words, words from the Bible, words of prayer that would save her soul if only she would let them. But she could not understand them any more, and she knew that was the devil in her.

And then: a miracle. Kenneth's voice, calling her name. 'Joanne,' he said. 'Joanne.'

Joanne opened her eyes. Kenneth's hand was in front of her. Hesitantly, knowing she didn't deserve this last chance, she took it. Kenneth drew her to her feet.

'Say it, Joanne. Say it,' he said. His voice was quiet and gentle, and she knew that if she could only do what he asked, everything would be all right. She fought back against the tears. Licked her lips.

'I . . .' Still the devil's hand choked her. 'I . . .'

'Say it.' That was Virginia's voice, from somewhere behind her. Forgive me, Joanne thought. She had done terrible things to that woman – tried to steal her husband, wreck her marriage – and still Virginia wanted to save her.

'Confess.' Kenneth's voice was firmer now. More demanding. 'Save your soul . . .'

Joanne tried again. 'I . . . I have . . .' She could feel them all looking at her. Willing her on; and *still* the words would not come. 'I have . . .'

'She can't,' Virginia said.

'She can't say it,' Norma agreed.

Michael said nothing. Neither did Kenneth, but the disappointment in his eyes was more than Joanne could bear. She sank to her knees, while the tears started to leak down her face again.

'It's her sin that's stopping her,' one of the women murmured.

Joanne didn't know which one it was, and cared less. All she knew was that Kenneth was watching her, and that she had failed him. She had to try again. 'I have committed –' She couldn't say the word. Fornication. Such an ugly word for something she had thought was so beautiful. She started again. 'I have sinned –' Kenneth, watching her. The words died in her throat. She had to admit how badly she had wronged him. 'I have corrupted,' she said. 'Corrupted. . . .'

And there it was, hanging in the air between them. She was evil, she had done a wicked thing, and she had tried to bring the person she loved most in all the world down with her.

She took a couple of deep, gulping breaths, understanding at last that now she had admitted it, she could be saved. But that if she were saved, she could never be with Kenneth again. Never touch him. Never hold him, or be held in that massive, enclosing embrace. Never feel his lips on hers nor know herself to be special above all women.

If that was what being saved meant, she wasn't sure she wanted it. She threw herself forward at him and grabbed at his legs. 'I love you,' she said. Tears flew from her eyes. 'Forgive me,' she whimpered. Forgive me for daring to think you might love me, forgive me for being so weak I can't give you up, forgive me for not being worthy of you. Forgive me for being myself, and not someone you can love.

Still crouching, she twisted round. The world turned above her. Faces stared down at her. Michael, Norma, Virginia. 'Forgive me,' she begged. There was no forgiveness in their hard eyes.

Kenneth's hand touched her burning brow like a benediction. 'It's God's forgiveness you must ask, Joanne,' he said. 'Not mine. Not ours.'

Yes, she thought. It was proof of her wickedness that Kenneth needed to point that out. Of course she should beg God's forgiveness. Kenneth and the others had surely already forgiven her. God would require more, because God knew what was in her heart; and in her heart, she had not given up her love for Kenneth.

Before God could forgive her, she would have to purge herself of that love. 'I must atone,' she said.

She turned back to Kenneth. He reached down to her, and took her face between his two gentle, loving hands. She could feel his breath on her face. His eyes held her.

'You must be punished,' he said.

'I must be punished,' she agreed, and for the first time in days, she felt free. Free of the dreadful weight of sin that had threatened to burden her soul for all eternity. 'I must be punished,' she said again, and rejoiced in the tears that burned down her cheeks.

Kenneth waited until Virginia and Norma came back from the cellar, where they had put Joanne.

Virginia clicked the door softly behind her. Before he could speak, she said, 'Punish her?' Her voice was gentle, but edged with hysteria. 'We can't punish her.'

Kenneth got up. He glanced sternly at Michael and Norma. He was sure of them: they would do what they were told.

But Virginia . . . her hands were already going to her mouth. He took them in his. 'Listen to me,' he said. He could feel her pulse, racing in her wrists like the heartbeat of a songbird. She was tense, pulling against him. That wasn't good. 'Listen to me,' he said again, using that trick of the voice he'd first learned as a teacher. It could quell an entire school, or bring a congregation to the love of the Lord God Jesus Christ. Virginia would certainly respond to it.

Trembling, she nodded, and relaxed slightly.

'You are right when you say we cannot punish her,' Kenneth said. He knew he was right, because he didn't know where the words were coming from. They burned in him, and he knew God had sent them to him. 'We cannot punish her, and we cannot judge her.' He looked from Virginia, to Michael, and then to Norma. 'Only God can judge her. Only God can punish her. You understand me?'

Virginia nodded. He let her wrists go. She brought her hands down to her sides.

'We must send her to God, so that He can do this,' he said. The words were shining and golden, and if beyond them there was darkness he did not need to look at that. Not yet. Perhaps never again. He would be rid of Joanne, who was the darkness incarnate, and all that would be left was God and his bright shining love. 'Are you with me?' he demanded.

'Yes,' Virginia whispered.

'Yes,' said Norma; Norma who was, in so many ways, the strongest of them all, with the love of God blazing in her eyes. 'Yes,' she said again.

Kenneth turned to Michael. Soft Michael. Michael who could only follow where Kenneth led. Michael who said nothing for a moment, and then gave out a little sigh and nodded.

'Good,' Kenneth said. 'I'll go and talk to her. We have to be sure she understands.'

All of them, together, he thought, staring at Michael. No single one of them more guilty than the others. Or less.

Penhaligon thought that going on television to appeal for Joanne to come forward was a waste of time. Her gut instinct was that they'd find the girl's body in a ditch

85

somewhere, or stuffed in a plastic bag in the woods.

Two things stopped her saying so. The first was the fact that she knew she was damn lucky Wise had agreed to let her continue to investigate as if a murder or abduction had taken place. She didn't want to jeopardise that.

The second was that tiny glow of hope in Mrs Barnes's eyes. Mr Barnes had continued to be cold and disinterested, but his wife had grabbed hold of the idea of the appeal like a woman offered a bottle of Perrier in the Sahara.

She obviously thought that the make-up and wardrobe staff were wasting their time, but she had borne their attentions patiently enough. Now Wise and Penhaligon flanked Mr and Mrs Barnes on one side of the familiar long table, facing the ranks of reporters and photographers, with the giant blow-up of Joanne smiling down from behind them.

Wise had done the standard intro, saying what had happened and describing Joanne. He was surprisingly good at it; the horror of the situation was laid bare more effectively by his flat Liverpudlian delivery than any amount of histrionics.

Mrs Barnes took over. She picked up her piece of paper, rattled it once and said, a little too fast, 'Come home Joanne.' She faltered. Go on, Penhaligon urged her silently. 'Wherever you are, come home to your Mum and Dad. Wherever you are, whatever you're doing, whoever you're with, we can accept it. All that matters is that you're well.' She hesitated. Penhaligon guessed that she was imagining all the things that could be happening to Joanne. 'Any other problems we can sort out: you, me and your dad.' She put the paper down.

'Is there anything you would like to add, Mr Barnes?' Wise asked.

'My wife has said everything,' Joanne's father said.

You don't say, Penhaligon thought. She believed Fitz's explanation – that the man could only cope with the situation by denying its reality – but she had found long ago that understanding something didn't necessarily mean forgiving it.

THIRTEEN

'You do trust me, don't you, Joanne?' Kenneth asked. The cellar was in darkness, except for the pair of candles he had lit. Their flames sent shadows jetting across the walls, and turned Joanne's face into a mask of light and darkness.

'You know that I do,' she whispered. Her hair was slicked down with sweat, and her face was blotchy with tears.

She repulsed him. How had he ever been confused into thinking she was the one for him, the gift of God's promise? All that was left was to make an end of it, to begin again in the sure hope of God's forgiveness.

Yet he must not be cruel to her. She was the unwitting tool of the devil, sent to test him. She must be punished, so that he might be made clean of the sin she represented. Yet even in this, God had his purpose: for how else could Kenneth be saved, if he had not fallen utterly and been forgiven, utterly?

He stroked her cheek with the back of his hand. It was soft to the touch, and cool. A little smile played briefly around Joanne's mouth.

'You know I don't want to hurt you,' he said. It was true. If there had been another way, he would have taken it; but God had told him what he had to do. 'But you yourself said you must be punished for what you have done.' She nodded. 'But only God can punish you.' Again, the nod. 'I must send you to God, so that you can be punished.'

'Yes,' she said after a moment. Her voice was little more than a sigh. Her eyes were shadowed pools in the light of the candles.

He reached into his pocket, and took out a handful of

Virginia's tranquillisers. 'Take this,' he said, 'and eat.'

'What?' she said.

He wondered if the reference to the Catholic Mass had been taking things a little too far; but they were the words that God's bright fire had put into his mind. A few pills now; more later; she would slip gently from the pain and degradation of this world into the glory of the next. It would be the best thing for her.

'Eat,' he said again.

She took one, and swallowed it dry. Then another, and another.

Not too many. The others must play their part. He closed his fingers over the remaining pills.

She was his, utterly his. He could see that now. God had sent her, not to be his companion but to carry the weight of the burden he could not bear.

Her breasts pushed against the thin fabric of her school blouse. Her cardigan, rather than hiding them, outlined them. She should have been innocent, but she was corrupt, had corrupted him. He thought of the pink hardness of her nipples, pressing against her bra, his hand, his lips.

Before he'd really thought about what he was doing, his hand moved to cup her breast.

'Don't,' she said.

But she was his. God had given her to him. She wriggled backwards. He grabbed her with one hand and ripped her blouse open with the other. She was still struggling. He lurched forward and pinioned her knees with his own leg.

'Don't,' she said again. 'You said it was wrong. You said I must be punished.' Her voice was just slightly slurred.

'And you shall be,' Kenneth said. His erection chafed him. Something in his mind was screaming that this was wrong, this was very wrong, this was nothing of God's will. But it was nothing to the urgent press of his desire, and the words that came into his mouth to serve that need. 'Don't you trust me?'

'Of . . .' she licked her lips: pink moist tongue against her

88

pearly little teeth. He wanted – 'Of course,' she said, and there was no mistaking the softening of her voice. Her pupils were huge, like those of some small nocturnal creature.

'Then you have to understand why you are being punished,' he said. It was the truth. He would have her, and punish her for it; and then he would be as degraded as he could be, and God would raise him up out of the depths of his despair. And Joanne would be . . . Joanne would be with her God, who would judge her and forgive her. Or not.

'Yes,' she said. And when he moved his hand up under her skirt, she didn't say anything to stop him; and when he peeled back her panties, and found the crisp mound of curls beneath them, and then the moist valley of warmth and softness, with its sudden hard core, she didn't stop him; and when he plunged himself into her, harder and harder until he was done, she moaned a little but she certainly didn't stop him.

And so, really, it was her fault, not his.

Afterwards, she lay there, and he couldn't bear to look at her. She was all the dark things he despised, all the things that separated him from God.

It was then that he remembered what he had thought of earlier: that he could be rid of her, be rid of them all, in one go.

He scrabbled around in one of the boxes on the basement shelving until he found what he wanted: a thick waterproof felt pen. Joanne was half asleep, eyes heavy with drowsiness and the aftermath of lust.

'Come on,' he said, fumbling at her skirt fastening.

'What?' she murmured; but she let him strip her.

Her body was pink and gold and shadowed. He had to make this right, so that he never had to do it again.

Not words. Signs. Signs and portents from the language of science that was bringing him down to his doom. Unless he could be rid of them, be rid of all his temptations in one.

The marker moved slowly and smoothly, over the flat

curve of her belly, between her breasts, across and down her arms. He made her roll over, while he worked out the sigils of damnation on the firm hard curves of her shoulder blades, and let them dip into the small of her back, and then up on to her buttocks and between her thighs almost into that place of delight and damnation that he must never know again.

She did not complain, or ask for any explanation: nor did he offer one. It was as if his hand belonged to someone else. The hand of the devil making him write out the terms of his own damnation.

But when it was done, and she was gone, the devil would never trouble him again.

There would be no more darkness, only God's perfect light.

'My God,' he thought. 'What have I done?'

They would be after him soon, wanting to know what to do next – beginning to doubt him. Hurriedly, he stuffed Joanne's clothes in a plastic bag. He found an old white dust sheet and wound it round her, like a shroud. She looked remarkably peaceful; and when she didn't complain or argue, but only followed him with her huge, frightened eyes, he knew he was doing God's work after all.

He left her lying there in the basement while he went to instruct the others.

Joanne lay in the darkness, staring up at the basement ceiling. She felt strange and heavy, as if she could sink right into the floor.

Kenneth loved her. Kenneth had loved her. Kenneth would punish her. Kenneth would never hurt her.

The two candles he had lit guttered in their holders, sending deep black shadows scuttling over the boxes and bags and shelves that filled the cellar.

Something had happened. Kenneth had said something, or done something, and she should worry about it. But it was too hard, when she could lie here in the lovely cool darkness and think about his face, his hands, his smile. . . .

She could hear the beating of her heart. Perhaps a little time went by, or perhaps it was a long time. She couldn't tell, but it didn't matter, because the door opened.

Kenneth came down the steps of the cellar. She tried to get up to meet him, but the sheet was tucked too tightly round her. She wondered what had happened to her clothes, but it wasn't important.

'No,' Kenneth said. He pushed her back down, and tucked the sheet round her. He said something else. She struggled to understand, and then relaxed as she recognised the Bible.

She would be punished. He had promised her that. She would be allowed to atone.

' "Be not afraid," ' Kenneth said. Joanne was not afraid, but she was sorry for the trouble she had caused him. God would see that, and would forgive her. ' "Say unto the cities of Judah, 'Behold your God'." '

' "Behold your God." '

The basement door opened, and a great light entered through it. For a heartbeat, Joanne thought that the angels of the Lord were descending the steps, and that the brightness fell from their wings and the aura of purity that surrounded them. Then she realised that it was Virginia, and Michael, and Norma, each one bearing a multitude of candles, so that the cellar was filled with light.

They came close to where Joanne lay, and put down their candles. Norma was also carrying a silver salver, which had on it a bottle of strong drink, and a chalice, and some more of the pills.

They knelt around her. Kenneth near her head, at her right hand, to help her to be strong; Virginia facing him, on Joanne's left, because she had been wronged by Joanne; and the others near her feet.

Kenneth filled the chalice with the drink. It smelled strong and sweet. Light glinted on his wedding ring, the ring she had seduced him into defiling.

' "Out of the depths have I cried unto Thee, O Lord. Lord,

hear my voice," ' he said. He shook a few more of the pills out on to the tray. ' "Let thine ears be attentive to the voice of my supplication." '

Kenneth helped Joanne to sit up. Then he placed a tablet on her tongue. She knew she should swallow it, but she lacked the strength. It was all right though. Kenneth put his arm under her shoulders, and then he put the chalice to her lips. She took a sip.

Gin! She recognised the sickly scent of juniper. And the chalice . . . it was a big, heavy, cut-crystal wine glass. 'No,' she tried to say. I don't have to do this, she thought. I don't. But it was too hard to think. Her head felt as heavy as lead, and fire burned behind her eyes.

But Kenneth was saying, 'Lord have mercy on this poor sinner.'

That was right, she thought. It was almost a relief to remember. She had sinned, had corrupted Kenneth and tried to ruin Virginia's marriage. But she didn't need to think about it, because soon she would be with God, and God would first judge and then punish her.

'Lord have mercy,' the others responded. Kenneth put the chalice to her mouth again, and she tried to swallow properly this time. Even so, she gagged a little, and the icy liquid ran down across her face.

He handed the chalice to someone. Virginia put a tablet on Joanne's tongue, while Kenneth said, 'She that hath committed iniquity –'

And the others responded, 'Forgive her, O Lord, and grant redemption.'

Virginia put the chalice to Joanne's lips.

Next the tablet came from Norma.

'She that hath sinned against Thee –' Kenneth said.

'Forgive her, O Lord, and grant redemption.' The chalice was cold and hard against Joanne's mouth.

Michael was last. He pushed the tablet hard against her teeth until she had to open them and take it in.

'She that hath done wickedly –' Kenneth said.

'Forgive her, O Lord, and grant redemption.'

Joanne wanted to whisper, 'Is it over? Is it over yet?' but she knew she must not speak.

Kenneth gave her the last tablet. Then he refilled the chalice, and poured the drink into her mouth. Joanne gasped, and swallowed, and swallowed again, but still the alcohol kept coming in a steady clear stream until she thought she would choke on it.

'That she may enjoy the blessings of eternal life,' Kenneth said.

'Eternal life grant unto her, O Lord.'

The words seemed to hang in the darkness.

Joanne closed her eyes.

FOURTEEN

Michael stared at the box in the back of his work van. The others were standing around waiting for him to say something, but he couldn't think of anything that didn't sound banal. He looked from Virginia, who seemed to be almost in shock, to Norma. She glared at him, as if daring him to protest. He knew she expected him to screw things up. She'd always thought he was a bit wet, a bit dim in comparison to Kenneth. And as for Kenneth, he smiled at Michael. That smile that said that Michael had his trust; that everyone was depending on Michael, and that Kenneth knew he could do a good job.

He could make you walk through fire to earn that smile, Kenneth could.

'Remember,' he said. 'All you have to do is put the box into the baling machine. It'll do the rest. Got that?'

'Yes,' Michael said. He smiled weakly, wondering if there were ever a time when he could have refused the unreasonable demands Kenneth made so reasonably.

'Good,' Kenneth said. 'Don't forget to drive carefully. No speeding. We don't want you pulled over tonight, do we?'

'No, Kenneth.' He wanted to say something else: to say, right, this has gone far enough; it stops here, before any permanent damage is done. But Virginia was near hysterics, and Norma had made it plain enough in the past that she would do whatever Kenneth wanted. And Kenneth . . . well, Kenneth was depending on him.

Michael got into the van and drove off into the darkness.

● ● ●

94

Mr Michael had asked Dean to come to the yard in the night-time. Mr Michael had never done that before, except one time at Christmas when there was a rush order on and they all wanted to get finished early, so they could have Christmas Eve off.

It was a funny old thing, too, that Mr Michael had phoned Dean from a coin box. Dean knew he had, because he had been trying to ask Mr Michael if he should get any of the machines ready, when the phone had gone beepbeepbeep, and then Mr Michael hadn't been on the other end of it any more.

Dean had hurried down to the yard. When he saw the van arriving, he opened the gates of the baler shed.

When Mr Michael opened the van, there was only the one box in it. That was funny. It was funny to run the baler for just one box.

'Come on, Dean,' Mr Michael said. 'Get the box.'

Dean ran to help Mr Michael. The box was very heavy, and Dean's hand slipped on it.

'Get the bloody box, Dean,' Mr Michael said. He never usually swore, so Dean knew he was upset.

Together they carried the box into the shed. They put it on the end of the conveyor belt. They both stared at it for a second. Dean thought he saw it move. He thought he saw the box move.

Before he could say anything, Mr Michael backed away. He turned and slammed the van doors. Then he moved forward again. He was still watching the box. 'I have to go now, Dean,' he said. 'No questions.' He backed off a little way, and repeated, 'No questions.' He ran to the van and got in it.

'No questions asked,' Dean said. He stared down at the box. He was sure it was moving – just sort of shivering where it sat on the concrete.

The van started away. Dean heard its tyres screech on the tarmac, but he ignored it. He went and got the control box for the baler.

He pushed the switch. The conveyor belt clattered to life. The box started its slow journey upwards.

The shredders clattered out of their bays and slammed into life. The blades began to whirl, quickly whizzing into a blur.

Dean watched the box move towards the shredders. It would be cut to pieces, crushed into a tight bale, tied up with plastic baling tape and shifted out onto the stack ready to go to the dump.

No questions asked. A nice bit of a bonus for working late, Mr Michael had said.

The blades whirred.

But it had moved. The box had *moved*.

It was almost at the top of the conveyor belt.

No questions asked.

The blades whirred.

Dean stopped the conveyor. He glanced back. The van had gone. No-one was watching. He tapped the switch that put the belt into reverse.

The box ground its slow way back to him.

He put his hands flat on the lid. The cardboard was cool to the touch, and it seemed to shiver slightly, as if a small animal were trapped inside and trying to find its way out. He pulled the lid off the box.

He thought he would stop breathing when he saw what was inside. He put his fingers up to ward it away, but it was no good. Even looking through the protection of his hands, he could still see her.

Joanne Barnes stared up at him. She was all wrapped up in a white sheet, and she was making little whimpering noises. He knew that noise. He'd made that noise when he was a kid and his mum had left him.

'Dean,' Joanne said. 'Help –'

How do you help someone? 'I –' he said, and then he couldn't think what to say.

He reached out to her, but she scrunched herself up into the corner of the box. The sheet fell away from her.

She wasn't wearing any clothes under the sheet. The thought of it made him feel sick and excited all at once. He knew he mustn't have bad thoughts. After that, he made sure he only touched the sheet, not her naked skin.

If he thought bad thoughts about Joanne, he might hurt her. He would never want to hurt her.

She clambered to her feet, clutching the sheet around her. Dean saw that her body was covered in signs and pictures and numbers. He had never seen anything like that. He knew he didn't have markings like that on his body, and there was nothing like it on the pictures of the ladies in the bad books he sometimes sneaked a look at in the newsagents. He was sure it wasn't right. He held up the sheet, so that she could cover herself better with it.

She took it and wrapped herself in it. Then she turned and stumbled away from him, into the darkness.

FIFTEEN

Lights came and went and came again. Tyres screamed on tarmac. The air was thick with the smell of petrol and the roar of engines.

Joanne's body felt as if it were made of lead. She put one foot in front of the other, over and over again. There was a dull, cramping pain in the base of her belly, and she was very cold.

All flesh is grass, she thought. All flesh is grass. I will be judged and punished by God, for I have corrupted. I must atone.

One foot in front of the other, until she came to a place of light and warmth. Its doors slid open in front of her, and she stumbled inside.

Up, she thought. I must go up. I must go to God in the Celestial City, and I must be judged, for I am evil and I have corrupted.

She stepped on an escalator, and it took her upwards. The pain in her belly was much worse now, and her head felt as if it were full of cottonwool.

She stepped off the escalator, took one step and then another, and then she collapsed against a plate glass window.

She tried to curl up, but the floor was too hard. She looked up, and saw her own face – her own face, but in another lifetime, when she had been young and well, and safe in God's love – staring down at her, repeated a dozen times.

Joanne breathed through the mask they had put over her mouth. She could hear herself breathing, hear the steady

98

double beat of her heart and the whoosh of the blood as it surged around her ears.

She thought she might be in hospital, but she wasn't sure. She was supposed to be dead. She didn't think she was in heaven.

'Oh Joanne,' a voice said. She knew the voice, though she couldn't have said who it belonged to. Whoever it was, they were nearly crying. Perhaps she had done a bad thing to them. She had done lots of bad things.

She opened her eyes. There were two people standing there, a man and a woman. She knew she ought to recognise them, but she didn't.

Dean liked copying. He got to the yard early and swept up. Then he went up to the office and got out some paper, and started to draw on it.

He drew Joanne. All the pictures and the patterns and the numbers that had been on Joanne. Over and over again. He used up all the scrap paper, and then he started on the headed notepaper. He wasn't really supposed to use that for drawing on, but he hadn't got it right before, and he had to get it right.

He glanced at the window just in time to see Mr Michael taking his jacket off in the yard below. Dean was lucky. Mr Michael had stopped to talk to one of the other men.

Dean crumpled up all the bits of paper and shoved them in the wastepaper bin.

That wasn't good enough. Someone would find them. Matches. Where were the matches? He fumbled them out of his pocket. He had to be quick. Mr Michael was coming. Mr Michael would see what he had done. He would know. . . . His hands shook, but on the third go he got a match to light. He dropped it in the wastepaper bin.

The papers flared up, whoosh. Dean waited long enough to make sure the fire wasn't going to go out, then he raced downstairs.

He met Mr Michael at the bottom of the stairs.

'Morning Dean, lad,' Mr Michael said. A couple of the other workers said hello as they passed by.

'Morning Mr Michael,' Dean said.

'No problems?' Mr Michael wouldn't look at Dean.

Dean knew there was a problem, but he said, 'No problems, Mr Michael,' anyway.

'I'll put the kettle on,' Mr Michael said. He started to fold his jacket over his arm.

Oh no, Dean thought. He started to panic, thinking the papers wouldn't all be burnt up; just as he was thinking what to say, Mr Michael's mobile phone rang.

Mr Michael answered the phone. 'Trant's Pack – oh, Ken,' he said, as he walked away. He threw his coat on the table. Dean thought maybe he wasn't supposed to hear what Mr Michael was saying, because the older man turned his back. But Dean didn't know what he should be doing, so he stayed where he was.

'All right . . .' Mr Michael said. 'Yes, all clear – no problems.' Dean wondered if Mr Michael meant about last night. About what had happened with Joanne. But he didn't think he was supposed to be listening, and thinking about Joanne made him uncomfortable. 'What? The church?' Mr Michael said. That was better. Dean liked the church.

He could smell something burning; and even over the factory noise, he could hear crackling.

He looked up. Smoke was pouring out of the office, and flames were leaping at the window.

Dean was scared. He made his sign at the office, but it just kept burning. He didn't know what to do. It was his fault, but he didn't know what to do.

Mr Michael ran past him to the steps. 'Dean!' he shouted, just like the teachers in school had been when he was in trouble.

That was when he remembered. *In case of emergency, dial 999.* There was a phone box across the road. He ran for it.

He glanced back. Mr Michael had grabbed one of the fire extinguishers, and was running upstairs with it.

By the time he got outside, the fire alarm had begun to jangle. He dashed across the road and into the phone box.

He rooted in his pocket for a ten pence piece then he remembered, *You don't need coins to phone the emergency services.* He punched the number. A woman's voice asked him something, but he didn't care. He had to make them understand. 'Fire. Fire fire. Ambulance. Police,' he said. That wasn't it. He glanced back. Smoke was pouring out of the factory. 'Quick,' he shouted. 'Fire . . .' But that wasn't it, wasn't the important thing. Someone was going to be hurt. She was standing all alone with the sheet wrapped round her, and Dean didn't know how to help her. The police, they helped people. 'She's hurt,' he blurted out. 'She's dying.' He was crying. He was so, so scared. The woman on the phone said something, nonsense words.

Dean dropped the handset and ran.

Someone was calling Joanne's name. She could hear them, and she knew the word was her name, but nothing made any sense. There was whiteness all around her. She liked the white. It was God's colour. She ignored the voice, and looked at the white.

But the voice didn't stop. It kept calling her, over and over again. 'Joanne?' She knew the voice. It was an important voice. She had been angry with the owner of that voice once, but she wasn't angry now. She was in her safe white space. The words kept phasing in and out. '. . . Hear me. Speak . . . please. You can . . . can't you?' What was there to say that was worth saying? What would be worth leaving the cool white space for? And yet they wanted her to talk to them so badly. Slowly, she forced her eyelids shut. There was darkness. She hated the darkness. In the darkness there were voices telling her things she dared not listen to. It was hard, but she forced her eyelids open again.

The other voice, the good voice, wasn't satisfied. It kept on talking, words that made no sense, things too complicated for Joanne to understand. '– all right. . . .

101

happened? . . . tell us?' The words came and went, like waves breaking on a shore. She wanted to catch one of the waves, to ride it back down to the ocean and become one with the water. But it dribbled through her fingers. '. . . all right now, all right, Joanne?' She forced herself to concentrate. '. . . ashamed or – it doesn't matter – just tell us what happened. . . . Can't you?'

She wanted to. She wanted to leave her white space and speak to them. She would tell them that she had been bad. That she had tried to atone, and that Ke– That He had punished her. Her mouth had forgotten the shapes of words. Her tongue was too thick, and she didn't know the names of things.

She stared up at the people staring down at her, and let the world fold back in on itself, until there was nothing left but whiteness.

SIXTEEN

It was all going terribly wrong, Michael Trant thought. He breathed deeply through the oxygen mask one of the firefighters was holding to his face.

God's punishment, he thought. If you believed in God's rewards – in Heaven and in being one of the Chosen Few – then surely you had to believe in His punishments as well?

He stared around at the yard, where business was slowly beginning to get back to normal after the fire. Dean was standing watching him. When the boy saw Michael look at him, he raised his hands in that irritating sign of his.

He would bring it all down round their ears, the boy would, Michael thought.

And maybe that would be no bad thing. Better to be punished by human law than by God. . . .

And yet, he thought, the fire hadn't spread. They had caught it in time. Perhaps that was God's will too. Perhaps He didn't intend for them to be punished by the law after all.

In any event, it wasn't for Michael to decide. All he had to do was to follow Kenneth's instructions, to the letter.

Fitz felt terrible. His head was banging and his mouth felt like an ostrich's armpit. It was his own fault – he should have known better than to go to bed without having so much as a half of bitter.

Work? Who needed it?

Well, you do, he told himself as he followed DCI Wise up the stairs to the hospital ward where Joanne Barnes lay. At least, he did if he wanted to avoid any more embarrassing ten pound notes from Judith.

So, he tried to concentrate on what Wise was telling him.

'We can't get anything out of her so you're here to find another way in.' Wise didn't seem bothered by the idea of bringing an outsider in on the case. Fitz missed Bilborough – he'd liked the guy well enough – but not his attitude: that edge that came from being promoted too young and needing to prove himself all the time. Wise was different. He'd paid his dues and knew it. Concentrate, Fitz warned himself. You can't do the job without all the information. Wise continued, 'She may have tried to top herself – she's three months gone and only seventeen.'

Christ, Fitz thought. That made her only six years older than his Katie. Or was it seven?

Wise was staring at him, waiting for a response. A question now would be good. Prove he'd been listening. 'Has she been sexually abused?'

They came out of the stairwell into the corridor. It was very quiet – there was no hustle of visitors up here, near the intensive care units.

'No,' Wise said. 'But she's been into something dodgy. Her body was covered in these daubings – signs, equations – you know.' He sounded resigned, rather than disgusted.

'Can I get some photographs?' Fitz asked. He was finally beginning to wake up, and the case sounded as if it might be more interesting than he had expected.

'Uh huh,' Wise said. Fitz spotted Panhandle sitting outside one of the intensive care units. No doubt she'd been assigned to look after the parents. Again. 'She's got nasty bruising on her arms and knees,' Wise went on. 'Could be an attempted abortion. She's got more pills inside her than Boots.' He stabbed the air with his finger, the only sign he'd made that the case was getting to him. 'We've got to find out where she's been this last week, and who with.'

That might not be so easy, Fitz thought. Suspects – suspects were easy. You found their weak spots, tapped in a wedge and then just kept hammering. Sometimes you were kind to them, or appeared to be. Sometimes you blazed away; but basically you did whatever it took. Witnesses you took a little more care with. But victims . . . with victims you never took the kid gloves off; and because of that, all you could do was manipulate them. It always left him feeling cheapened.

Panhandle stood up as they approached. The ward door opened. Mrs Barnes came out. She wasn't so much crying as coming apart. Mr Barnes followed her. His jaw was clenched, and he stared straight ahead. With a little imagination, Fitz thought, you could see the lines of power with which his mind held his body together. If he didn't talk soon, he would be in trouble – like an oak that could not bend in the storm, he would simply shatter.

But for now, Mrs Barnes had to hold his attention. 'I know she can hear me,' she said. She took a huge, gulping breath. Her hands worked at each other, as if she got comfort from the feel of her own flesh. 'But no, she – she still won't say anything.' She rubbed her eyes with the back of her hand. 'As if we're to blame. Are we to blame?' She looked straight at Fitz, as if she thought he was like a priest and could absolve her of whatever sins she imagined she had committed.

They made the usual comforting noises. It wouldn't do any good, Fitz thought, even as he joined in. The only way they could ever get free of the guilt-demon was by looking it in the eye; and they wouldn't do that alone.

Later, he would help them; but for now, he had to concentrate on Joanne.

'See her again tonight,' Panhandle said. Mrs Barnes nodded. 'Can we give you a lift home?'

Mrs Barnes looked shocked. 'Oh, we're not going home,' she said.

'No of course not, love,' Wise said. He took Mrs Barnes by the arm, and drew her away to the side. 'Let's get a cup of tea.' Mr Barnes followed them.

As they went, Wise threw Fitz one last glance. Go on, he seemed to say. This could be your only chance. Don't blow it.

Fitz followed Panhandle into the ward. Christ, but he hated hospitals. They had a stink about them of mortality. Funny thing was, it came not of the stench of dying, but of disinfectant, that half-hearted attempt to keep death at bay.

It made him long for a fag, and a triple scotch. Anything to prove he could still laugh in the face of Old Nick, instead of running scared behind hospital greens and a cloud of Dettol.

Yet it was hard even to think that when he stared at the waxy face of Joanne Barnes. He stood at the end of the bed and watched her. They still had her on a drip, and her eyes were dilated. Most likely the tranks weren't out of her system yet.

She should have been able to talk, though, if she hadn't retreated into some safe fantasy-land, where whatever had hurt wasn't allowed.

'Hello Joanne,' he said. No response. The eyelids didn't so much as flutter. He went round to the side of the bed, and sat down. 'My name's Fitz,' he said. 'I'm not a policeman. I'm a shrink. I don't suppose you want to talk to me, either.'

Still no response. For a second Fitz wanted to walk out; to leave her to whatever peace she had been able to find within herself.

What he was going to do would hurt her. What he was going to do would rip her from that safety, and make her relive whatever hell she had so recently escaped from.

Sometimes Fitz thought he wasn't so different from the villains. It was all just a matter of intent. And sometimes that didn't feel like so very much of a difference.

SEVENTEEN

The fire was rotten luck, Michael Trant thought. It wasn't enough that he'd lost all the company's financial records, and a full day's production, but now the police were sniffing around as well.

He strolled round the factory, getting close enough to the uniformed police constable so that he could hear what the man was saying to the detective.

Bit over the top, that, Michael thought. Maybe it was standard procedure. Mustn't panic, that was the thing. If God intended them to get away with it, they would. And if not, they would not suffer nearly so much at the hands of the law as they would when God punished them.

Then again, maybe Dean had found Joanne and let her go. There was always that possibility – the one he'd planned on when he told Dean to put the box in the baler. Or had he planned it? It was hard to be sure: hard to know what he'd thought at the time, and what had occurred to him later.

All he really knew was that he couldn't have started the machine himself. Not and watch the cardboard turn red with her shredded flesh and blood.

He was beginning to panic again. Any minute now he'd be in the middle of a full-scale panic attack. He forced himself to breathe slowly and calmly, and to listen to what the two policemen were saying.

'– accidental,' said the uniformed officer. The detective noted down what he said. It seemed like a duplication of effort to Michael, a real waste of tax-payers' time and money, but he supposed they had their reasons. The uniformed constable went on, 'No-one's hurt. There's nothing suspicious – just plain bloody carelessness.' The two of them stared up at the office for a second. 'No body,' the uniformed officer added as an afterthought.

The detective nodded, and made another note. 'Who called you?' he asked.

The constable jerked his thumb at Dean. 'Lad over there,' he said. Oh no, Michael thought. Not Dean. If they start questioning him, we're done for. 'Goalkeeper short of a full squad if you ask me,' the constable said.

It might be all right, Michael thought. If they thought Dean was crazy – let's face it, Dean *was* crazy – they might not pay much attention to anything he said.

'Cheers, pal,' the detective said. He strode towards Dean. He was very young, Michael thought, and he didn't look too bright, if looks could tell you anything. He stared at the stock sheet he was holding. If he interfered, he might seem suspicious; but if he did nothing, Dean might start talking.

Too late. It was too late. The detective was talking to Dean, who was sitting on one of the bales of finished boxes. Michael licked his lips and waited, knowing it was too late to do anything but watch.

'I'm Detective Constable Harriman,' the police officer said. Dean's hands came up in his special sign. Harriman sighed, impatient already. Michael relaxed slightly. 'You work here?' Harriman asked.

Dean nodded.

'What's your name?'

Dean didn't answer. He slid off the bale and turned to face Harriman. 'No-one. Nothing,' he said.

Who knew what that meant? Michael certainly didn't. As for Harriman, he seemed to think Dean was winding him up.

'Shall I start with something a bit easier?' he said.

Dean looked sideways, then at his feet. He took a big breath. Michael knew that reaction: it was what you got when Dean thought he was in trouble. 'Dean Saunders,' he said at last.

Harriman wrote that down. 'You reported the fire?'

Dean thought about it. 'Yes.'

'You said someone was dying.'

Dean's face took on that weird intensity it had sometimes in church, when Kenneth chose the readings from the Book of Revelations. 'The first angel sounded,' he said, 'And there followed hail and fire mingled with blood. All flesh is grass.'

Any minute now he would be talking about his very own angel: Joanne, with her body covered with those strange daubings of Kenneth's. Michael knew it. The only question would be whether he would say it in a way this Harriman would understand.

Harriman clearly didn't understand what Dean had said so far. 'Anagram, eight letters?' he asked. He leaned back against one of the bales, grinning.

Michael hurried over. 'I'm sorry constable,' he said. He managed to get himself between the two of them. 'You're unlikely to get anywhere with Dean.' He turned to Dean. 'Put your coat on and go home, lad. I'll pay you for the day.'

Dean nodded slightly. He stared at Michael for a long moment, as if to ask whether he had done something wrong.

'Is everything all right, sir?' Harriman asked Dean.

'All flesh is grass,' Dean said, as if it were an answer to the question.

That was enough, Michael thought. Far better to get Dean out of it all together, where he couldn't do anyone any harm. 'Dean!' he said sharply. 'Home.'

Dean made his sign at Harriman. Or perhaps at Michael. He backed off a couple of paces, then he turned and ran.

Harriman said, 'What's all –' He made Dean's sign, while still holding his pen and pad.

'My nod towards equal opportunities,' he said. It felt

good to be saying something that was one hundred per cent true. 'Have to do one's bit,' he added.

'He called us as well as the Fire Service,' Harriman said.

'The boy panicked,' Michael said, knowing he was speaking too quickly, sounded too glib. 'He threw a cigarette in the waste bin.' He couldn't look Harriman in the eye. 'He panicked.'

'You sacking him?' Harriman asked.

Michael supposed it must seem the logical thing to do. In other circumstances, he might have considered it. 'How could I sack him?' he asked, thinking, how can I sack him when he knows that I – not Kenneth, not Norma nor Virginia as far as he's concerned, but I – killed Joanne? 'Who else would give him a job?' he said. It sounded right. The kind of thing a pious, God-fearing man should say, and mean. Up till now, it was the kind of thing he always had said. 'I will not pass by on the other side . . . you know.'

Harriman stared at him blankly.

Dear God, Michael thought. Help me get through this. Just help me find a way through it. The trouble was, he knew he didn't deserve God's help, now. Perhaps he never had.

They were good people, God-fearing people, Virginia thought. What they had done didn't change that. She glanced at Kenneth, at his firm hands on the steering wheel as he drove. They had done what Kenneth had said, and they had done the right thing. The thing God had wanted them to do. It was impossible to doubt that on such a day as this, a day of bright sunshine and just enough of a cooling breeze to be pleasant. Even the music on the car radio was soothing.

It was like the Biblical tale of Abraham and Isaac. God had demanded that Joanne atone for her sins – she knew this, because Kenneth had said so – and they had been the instrument of that atonement.

With one part of her mind, she noted that the music had

110

stopped and the news had come on. But it held no interest for her. She went back to her musings.

Others would see their action as retribution, perhaps even as an attempt simply to keep their homes and careers together. But they would be wrong. If God had not wanted them to do it, He would have sent down a sign to stop them, as he had when he had stopped Abraham from killing his son Isaac. Oh, not an angel of fire, brandishing a sword. But something. Some doubt that would have caused one of them to speak out against what they were doing, against Kenneth's instructions. But none of them had, so she knew their actions were righteous.

As for those others . . .well, they would never know what she and the others had done to Joanne, would they?

'– Joanne Barnes –' the name cut through Virginia's reverie the way the crying of her hungry infant wakens a mother from deepest sleep. What? she thought. '– found in a shopping centre near her home, semi-conscious . . .' said the flat Liverpudlian voice on the radio.

'What?' she asked aloud.

Kenneth motioned her to be quiet.

'– seriously ill but we understand that her condition is stable,' the voice continued. Virginia listened, but she could hardly make sense of the words. 'We would again appeal to anyone who may have seen her over the past week, or who has knowledge of where she was, to phone the incident room . . .'

Kenneth pulled the car over to the side of the road.

Virginia's heart was pounding. She felt as if the world were falling in on top of her. 'I thought Michael said . . .' She couldn't bring herself to finish the sentence: that he'd made sure she was dead, disposed of the body. Finished things, as she'd been thinking of it.

'Yes,' Kenneth said. He sounded calm, reliable.

Even with him there, Virginia couldn't ward off the panic. 'We'd better go back,' she said. She thought, thank you God, for not letting me hear this terrible news alone.

111

They were to be tested further. That was what it meant. They must stand firm, in the eyes of the law and God.

'No,' Kenneth said. He took her hand. She was trembling, and she couldn't stop it. 'No, we must go to the Fellowship –'

He was right, of course. He would make it be all right.

EIGHTEEN

Fitz looked down at Joanne's face as she lay in the hospital bed.

She hardly knew he was there. You gazed into her eyes and no-one looked back at you. He had tried talking to her, asking her what had happened, and she hadn't responded.

His little dictating machine lay on her pillow, ready to catch her words the moment she spoke.

He had to make her respond. To do that, he would tear into the quiet space she had built for herself, force her to face the awful things that had been done to her.

He glanced at Panhandle. She stared back at him levelly. He wondered if she would think less of him – *even* less of him – when this was all over. Or would she think he'd done well, to force Joanne to speak when even her parents had failed?

Fitz the hero. Fitz the superman.

He fiddled with the edge of the sheet. It wasn't significantly paler than Joanne's waxy skin.

Go on, he told himself. Do it. Do it for her, so that eventually she can find peace. Do it for them, all the other Joannes who might be in danger from whoever did this.

Do it for yourself, you scummy, manipulative bastard, so you can look good in front of a woman you've already hurt beyond measure.

All right then. 'They blame themselves, you know,' he began. His voice was low and beguiling. Nothing. He knew what the key was. He knew the guilt that had driven Joanne, the ideal that she couldn't live up to. He'd known it the moment he'd walked into the neat suburban semi, and seen the desperate pride with which Mrs Barnes displayed the photos in her album, and the tight despair that lined her husband's face: the anger he thought he was hiding so well, when he clicked his way through that boxing video, when all the time he wanted to be pounding the face of anyone who had hurt his girl into the ground. So say it, Fitz told himself. Let it begin. 'Your mum and dad. They think they're to blame for what happened to you. . . .' That got her. The eyelids fluttered. Her tongue flickered across her lips. Right first time, Fitz told himself. Doesn't that feel great? Doesn't that make you feel like a superstar? Irrelevant, he told himself savagely, and murmured, 'Do you, Joanne? They love you so much, they're so proud of you, they can't understand what happened . . . they think it must be their fault.'

Panhandle was watching him. Her expression was unreadable, even to Fitz.

Joanne turned her head, slowly, from time to time. Then she was still again. A pulse fluttered at her throat. So vulnerable, he thought. Fragile as a child – Christ, he thought, she *is* a child, pregnant or not – and as in need of protection. She had been a good girl, everyone said it. She wouldn't be used to trouble, to having other people's anger directed at her. He let irritation creep into his voice. 'I don't know what they've got to feel guilty about, your mum and dad. Maybe they feel they were too strict with you.' Time for the big lie. 'Maybe they regret hitting you.' He was sure Joanne's parents had never so much as slapped her in her life, whatever Sarah said. She had clearly been afraid of the police and willing to say anything she thought they wanted to hear.

Joanne shook her head. Her breath came out in urgent little sighs that were not quite words.

Push, he told himself. Push you great fat bastard, and never mind how it makes you feel. 'When they were angry with you – they did hit you, didn't they?'

Joanne became even more agitated. 'No,' she said, quite clearly, and then, 'Mum. Dad. . . .'

114

Panhandle glared at Fitz. She obviously thought he ought to stop. Maybe she was right. But if he did, they might never get Joanne to talk.

'Not even when you told them you were pregnant?' He kept his voice so low the words were hardly there at all.

'No – no –' Joanne said. Her fingers scrabbled convulsively against the oversheet, making the saline drip in her arm jounce. 'Mum,' she swallowed hard. 'Dad. Dad's little . . . little angel. Can't –' Sweat slicked her skin. She seemed to search for breath. 'Can't.'

'Couldn't tell them,' Fitz said. He looked away from her, and away from Panhandle's accusing eyes. He wanted to weep with frustration. All that love gone to gall and ashes because she couldn't talk to them.

Any minute now, Panhandle would say something soothing born of guilt, and he would lose Joanne again.

Guilt. Somewhere out there, there was someone who ought to feel very bloody guilty indeed. And Fitz was going to find him and make him pay. And then maybe Fitz would be free of it.

Michael had screwed up. Norma glared contemptuously at him as she got out of the car to go into the Fellowship meeting. All he'd had to do was one simple little thing, and he'd messed it up.

She might have known.

She smoothed down her skirt and prepared to put a good public face on things. Kenneth had said they must show just enough shock and sorrow over Joanne. Not too much, or it would appear stagey. Certainly not too little, or it would seem uncaring, and that would never do.

Kenneth's car drew up, and he got out.

Don't stare, she told herself; but she couldn't help it, especially not when she knew Michael was watching her. He was so feeble, such a burden to her. He would never stand up to her. Kenneth now. . . .

He helped Virginia out of the car. She looked shaky,

almost on the verge of tears. She was going to be a problem. Norma could see that very clearly.

Kenneth took her hand and murmured something to her.

Norma felt her nails dig into her palms as she clenched her fists. Kenneth should have married someone more suitable, she thought.

Virginia was her best friend. But there was no way she was fit to be Kenneth's wife.

Joanne was safe in the cool white space she had made. As long as she didn't look at the shadow. It hovered over her, but she didn't have to look at it.

She knew what it was. It was the angel of death, and it was the devil, and it had already said the bad word that had led her to the place.

Pregnant. Pregnantpregnantpregnant. The sound of the word was ugly. It made her want to scream and beg for mercy, but the angel of death was holding out his hand to her. Big hands, looming. Wanted to touch her where she must not be touched. His mouth opened, and she knew he would say that she was God's gift to him.

God's gift to the angel of death.

'No,' she said. 'No no no.' She was pregnant but she was not to be touched because she was a good girl, her mother's little angel, her father's little angel. Perfect in every way. Immaculate, like Mary. 'Hail Mary, full of grace,' she said. That was better. The angel of death could not touch her when she spoke the name of the Virgin. Could not give her pills and strong drink, and make her open her mouth and swallow them. She was in the basement now, with only a thin line of light bleeding under the door to illuminate the darkness. 'The Lord is with thee. Blessed art thou amongst women and blessed is the fruit of thy womb, Jesus –'

The fruit of thy womb, the fruit of thy womb was Jesus come to save mankind, but the fruit of her womb, Joanne's womb, would be death and destruction and her iniquities would be remembered by the Lord God who would judge

116

her. 'Not judged,' she begged. But she would be judged, and utterly burned with fire.

'They didn't know you had a boyfriend, did they.' The voice was infinitely patient, but it was still the voice of the angel of death; and it was infinite only in its deceit. 'Who is he, Joanne?'

Kenneth's face leaned down out of the shadows at her.

He would touch her and she mustn't be touched. 'You mustn't tell anyone,' he said. 'The universe begins and ends and beyond it all there is nothing . . . snowflakes and madness and no God at all –' he opened his mouth, and began to laugh. His lips stretched back from his strong white teeth and there was nothing in the universe but Kenneth telling her she must tell no-one.

But she wanted to tell. Wanted to speak. But she hardly had a voice at all. 'Holy Mary Mother of God,' she said. 'Pray for us sinners –' I have sinned, I have sinned I have defiled and corrupted. 'Pray for us sinners now and at the hour of our death . . .'

Kenneth reached down to put his hand over her mouth. She had to get away, to be safe. He wanted to smother her, to make her keep silent.

But the angel of death was at her side. Or maybe the angel of death was Kenneth, testing her, testing her.

'You don't want to die, do you, Joanne?' he said. His voice was like a whiplash, scourging her flesh. She must atone, must be punished. 'Someone's done it. Who was it?' Kenneth, she wanted to say. She wanted to tell, to stop the voice tormenting her. She wanted to cry out to Kenneth to come and save her, to help her atone so that she could be saved.

But he'd told her to be silent, to tell no-one, or else be consigned to the timeless chaos that came before the universe and after it: that most terrifying place where God was not. She tried to speak, but she could not make the lips and tongue obey her, and all that came out of her throat was a wordless cry of supplication.

117

And still the voice persisted. 'Who made you take those pills? Who gave you the drink? Who wrote those things on your body? Who is it?'

She wasn't supposed to die. She didn't want to die, only to be made clean in the sight of God. If she could make the angel of death understand that, perhaps he would go away. 'Not die,' she said. 'Not die.'

But the angel didn't go away. She could feel his shadow hanging over her, feel his cold breath on her flesh. He would come for her at the end. At the end, when – 'All flesh. All flesh is grass. Is grass.' They had said that at the Fellowship. Snowflakes, her Kenneth had said. Had said that unbelievers would burn in the cleansing fires of the Lord God. He had to forgive her for corrupting him. Had to. But not his forgiveness. Not theirs. Whose? 'Judged,' she said. 'Judged, judged, judged.' The face of the angel of death pinwheeled in front of her, became Virginia. She put her voice into Joanne's mouth, so that Joanne could know the great evil she had done. 'Evil little bitch.'

She was evil. Was a bitch. She knew that now. She had seduced Kenneth, put evil thoughts in his head. But she would keep her promise to him, and not speak his name to the angel of death. God would forgive her. She would make her act of contrition, and He – God, Kenneth – would forgive her. 'Bless me Father for I have sinned,' she began. This was right. She had her voice back now. But to be shriven she had to name her sins. The world turned above her. Kenneth glared down, and Michael, and Norma . . . and Virginia.

'She can't say it,' Virginia said.

'I have committed –'

'She can't say it,' they all said.

'I have committed –'

'Her sins stop her,' Norma said, and smiled.

'No!' Joanne cried out.

'Who is it?' demanded the angel of death.

'He –' Joanne said, but Kenneth smiled sadly at her and shook his head.

'Who?'

'He,' she screamed. 'He – he – he –' but she could not, on peril of her immortal soul, say more.

'Who is it?' The fury of God was in the voice of the angel of death, but Joanne still couldn't answer him.

'Fitz –' said another voice.

'Who, Joanne?'

'Help,' Joanne cried out. 'All flesh is grass.' It was the only thing she knew for sure. 'All flesh –'

'Fitz, lay off –'

'– is grass. Is grass. Help me, please help me . . .' Her body arched and spasmed. Her jaw locked open and her screams filled her throat and convulsed her body.

Hands soothed her then, and made the angel of death go away. And a little time after that, there was sleep, and the dark, and quietness.

NINETEEN

Kenneth Trant surveyed his people, his Fellowship. They were good people, and until now, they had been unquestioningly loyal to him, and to his teaching.

But they had never been tested, never been called upon to face the fire and fury of public opinion. Kenneth Trant had been careful to keep the doings of his Fellowship out of the glare of tabloid publicity that had proved the undoing of so many other, less careful, religious leaders. There was so much more freedom in secrecy – freedom which he knew God intended him to have, but which the petty minds of Middle England would rather he did not have.

With God's help, he would continue to enjoy those freedoms. After all, how else could he continue to lead his people – God's people – out of the morass of decadence and deceit that was the late twentieth century?

Norma finished the reading. She glanced at Kenneth, and gave him a hard little smile. Then she sat down. A good woman, Norma. She would not fail him. He wished he could be as sure of Michael, and of his own dear Virginia.

He stood up, and, restraining the impulse to lick his lips or adjust his clothing, began to speak. 'I know you will all feel the deepest pity and sympathy for Joanne Barnes, who is at this very moment lying dangerously ill in hospital,' he said. A murmur ran through the congregation. Apparently, some of them had not yet heard. He carried on. 'Whether she was the victim of an attack, or whether her wounds were self-inflicted, is yet to be determined.' That was a neat touch. Whatever happened, he had to be wary of appearing to know things he could not know. 'The police are now investigating the matter and they will, no doubt, be appealing for information from anyone who knows Joanne.' He paused, and let his gaze sweep across them. Many of them were already working out what they would say when the police talked to them. He knew them. He could see it in their faces. They were good people. They would want to help. 'Brothers and sisters,' he continued, 'while we wish them every success with their enquiries, I believe we would be wise to keep our distance.' He smiled, a precisely calculated smile intended to convey his sorrow at the terrible world they lived in, which would not even allow them to aid the search for Joanne's attackers. 'You all know how deep and widespread is the prejudice and bigotry against a non-established church such as ours –' It was true. He would be pilloried, stripped of his post at the school, and the Fellowship would turn on him like wolves bringing down a lamb. He went on, ensuring there was no hint of desperation in his voice. The weak would fall by the wayside. But Kenneth Trant would not be weak. 'The tabloid newspapers delight in encouraging such bigotry. Let us protect ourselves, and our church, from the scandalmongers,' he concluded.

He led them in a prayer for Joanne's well-being. The Fellowship were good people, and he had led them well. They deserved as much truth as they could understand. But that did not mean that Kenneth had to become a martyr for them.

Michael had known he would have to face Kenneth as soon as he realised that Joanne had been found.

He should have expected it – that the police would find her; but somehow he wasn't ready for it when he heard the news on the radio. He'd thought it would take longer, that he would have time to explain things to the others.

But now there was no more time. There was just Kenneth standing too close to Michael, his face hard with anger. He had erupted the moment the congregation had left the church. Now they stood, all four of them, on the speakers' platform in the otherwise empty hall, with only the plastic

121

chairs to listen to them argue as they faced the fact that they might be about to lose everything.

'You left that idiot to do it –' Kenneth said. He was so close that Michael could feel his breath.

'He's not an idiot, he's –' Michael started. It had been this way since they were boys: Kenneth would try some wild scheme; when it failed, he would expect Michael to help him sort it out – and to take the blame, if things came to that.

Norma was just as angry with him. But then, Norma was always angry with him.

'You didn't tell *me*,' she said. Her voice was full of contempt. She looked from him to Kenneth, and he knew she found him wanting.

Michael wanted to say: I couldn't do it, all right? I thought about it, and I just couldn't believe that killing that girl could be right – not before the law, and not in the eyes of God.

He was a coward, like Peter denying Jesus. He couldn't stand against them. 'He knows how to work the machine,' he said. 'It's his job –'

'He's always had a soft spot for the girl,' Norma snapped. 'You must know that.'

Even you must know that, she meant. 'I thought it would be all right,' Michael said, and that was the second time he had betrayed himself.

Kenneth slammed his hand down on the table. 'Well, it isn't all right, is it?' He paced the platform. One stride, two, and he turned and came back again. 'You bloody fool, Michael!' he said. 'If that boy starts blabbing –'

If he did, they were done for. I was stupid, Michael thought. A bloody fool, just as Kenneth said. He should have done what he was told. They would be safe. And Joanne would be dead.

'Why isn't Dean here?' Virginia said suddenly. She looked pale, and she played with the cross around her neck. 'Where is he now?'

● ● ●

Dean ran. His feet pounded the pavement, sending jolts up his spine and making his head hurt. He gulped for air, and tried to make the pistons of his legs move faster.

Faster.

They were coming for him. The police were. He had done a bad thing. He had seen what he was not supposed to. The memory of Joanne's body, etched with those dark signs and outlined by the actinic glare of the street lamps, was burned into his retinas.

He wasn't supposed to see things like that. They weren't for him. That was what Miss Jefferies at the home had said. He mustn't think of them, think of touching. . . . He couldn't put his hands up to make his sign and keep the world at bay, so he muttered to himself over and over again as he ran, 'We see through a glass . . . through a glass . . . glass . . . through a glass darkly.'

And then it was all right, because he was home. He slammed the door open and took the stairs three at a time. One flight. Two. They were coming for him. Might be behind him now. His floor. He fetched up against the wall, almost sobbing in his fight for breath. His keys . . . he had them in his pocket. Spare set at the factory in case he lost this set, but this set always in his pocket.

He found them. Key in the lock. Door open. He stumbled into his bedsit, and turned to double-lock the door behind him. He put the chain on too. Safe now. Safe.

There was a noise behind him.

He turned. Mr Kenneth came at him from the far side of the room. His eyes blazed with anger. Dean put his hands up, not to make his sign, but to protect himself from the blows he knew he was going to get.

He was bad. He knew he had been bad. He began to cry. Mr Kenneth grabbed his hands. 'Please don't,' Dean said. But he knew that Mr Kenneth was going to punish him.

'What happened with Joanne?' Mr Kenneth demanded. He shook Dean hard, and swung him round till he could hardly think.

'She –' he said. What had happened? He couldn't really remember, except that she had been all naked under the white sheet, and that she had been crying. Had he made her cry? He couldn't really remember that, either. He did know that he had tried to touch her, and she hadn't liked it. He knew Mr Kenneth would be really angry with him if he found that out. 'She ran,' he said at last.

Mr Kenneth slapped him, hard enough to make his ears ring. 'What do you mean, she ran?'

Dean stumbled back. 'Ran,' he said. 'Ran. I'm sorry, Mr Kenneth.'

Mr Kenneth grabbed Dean by the shoulders. He forced Dean back, until he fell on to the bed.

'She couldn't run,' Mr Kenneth said.

Dean tried to get up, but Mr Kenneth was bigger and much stronger, and he pinned him to the bed.

'I'm sorry, Mr Kenneth,' Dean said. He couldn't think of what else to say, so he said it over and over again.

'Where did she run?'

'Away,' Dean said. He didn't really know where she had gone, but he knew if he said that, Mr Kenneth would get angry again. He might hit Dean, and Dean didn't want to be hit any more. 'Run away,' he said. 'Out. Away.'

'Out of the factory?'

That was easy. Dean was sure of that. 'Yes,' he said. 'Out. Away.'

Dean wanted to get up. He wanted to go to the toilet. He wanted to put the kettle on for tea. He wanted to think about Joanne, and the strange markings on her body, and the way she had looked in the white light, without any clothes on. But he knew that was bad, and anyway, Mr Kenneth was still standing there, still asking questions.

'Was anyone around?' Mr Kenneth said. He put his face right up close to Dean's. 'Did anyone see her?'

Dean started to shake. He was quite sure that Mr Kenneth knew that he had been thinking about Joanne. Thinking bad thoughts about her. Dirty thoughts. 'No.' But Mr Kenneth wanted to know if anyone else had seen her. Not just Dean. 'No-one see her. No-one. No. Nothing.' He began to shake and cry, and he couldn't stop it, couldn't stop the words that came tumbling out of his mouth.

And then, suddenly, it was all right, because Mr Kenneth wasn't angry any more. Dean stared up at him, with tears dribbling down his face.

'All right, Dean,' Mr Kenneth said. He put his hand on Dean's head, like when he gave the blessing at the Fellowship. 'All right. It wasn't your fault. I know it wasn't your fault.' But Dean couldn't stop the words coming out of his mouth, or the shaking of his body. He wanted to, though, so Mr Kenneth would be pleased with him again.

But Mr Kenneth wasn't pleased with him. 'Stop crying, Dean,' he said sharply, and when Dean still couldn't stop, he said again, 'Stop it, will you?'

He sounded really angry now; but it was easy for Dean to do what he wanted. Easier than telling him about Joanne, anyway. He wiped the back of his hand across his face.

'Good,' Mr Kenneth said. 'Good boy, Dean.' He turned and walked to the other side of the room. Dean stared at his back, wondering what he would want next.

Mr Kenneth turned back to Dean. He took a handkerchief out of his pocket and wiped his hands. Dean stared at the bedspread. Mustn't think of Joanne, he told himself. Do what Mr Kenneth says. Be all right, just –

'Listen to me, Dean. If anyone asks – Are you listening?'

Dean jerked his head up. 'Yes, Mr Kenneth.'

'If anyone comes and starts asking questions –' he stared at Dean. Dean wanted to look away, but he knew he mustn't. '– you tell them Dean. Tell them about Mr Michael who's always looked after you, cared for you.'

Dean scrambled up off the bed. He stood facing Mr Kenneth, but he couldn't stop his hands coming up in front of him. Mr Kenneth reached out and took them, but he didn't seem angry any more. He pulled Dean's hands together, as if they were clasped in prayer. It made Dean feel safe. Mr Kenneth would keep the police away. All Dean had to do was make sure he did exactly as Mr Kenneth said. 'And Mr Kenneth, Dean.' Dean nodded. He wasn't quite sure what Mr Kenneth meant, or why it was so important. He would have said all these things anyway. They were all true, weren't they? Mr Kenneth's hands moved to cup Dean's face. 'A good man,' Mr Kenneth said. 'A man of God – your minister. You understand Dean?'

Dean nodded. He had never been so scared, not even when he was at school. But he would do exactly as Mr Kenneth said, and Mr Kenneth would make everything all right.

TWENTY

The key to what had happened to Joanne Barnes lay in the strange markings written on her body. Fitz had tried to tell Wise that, but the damn man hadn't been interested in listening, only in relaying the ward sister's complaints about his badgering of the girl.

Badgering! As if he hadn't been doing it to try and help her.

Ah well, at least Wise had let him bring a set of the photos home with him. They showed, in stark detail, every symbol, number and line that had been drawn on her, from shoulder blade to lower thigh and from breast bone to pubis.

Fitz was sure they held the answer. He dropped them on the living-room sofa, next to an old kebab wrapper and an ashtray he didn't remember filling.

He poured himself a triple whisky, straight up, no soda or ice, and put a record – none of your compact discs, too perfect to be interesting modern crap, but a good old-fashioned vinyl 33r.p.m. record – on the turntable, and sat down to contemplate what it might all mean.

Ray Charles, with his voice like a broken dream, a decent blended malt – singles were a bit beyond Fitz's pocket these days, more's the pity – and a problem to solve. All was right with the world. Unless you counted the loss of Judith and Katie, and persistent niggle in the groin area every time he clapped eyes on Panhandle. But he really wasn't thinking about that just at present.

He lowered himself awkwardly to the floor, and started laying the photos out. It was damned difficult to make out what was on some of them. He thought about it for a second, and then looked up the transcriptions in the folder Wise had given him. Some clerical officer had spent a lot of time painstakingly working out what each bit of graffiti meant, but it wasn't good enough. The transcriptions were devoid of context, and therefore almost useless: the significance might lie, not in the individual symbols, but in the relationship between them. Besides, the clerk might have made all sorts of mistakes. Fitz would much rather make his own.

He grabbed a handful of file cards and started copying out the numbers. 10. −1. −13 . . . Negative numbers. Christ, it was worse than his bank balance, and decreasing just as fast. 10. Each of the negative numbers seemed to appear next to a 10. Was that significant? He didn't know. 1·40·6: that caught his attention because it was different from the rest. But then there was a rat's nest of an equation, all curly brackets and sub- and super-scripts.

Somewhere in all this, there would be something he would recognise, something that would knock all the bits of the jigsaw and make them fit together.

He took a sip of whisky, and noticed with a jolt that it had got dark outside since he took the last one. Too much thinking, he decided: bad for the brain. He sat down in the armchair and lit up a cigarette. It didn't help. What have we got: a slew of numbers, mostly disconnected. An equation. No, two equations. He pulled out the card he'd written $E=mc^2$. That one stirred memories. Something about the speed of light. Einstein. Dammit, you'd need an Einstein to understand this lot.

He passed a hand over his gritty eyes. Got up. Paced round to the other side of the room. All right, if he couldn't understand the numbers, what about the drawings? Lines connecting the numbers, running all over her belly and breasts. Not particularly interesting lines, just inartistic squiggles. On her shoulder, there was what seemed to be a clock face. On her knee, a thick, stubby line, branching into others, like several 'Y's melded together. 'Y's Whys? A clue? Maybe. But why were they so ugly? And why on her *knee* of all places?

On her back, there was a spiralling line of circles and part circles, like a worm retreating to infinity. Something about that dragged at Fitz's attention, but apart from its obvious phallic significance, he couldn't make anything of it.

It was light outside. Dawn. He had to think it through. Had to. But he couldn't, and in the end he gave up on it, pushed the mess off the sofa and sprawled out with his fingers trailing on the carpet, almost touching the photographs.

Dean remembered Joanne. He lay curled up on his bed, with his face still stiff with tears, and he remembered the dark markings on her body as she walked away from him into the night.

He shouldn't think about her. Mr Kenneth would know. He would come back, and shout, and grab Dean by the shoulders and shake him and hit him.

But she had smiled at him. Not that night. Not when he had tried to help her, but before. His hand reached for the dull aching place in his groin. He wanted to . . . but he wasn't supposed to do that. If you did that, you would get sick and die.

He thought about the markings instead. Such strange markings, numbers and letters that Dean didn't understand. But lines, too, and stars and suns and a clock face.

He wanted to draw them, so that he could look at them better. But when he'd drawn them at the factory, he had made the fire. That had been bad trouble. Even Mr Michael, who didn't lose his temper with Dean very often, had been angry. . . .

But if he drew them here, there would be no-one else to see. He decided to do that. He had some markers, but no paper. Now that he'd thought of it, he couldn't not draw the pictures. They were an ache just like the one in his groin.

129

Where to draw, where to draw? 'We see through a glass, darkly,' he muttered to himself. Black ink on her white body. White paper to draw on. What else was white? And then he knew.

Quickly, he moved the bed away from the wall. Yellow paint, peeling to white, but that was all right. Lines, he thought. Lines here and here and here, curving round over her leg up her back . . . round and across her . . . across her . . . across her breast. He almost stopped then, but he couldn't stop, didn't dare stop because stopping meant he would have to lie in the dawn light thinking about her . . .

He needed more space, so he clambered onto a chair, to reach up higher. Swirls of lines, over her creamy skin. A spiral, a clock face, her frightened eyes, the numbers and letters and lines all sharply picked out in the white glare of the street lamps, and he wanted it, wanted her and there was only the wanting and the line, following the line across the wall into a place where there were no words and no need to explain what he could see so clearly and no-one else could see at all.

There was a thunderclap near Fitz's left ear. He jerked awake. Mark was sitting staring at Fitz's carefully arranged piles of cards.

He'd opened the curtains, letting in the sunshine. Little sod, Fitz thought. I'll have to have a word with your mother, when I see her. If I see her.

It wasn't the best start to the day.

'Want your Paracetamol?' Mark asked.

Cheeky little tyke. 'I wasn't drunk,' Fitz said. He massaged the bridge of his nose and considered sitting up.

'Yeah,' Mark said. He looked away, with something close to contempt in his eyes.

'I wasn't!' Fitz said.

'Why don't you sleep upstairs?' Mark leaned forward and picked up one of the cards. Almost without looking at it, he dropped it again.

'That's your mother's bed.' Fitz rolled to a sitting position. He wanted a fag and a drink, but he'd be damned if he'd give Mark the pleasure of seeing him do either. He leaned back and squinted against the light. 'Where was I?' he muttered.

He knew very well. He had been on the point of admitting defeat over the graffiti scrawled all over Joanne Barnes; but he wasn't going to admit it with Mark in the room.

'Good puzzle this.' Mark glanced at Wise's folder, then moved one of the photos. 'There's not one answer is there?'

Fitz suddenly realised what Mark was doing. 'Oh you haven't. Tell me you haven't,' he said. He leaned forward, suddenly fully awake. Sure enough, Mark had moved most of the cards. 'You have. I was up all night on this.' He waved his hand at the cards. Christ knew, he didn't want to argue with Mark, but this was too much. 'You mind your own business.'

'I was helping,' Mark said, sounding much younger than he actually was.

'Yeah, well I don't need your help,' Fitz said, thinking, that's it; why don't we bring this right down to the playground? Count to ten, he told himself. But before he'd got to two, he said, 'What do you know?'

'The big bang. The big crunch.' Mark glared at Fitz for a second. 'But you don't need my help,' he said. He got up and left the room.

'Try me,' Fitz called. Mark paused by the kitchen door. 'Don't play games,' Fitz said. 'Try me.'

All right then, Mark's expression said, I bloody well will. But all he actually said was, 'The universe begins at the ten to the minus forty-third second after the big bang.' This wasn't anything Fitz had expected, Einstein's equation or not. Well, he'd follow anywhere Mark chose to lead. He got down on his hands and knees to look at the cards Mark was pointing to. 'Planck time –' Mark said.

'Walking, or warping?' Fitz deadpanned. It was always good for a bit of thinking time.

'Max Planck,' Mark said. He almost sounded amused. 'Before that instant, the normal laws of nature simply don't apply. There's just a boiling mass of space and time –'

'Anarchy?'

'Cosmic anarchy.'

'Ha!' Fitz said. What the hell else could you say to something like that.

Mark almost grinned. 'Then the core bursts and the rips in space and time appear as these – cosmic strings.' He leaned over and picked up one of the photographs that showed Joanne's skin covered in thin, curving lines.

Fitz couldn't resist it. 'You've got to stop smoking those bus tickets.'

Mark pointed to the photograph of Joanne's leg – the one with the Y-like branching. 'Then the four known forces separate.'

'Enlighten me.' Fitz thought, he could be talking a load of bollocks. I'd never know the difference.

Mark tapped various cards. 'They divide into nuclear, electromagnetic –' he hesitated. 'Something else, and gravity.' He turned to Fitz and grinned. 'The universe is under way – expanding, evolving –'

'Leading to me?' Faced with those cold equations, the only sane response seemed to be utter solipsism.

'Only from where you're standing –'

Oh great. I'll remember to talk to you the next time I'm suicidal, Fitz thought. He grinned sourly at Mark.

'So, what came before the big bang?'

'Nothing,' Mark said, as if it were the most obvious thing in the universe.

'Or God?' Fitz asked. He didn't believe in God. He didn't. He believed in what he could see, feel, taste and hear. And deduce, about people's motivation. About what made them go. And religion was part of that. That was all it was.

'Yeah. God or nothing.' Well, Fitz could go for that. 'But then,' Mark said, 'the big bang theory itself is probably past its sell-by. Some physicists see it as just another clapped-out old creation myth like the Bible.'

Christ on a bicycle, Fitz thought. My son the rocket scientist. 'I can't believe you packed in your A-levels,' Fitz said, and meant it. 'I'll pay you a grant.'

'You've got no money,' Mark said; but he didn't seem pissed off about it, just matter of fact.

My God, Fitz thought. We're having a warm and fuzzy, father and son, male-bonding moment. Any minute now the end credits will roll and I'll know my life's been a sit-com after all.

Couldn't have that. 'Well I'll earn some,' he snapped. And then he thought: that's it, Fitz. Ruin even the best moments. 'It's worth it to me – I don't want you wasting your life.'

'On the scale of these equations my life makes no odds.'

Gawd, Fitz thought. I was at least twenty-five before I got that cynical. 'Nor any life,' he said.

Mark grinned. Warm fuzzies, Fitz thought. Maybe it wasn't so bad.

He stared at the cards, wondering if he'd learned everything he possibly could from them. He checked them off mentally. All but one. 'What does this mean to you?' he asked. '1·40·6?'

'I'll pass on that,' he said, without any hint of defensiveness. 'But they're all saying something about the beginning of life . . . and the end –'

'Birth and death,' Fitz said.

'You would see it that way.'

Yeah, well, Fitz thought. You get sex and death in there and you're well on the way to understanding everything. 'The works,' he said.

Joanne, in the dark, unclothed, but with her body covered in dark graffiti.

Dean, in the dawn light, staring blankly ahead of himself, pinioned against his wall by his own desire, outlining himself with black marker, letting the pen travel around his body and over his arms and down and around and across his chest and up and around and over his face.

Dean, pinioned against the wall that was covered in the markings he had copied from Joanne's creamy flesh.

Dean, dreaming of that flesh, hating himself for thinking wrong thoughts, but unable to stop, and the pen, moving, moving.

TWENTY-ONE

Joanne Barnes's sightless eyes stared up at the ceiling of the intensive care unit. Her mother stood by her bed, clutching at her hand as if she could will life back into her daughter's body.

Behind her, Mr Barnes stood impassively, as if waiting for something, some signal that would enable him to move or speak. Cry, she thought at him. If you don't cry now, you'll be in big trouble later.

No-one knew it better than she did.

Time will heal you, Penhaligon thought. It had healed her, after her father had killed himself. At the time, she hadn't thought it possible, but it was true.

She no longer cried herself to sleep thinking about him. She hadn't thought that was possible, either.

But a child . . . she thought. A child, dead of her own hand or someone's else's. That was worse. That was the universe falling apart.

She longed to go to Mrs Barnes, to say something or to hug her; but that was her husband's place.

Go on, damn you, she thought. But Mr Barnes just stared at his daughter with eyes seemingly as sightless as her own.

Mrs Barnes let her fingers slip free of Joanne's hand. Her face crumpled, and she stifled a sob. Behind her, Mr Barnes clenched his jaw. His mouth worked. For one moment he seemed to be about to reach out and touch his wife.

Go on, Penhaligon willed him. Cry, damn you. But he didn't.

He sobbed, once. Mrs Barnes half turned towards him. He fell to his knees, his mouth stretched wide in a silent scream

135

of desperation. A moan came out of him, like the sound of a person being torn in two.

Thank God, Penhaligon thought. He would be all right now.

Mrs Barnes turned. She sank to her knees beside him. He rocked backwards and forwards, backwards and forwards. Mrs Barnes took his hand, and then drew his head towards her like a mother comforting a sick child. He reached for her, and together they wept.

Fitz sat amid the debris that littered his living room, with a cigarette in one hand and the telephone receiver in the other. He was in big trouble with probably the most important people in his life, and this time he didn't seem to be able to talk his way out of it.

It was bad enough when he really had brought it on himself. Knowing that this was one of the few times when he didn't actually deserve it made taking a bollocking from Katie almost more than he could stand.

'Katie, please listen to me,' he pleaded.

'You could have phoned,' she said.

'I know.' What could he say? I was down at the hospital badgering a near-comatose girl into a state of hysterics? I was out trying to make the world a better place for you to live in? He didn't even want to make her think about the kinds of things he had to deal with on a day-to-day basis. 'I had the tickets, all right? They were in my wallet. You can see them if you want to.' Christ, he thought. Here I go, on the attack because I'm in the wrong. Just like old times. Only it doesn't feel so good when the target's the light of my life. Time to change the subject. 'How did they do, anyway?'

'Don't change the subject, Dad,' Katie said. Sharp as a pin, that's my daughter, Fitz thought. 'I bet you were pissed.'

He hated hearing that tone of near-contempt in her voice. There was only one place she could have learned it from. Score yet another one to Judith.

'Katie I was *not* pissed,' he said, almost managing to keep his patience. She started to say something angry, something about other kid's dads not being drunk all the time. Restraining his temper wasn't worth the effort. 'Katie where'd you learn that word?'

'Off you, I should think,' she said; and now she was being deliberately, provocatively rude.

He wouldn't want to disappoint her. 'That's right, blame me for everything.'

'If you want,' she said, suddenly demure.

'I was not pissed, I was working.' He was raising his voice. Bad idea. 'Ask Mark.' The doorbell rang, followed immediately by hammering on the door.

Bloody hell, just what he needed. He held the receiver away from him, and yelled, 'All right. All right.' The hammering continued.

He heard Katie mutter something – something smart-arsed, if the rest of the conversation was anything to go by – but he couldn't make out what it was. Then she said, 'Well, if it's really all right –'

'No, not you,' Fitz said quickly, wondering what she thought he'd agreed to. 'There's someone at the door. Look, I'll have to go –' The banging hadn't stopped. 'It might be urgent.'

'I suppose so,' Katie said. She sounded genuinely upset. 'You think everything's more urgent than me.'

'No, obviously not more urgent than you.' How could she think that? he wondered. He'd spent a week chewing the carpet because he hadn't seen her, and she thought that. The doorbell rang again and didn't stop. The telephone clicked and the line cleared. 'Katie –' Fitz said. Too late. 'Shit,' he said, and slammed the receiver into its cradle.

Too late. Story of my bloody life, Fitz thought, as he levered himself to his feet and ambled through the hall to the front door. Whoever it was, they were damned persistent. They were still leaning on the doorbell.

'If you're Jehovah's Witnesses I've got a Rottweiler,' he yelled. 'And it's hungry.'

137

He could see Panhandle, standing on the porch, shaking water from her umbrella. It was raining. He hadn't realised. He opened the door.

Panhandle didn't speak. She just stared at him with those huge eyes he could so easily have drowned in. Christ, he thought, I wonder what I've done now?

'Sorry, that was Katie,' he said. Damn, he thought: she hated hearing about his family. I've started, he decided, so I'll finish. 'I was meant to take her to the football yesterday.' Still Panhandle stared at him. 'I had the tickets in my back pocket. She didn't know how to get hold of me.' Still nothing. He put on a silly voice, to try and lighten the mood. 'She thinks I was gambling or down the pub.' Panhandle nodded, as if she'd hardly heard him. 'Are you all right?'

Silence. Just those eyes, staring at him. Then: 'Joanne's dead.' Her voice was flat with grief. He knew she wouldn't have let it show around the family or Beck or any of the rest of her colleagues.

'She was murdered,' he said. Fury mingled with flat despair at the thought that his Katie was growing up in a world where such a thing could happen.

He stepped on to the porch just at the moment she came forward to meet him. They clung to each other then, and their tears mingled with the sheeting rain.

Dean sat on the top deck of the bus. No one sat near him. He was used to that. His face tingled, where he had scrubbed it to get the magic marker off.

Clean. He had to be clean. He mustn't think of dirty thoughts, bad thoughts, Joanne in the darkness with the sheet wrapped round her, Dean in his room with the marker in his hand, copying Joanne. Becoming Joanne, because that was the most of her he could ever have.

It had made him feel strange and warm and comfortable, but it was wrong. He mustn't think of it. So he looked out of the window instead. But the rain had smeared across the window, and he couldn't see out.

He looked around for something else to look at. The woman in front was reading a paper. She turned the page. Joanne's face stared out at him. Pretty Joanne, in her school uniform.

And then he saw the headline. He spelled it out laboriously, sounding out the words the way they'd taught him in school. GRAFF-IT-I. Graffiti. He knew what that was. Writing on walls. He'd been shouted at, at school, for doing that. GIRL. Joanne was a girl. Joanne's picture was in the paper. Joanne's body had been scrawled all over with writing. GRAFFITI GIRL. Joanne. DIES. Dead. Burned utterly, laid in the ground. Dust to dust, ashes to ashes. We see through a glass darkly, then face to face. He put up his hands in his special sign, but it didn't make the headlines go away.

GRAFFITI GIRL DIES.

Joanne was dead.

Joanne was dead, was burned, was ashes.

Before he knew what he was doing, he had run downstairs. He pushed past a woman with a child in a sling, ignoring the people who shouted at him.

The bus stopped. Dean leapt off it. He started to run.

He had to get to somewhere safe. But where was safe? Joanne was dead.

TWENTY-TWO

Fitz, that smug fat bastard, was at it again. Jimmy Beck took a drag on his cigarette and settled back against his desk. Look at him. Holding forth like he was the only person who ever had any insight into a crime at all.

Like he was a policeman, for Christ's sake.

And Wise was letting him do it. Had them all in the incident room, so Fitz could tell them what was as plain as day.

The bastard that killed poor little Joanne Barnes was a raving pervert. How much of the tax-payers' money were they paying Fitz to come here and lecture them and leer at Penhaligon as she pinned up the pictures of Joanne's nude body? Too much, that was for sure.

Penhaligon pinned up the last photograph: Joanne's back, covered in swirling lines, just where it curved in and then out into the sweet swelling of her buttocks.

Beck looked away. It was disgusting. Perverted: though it held a certain attraction, that was for sure. You could go blind, looking at a thing like that. Not that there was a man in the room who wasn't affected by it. And some of the women too, if he was any judge.

Penhaligon moved out the way. Wise nodded to Fitz, who hit the play button on his dictating machine. Joanne's voice, whispered ghost-like through the incident room. 'Holy Mary Mother of God, pray for us sinners . . . pray for us sinners now and at the hour of our death . . .'

Fitz walked to the place he liked to be – centre stage. He waved his cigarette towards the photographs, sending cigarette smoke wreathing across the room. He stopped the tape. 'What do you notice?' he asked. No-one answered. But then, Beck thought, he really didn't want one. He just wanted his chance to play the big man in front of his bit on the side. Sure enough, Penhaligon was watching him, with that secretive little smile playing round her lips. 'They're not smudged,' Fitz said. He sat down heavily, on a chair in the centre of the room. Tell us something we haven't already figured out, Beck thought. 'So we're not looking at some elaborate foreplay. She is naked. Willing obviously – you couldn't do those drawings on her if she was struggling.'

Yeah, Beck thought. He bit at his moustache with his bottom teeth, thinking about it. That innocent young girl, with some pervie wanker working over her. . . .

'After sex maybe? Well, in that case we're not looking for a wham-bam-thankyou-ma'am sort of individual. He lingers.' If you say so, Beck thought. He made himself concentrate on what Fitz was saying. He could think about the other thing later. Fitz went on, 'He talks to her. Explains what all the symbols are about, maybe shows her them in a mirror.' He leaned back and took a long drag on his cigarette. 'This is no spotty adolescent.' Fitz paused. Just for once he seemed short of words. 'Or even,' he said as if he were thinking it through as he spoke, 'he did the drawings after he'd made her take the pills, in which case she couldn't struggle at all. Did all those drawings on her dying body.' Now that was truly perverse, Beck thought. He repressed a grin, thinking, takes one to know one. Fitz carried on, 'Now that's power. That's arrogance. A dying girl – and she was just a canvas for this man's artistry, and his so-called intellect.'

An almost inaudible murmur ran through the room. You had to hand it to Fitz sometimes, Beck thought. He could give you the willies when he had a mind to.

Harriman went up to the photographs. He pointed gingerly at one of the photographs, as if even looking at one of them would infect him. 'What is all this?'

Oh no, Beck groaned silently to himself. Don't give him an opening. Don't –

141

But it was too late. Fitz was on his feet, smiling smugly. 'You don't know about Planck time then.' It wasn't a question, it was a statement. Beck wondered how long it had taken Fitz to dream up this particular load of crap, and how far Wise would let him go before he shut him down. Fitz went up to the photographs and tapped one that showed Joanne's shoulder. A fine black line, divided into numbered sections, snaked across it. 'The instant just before the universe was created,' Fitz tapped the photograph. 'Just after the big bang, when there was nothing but a boiling soup of space and time – no rules and no law, just anarchy and chaos.'

Oh for fuck's sake, Beck thought. He couldn't imagine what this was supposed to have to do with finding Joanne's killers. He shifted around against the desk. No doubt Fitz would tell them.

Fitz walked forward, making sure all eyes were on him. 'Joanne's lover was a man who saw sex in death and vice versa –' Yeah, yeah, yeah, Beck thought. It was the same old song Fitz always played. He just changed the tune occasionally. ' –a morbid, manipulative lover, who in the end wanted to combine the two in one moment of perfection.' Fitz sat back down again. He clicked the dictating machine on again.

'You don't want to die, do you, Joanne?' Fitz said through the hissing of the tape. 'Who made you swallow the pills? The drink? Who wrote those things on your body? Who was it, Joanne?'

Christ, Beck thought. If I'd had that fat bastard badgering me like that, I'd have given up the ghost. He looked around at the others – Harriman, Wise, Penhaligon, the other officers assigned to the case – and wondered if the same thought had occurred to them.

Whatever, Wise sat down right next to the dictating machine and listened hard. Everyone else did likewise.

'Not die,' Joanne whispered, living again for the brief duration of the tape. 'Not die. All flesh. All flesh is grass. Is grass.'

Harriman's head jerked up. 'I've heard that before.' At the moment he was a long streak of nothing much at all, Beck thought. He'd certainly made enough mistakes – like telling that reporter that the Asian shopkeeper Albie Kinsella had killed had been done in by a skinhead. That might very well have been the first mistake – the first of many, Beck had to acknowledge – that began the chain that led to David Bilborough's death. Not that Beck could talk – he closed off that line of thought pretty damn quick. Nah. Given time, and Harriman would make a good, solid copper.

'What?' Wise asked.

'All flesh is grass. I've heard it before.' He went over to his jacket and pulled out his notebook.

'Which is Joanne's church?' Fitz asked. Beck scowled. He just couldn't bear to lose the centre of attention. But then no-one had ever accused Fitz of being a team player.

Penhaligon checked her records. 'St Timothy's.'

Behind Fitz, Harriman flicked through his notebook. 'Dean Saunders.'

'Who?' Wise demanded.

Harriman went over to show him the notebook. 'He started a fire. Dean Saunders. Community care case.' He flipped over to the next page. 'He kept talking weird.' He nodded towards the dictating machine. 'Like that, like that. All flesh is grass. He said it.'

Wise jerked his thumb in the direction of the interview rooms. 'Bring him in for questioning.' He looked round the room. 'Take Beck with you.'

Harriman was out the door like a whippet after a hare. Good lad, Harriman. Beck followed. All right, he thought. We're on.

Michael Trant was trying to gauge the water damage for the insurance assessor when he saw the two men striding purposefully across the yard. He knew who they were immediately.

They were back. The police were back. Two of them this

143

time. The young one that had been around before – what was his name? Harriman, that was it – and another one. An older one, who didn't look anyone's fool.

Michael Trant pushed his hair back out of his eyes. For a split instant he thought about putting his clipboard down, but he decided against it. Best to look busy. It might help to get rid of them more quickly. Besides, it gave him something to do with his hands.

They were talking about something. As he hurried across the yard to them, he quite clearly heard the younger one say the word, 'Saunders'. But it had to be all right – they were staring at the office. He had to assume they were here about the fire, not about Joanne.

'Can I help?' he said.

'Afternoon Mr Trant,' Harriman said. The other one, the one with the bald head and the moustache, nodded a greeting.

'I'm impressed,' Michael said. 'One small fire, two visits, two officers.' He thought, keep it light. Keep calm. We just have to stand together and they can't touch us. He led them between the bales of boxes, heading in the general direction of the office but without a clear purpose. It just seemed easier to deal with them on the move – less eye contact, for one thing.

'Is Mr Saunders around?' That was Harriman again. Michael got the strong impression that Beck was keeping score of everything he said, every move he made.

'Dean? Why? No.' Too fast, Michael thought. I've got to relax. 'He's not in work today.'

'Is he sick?'

'Oh, a touch of this bug that's going around, I think.' That sounded right. Suitably vague. Not something you could check up on easily.

'Could we have his home address, sir?' That was Beck, from behind him. His voice was flat, no-nonsense, with a heavy Liverpool-Irish accent.

'Why on earth would you –' Michael's voice faltered.

Not the fire, something screamed in his head. Not the fire, you idiot. Not the fire, Joanne. He stopped walking and turned to face them. 'Really,' he said, weakly. He grinned. 'One small fire.'

Harriman kept walking for a second, so that by the time the three of them had stopped, Michael was flanked by the two policemen, with his back to a high bale.

'We need to question him concerning another matter,' Harriman said, as if he were reading it straight out of some police cadet's training manual.

'What's that then?' Michael asked. He tried to sound casual, but the voice in his head was screaming, I know you do, I know you do.

He thought of Joanne, as they bundled her up and bent her compliant body to fit the cardboard crate. Dear sweet Jesus, he thought, I couldn't have killed her. But Jesus would have forgiven him for killing her. He doubted very much that Kenneth would forgive him for letting her go.

If they were caught. He would just have to do his best to make sure they weren't. Not that his best was ever good enough.

'His address?' Beck wasn't going to stand for any nonsense, Michael could see that. But he couldn't have what didn't exist.

'Well, I'm not sure I –' Michael ran his hand through the back of his hair. He wished Kenneth were there. Kenneth would have been able to deal with this upstart policeman.

'You got to have his address for National Insurance.'

'Well yes.' Inspiration came. 'The fire. My records.' He waved his hand vaguely in the direction of the gutted office. 'My filing cabinet's ashes, I'm afraid.' He shrugged and crossed his arms.

'You must know where he lives.' Beck again, getting bolshier by the minute.

Michael shrugged a feeble no.

Beck changed tactics. 'How many employees on your books?'

What's he getting at, Michael wondered. But he couldn't not answer. 'Thirty-four,' he said. He turned to Harriman. 'Look, he should be in tomorrow –'

'Burns your office down you give him a day off,' Beck said. He shook his head. 'This is wasting our time –' There was an implied threat behind the words that was more worrying than any direct statement could have been.

'He's not in any trouble,' Harriman put in, soothingly.

'– that means wasting police time,' Beck finished. 'Which is a criminal offence.' He crossed his arms, and despite the fact that he was the shorter by a good two inches, Michael felt Beck was somehow glaring down at him from a height. 'Now a law-abiding citizen like yourself, sir, wouldn't want a criminal record – so just tell us where he lives or we're having you in.'

Michael stared at Beck for a second, unsure how the situation had come to this quite so quickly.

He turned to Harriman.

'Please,' the younger officer said.

Michael wasn't sure if he was being sarcastic or not, but at least it allowed him to save a bit of face. 'That's better, isn't it?' he said. He looked at Beck, who glared back, profoundly unimpressed. 'A bit of politeness gets you further in the end.' He shifted his weight from foot to foot. 'Now I come to think of it, I may have Dean's address in my Filofax.'

He went to get it.

'Thank you, sir.' Harriman's voice came from behind him. 'We'd be most grateful.'

Sarcastic little *shit*, Michael thought.

TWENTY-THREE

Beck pounded up the stairs to Dean Saunders's flat. Harriman was just ahead of him. Time to show the kid how an experienced policeman made a collar.

Harriman had been incredibly excited on the way over. They'd pull Dean in – maybe find some piece of incriminating evidence in his flat – and it would be promotions all round. Well, commendations, anyway.

Beck had had to set him straight on that one. They'd have to take it a bit slowly, make sure they nailed the bastard good and proper. But that was as much for his own benefit as the kid's. He had that gut-clenching feeling that they were on to a winner all right. He just wanted to be sure.

And now here they were, taking the stairs two at a time. The place was a pit, all peeling paintwork and piss in the corners of the stairwells. It stank of it, with an overlay of cheap disinfectant.

Somewhere, a baby was screaming for its mother.

Well, when they got their hands on Dean Saunders, it wouldn't be the only one.

Third floor. The stairs opened out onto a landing with half a dozen identical maroon coloured doors. Number 3d was straight ahead. Harriman got there first, and started hammering on it. One of the doors was open. Beck glanced through it as he passed: a lank-haired woman sat on the edge of an unmade bed, nursing her screaming child. A line of washing hung in one corner. The place smelled of damp and despair.

'Hello? Dean?' he shouted. No response. He hammered with the side of his fist. Nothing. He shrugged and turned away. 'What now – ask the neighbours or back to Anson Road?'

Beck considered. He was tempted to shake the neighbours up and see what fell out: but he didn't think they'd know anything, and he didn't want them putting the wind up Dean. 'Christ no,' he said, just to make sure Harriman knew he'd jumped in the wrong direction. 'Now we wait.'

Saint Timothy's Roman Catholic Church was a neo-Gothic pile of stonework parked ludicrously in the middle of a modern housing estate. Fitz supposed they were lucky to find it open: or maybe the priest was prepared to take his chances with vandals and thieves in the hope of making a few converts.

He went in, with Panhandle at his side. The place was full of the smell of incense and melting wax, and that peculiar chilly silence that churches specialise in. The aisle stretched between rows of pews down to an ornate altar, where unlit candles stood sentinel on either side of the crucifix. Above it, stained-glass saints looked down from the jewel-like splendour of their windows. By comparison, the priest who stood facing the altar seemed small and dowdy.

How long since he'd been in a church? Not counting births, deaths and marriages, a good twenty-two years. He glanced at Panhandle. She was staring blankly at the vaulted ceiling with its buttresses and cornicing. He realised that she was trying hard not to let her thoughts show. Then it came to him that the last time she had been in a church was almost certainly at Bilborough's funeral. But that had been a modern box of a place, not this magnificent folly.

Their footsteps rang on the floor as they walked towards the altar, but the priest didn't turn round until they were almost upon him and Panhandle said, 'Father O'Ryan?'

He turned. He was a mousy owl of a man compared to the peacock glories of the stained glass that surrounded him. Fitz smiled down at him. O'Ryan was shorter than he was, but not much thinner. He had a double chin so magnificent it made Fitz's look like Sting's cheekbones, and a mess of grey hair that stood out round his head like a greasy halo.

'DS Penhaligon,' Panhandle said. 'This is Doctor Fitzgerald –'

The priest blinked at them from behind his glasses. He nodded a hello. 'It's about Joanne? I was about to –' Sharp, Fitz thought. . . .

'If we could have just five minutes of your time . . .' Panhandle said.

'Come into the sacristy.'

He bobbed a genuflection as he crossed the altar. Fitz restrained himself from doing likewise; a memory of a screaming row he had had with one of the Jesuit fathers who had taught him flashed through his mind – not a row, really, a bollocking that had ended with the tawse, as so many of them had. He glanced round to force the memory away. A plaster angel stared down at him, with a smile as enigmatic as the Mona Lisa.

He whispered to Panhandle, 'Why do churches always make you feel you're being watched?'

O'Ryan stopped and turned. 'Because you are, Doctor Fitzgerald.' He sounded faintly amused.

Fitz grimaced. He liked this priest – liked his sharpness, his sense of humour and his timing – despite himself.

O'Ryan led them through one of the smaller side-arches, and unlocked a door. As she went through, Panhandle glanced back.

'Thought I heard something,' she said in response to Fitz's raised eyebrow.

The room on the other side of the door was small and cosy, like something out of C. S. Lewis, though the fireplace was filled with dried flowers. O'Ryan started to pull on one of his vestments, a plain white smock that went straight over his ordinary clothes. A chasuble? Fitz wondered, and was irritated that he could no longer be sure of the name.

'I saw you lecture once,' O'Ryan said.

'Oh,' Fitz said. He smiled, wondering whether to expect roses or raspberries.

'That level of cynicism must be hard to sustain,' O'Ryan said. He sounded almost sorry for Fitz.

'Not at all,' Fitz said blandly. He was not going to get into a religious debate. He was not going to embarrass Panhandle. He was going to stick strictly to the point.

'At times like this,' O'Ryan said, 'I can only remind myself that there is a purpose to everything – that God's love reveals itself in all our fates.'

Tell that to a spina-bifida baby or a mother in Rwanda watching her baby die for want of clean water, Fitz thought. 'That level of idealism must be hard to sustain,' he said, then cursed himself for letting himself get involved.

Panhandle watched them both, impassively. Sometimes Fitz thought she got harder to read the longer he knew her, not easier.

'It is.' Father O'Ryan paused. Fitz got the impression it was more for effect than anything else: that was what years of pulpit thumping would get you, he supposed. 'Extremely.' The priest turned and picked up a white cord belt. 'But you, Doctor Fitzgerald – as an unbeliever, how do you reconcile yourself to such tragedies?'

'I don't!' Fitz said. He'd never understood the need to make sense of the world. As far as he was concerned, shit happened, good things happened. There was very little you could do to influence what you got. All you could do was deal with the aftermath, in the sure knowledge that the universe didn't give a damn either way. Mark was right. On the scale of astronomical time, human lives meant very little. 'I don't even try,' he said. 'As a psychologist, my job is to listen – and to understand.'

O'Ryan tied the cord round his waist, turning himself into a fair impersonation of a sack of flour. 'That must be difficult –' he said.

Fitz had meant to rile the man. Now he realised the priest was genuinely interested in understanding a viewpoint that was clearly alien to him, and he felt slightly ashamed. 'Well, your job is to listen and to forgive. That must be even harder.'

'I'm not the one who forgives,' O'Ryan said. He stared levelly at Fitz. If anything, he seemed vaguely amused.

'I wish I could believe that,' Fitz murmured, and realised that for the first time in two decades it was true. He dealt with it the only way he knew how – with a challenge. 'But we're both confessors, Father. You're as exposed to the dirty realities of life as I am. Does that not disturb your faith?' Let's see you get out of that one, he thought.

'In man,' O'Ryan said. 'Not in God.' He picked up a scarlet and white sash, kissed it and put it round his neck.

'Well –' Fitz said.

Before he could get any further, Panhandle cut in, 'Father . . . could you tell us about Joanne, please?'

'Of course,' the priest said. 'She was always a very devout girl – regularly attended Mass *and* Benediction.' He paused. This time it wasn't for effect, Fitz thought, but to damp down his anger, which was clear in the set of his jaw. He pursed his lips, and then went on, 'But we haven't seen her here since Christmas. I believe she was recruited into a local sect.'

He said the word as if it were blasphemy. Fitz sucked on his cheek and thought, well, from his point of view it might not be so far off, at that. At the very least, it seemed like a better clue to Joanne's mindset than her friend Sarah's tale of rows at home and plans to abscond.

'Who recruited her?' Panhandle asked, cutting to the chase as usual.

'Her headmaster, I believe.'

Fitz and Panhandle stared at each other. One more piece of the jigsaw, Fitz thought. It was coming together. Slightly askew, but coming together. 'Trant –' he muttered.

Panhandle scowled.

'You know him?' O'Ryan sounded shocked.

'Yes,' Fitz said. 'Do you?'

'No.' The priest had stopped robing. 'But I'm not entirely happy about the way he uses his position at school –'

'To do what?' It was a rhetorical question. It was as plain as day: that charismatic smile, that easy avuncular manner. What else would a man like Kenneth Trant be doing if not persuading people to his way of thinking?

'To recruit young people into his sect.' From his tone, he was surprised Fitz even needed to ask.

Fitz hated to sound stupid, but he had to be sure. 'These young people. . . . How would you describe them? I mean – do they have anything in common?'

'Yes' the priest said sourly. 'They're all rather lonely individuals – and they're all girls.'

There wasn't anything to say after that, and certainly no time to lose. O'Ryan led them back out into the church.

Sunlight shafting through the stained glass turned the old stone silver and gold, and leached colour from the candle flames.

'I take it, doctor, that you're a lapsed Catholic?' Father O'Ryan said.

Bloody hell, Fitz thought, the man was sharp. He was more used to handing out the startling insights than receiving them, and he didn't like it one bit. 'Why?'

'Because you're so serious in your mockery.'

Fitz glanced at Panhandle. She was grinning.

'Don't knock the mock,' he said. It was the best he could come up with in the way of a smart comeback. 'But you're right, anyway.' He sniffed, wondering whether he should shut the conversation down before it got any more uncomfortable. What the hell. 'Bless me, Father – it is about twenty-two years since my last confession.'

O'Ryan grinned. 'Then the next one should be worth hearing. I shall look forward to that.'

A priest with a sense of humour. Fitz really didn't think it ought to be allowed.

'Fat chance,' he murmured as Panhandle thanked the

priest for his time; but this time he made sure he said it too quietly to be heard.

Father O'Ryan was busy. Dean watched him from one of the side chapels near the altar. He was speaking to two people Dean didn't know. He said Joanne's name. Dean heard him. They all looked very serious, and then they went into Father O'Ryan's special room.

The two people must be police. They would come and they would take him away and lock him up in a little room without a light where you could hear the rats scuttling around, and there wouldn't be any food and he would have to stay there forever.

That's what they'd said at the home. If he was bad, the police would come for him.

But he would be good. If they asked him, he would tell them how good Mr Kenneth was, and Mr Michael too, and Mr Kenneth would come and get him from the police station.

It would be all right. He would wait until they had gone, and then he would talk to Father O'Ryan. Father O'Ryan was a priest. That meant he couldn't tell anyone what you said to him.

Dean settled back in the shadows of the chapel, quiet as a little mouse, and waited for the people to go.

When they came out, the two people looked even more serious than when they went in. Dean watched them go. Father O'Ryan walked to the back of the church with them.

Dean stepped out. He made sure they were really going. 'Father,' he said. 'Father –'

Father O'Ryan turned. 'Dean?'

Dean started to cry. He didn't mean to, but he couldn't help it. He kept seeing Joanne's picture in the paper. He could feel the bus lurching along underneath him as he worked out what the words meant. GRAFFITI GIRL DIES. He felt like he would stop breathing at any minute. 'She –' he started; but he couldn't get the words out. 'She –' he tried again.

Father O'Ryan came and stood close by. 'What is it, Dean?'

I have to say, Dean thought. He's Father. He can't tell anyone. He tried to make his mouth shape the word, *dead*, but he couldn't do it. Jesus was here in the church. Jesus was watching him, and Mary and the saints. He couldn't say that word when they were all watching him. He swallowed hard. His throat hurt from crying and running. He said, 'She's in Heaven now.'

'Who is?'

He didn't know. Somehow, Dean had thought that Father would know, like God knew and Jesus knew and Mr Kenneth knew. He couldn't say her name. He couldn't. The people had been talking about her, and he was scared if he said her name they would come back and get him. He looked at the door, hoping they had gone.

'Joanne?'

Father O'Ryan sounded shocked. Dean was scared he would be angry. 'Help me,' Dean said. He couldn't think what else to say. They would find out he had wanted to touch her in the dark. They would think he had hurt her. They would say he should have phoned. They would say it was his fault she was dead. 'Help me,' he said again. 'Please. Please, Father –' He started to tremble.

'What's wrong with you, Dean?' Father O'Ryan asked. He took Dean's arms gently, not to hurt him but to stop him shaking.

Father O'Ryan might tell, Dean thought. Just because he wasn't supposed to tell . . . if the police came and asked him. 'You. Me,' he said. There was a place, a special place. He tried to remember the name of it but the word wouldn't come. He stared desperately at Father O'Ryan, hoping he would understand.

'What were you saying about Joanne?'

He was going to be angry with Dean. Any minute now, he would be, and then there would be no-one in the world that Dean could talk to.

154

Dean fought for words. 'The box –' he said. He twisted round, to look at it. You went in and you said, 'Bless me Father for I have sinned,' and then you told Father all the bad things you had done, and then he gave you penance and then it was all right. And Father could never, never tell anyone what you had said. In the box, it was just you and father. And God. 'In the box –' Dean said.

Father O'Ryan stared at Dean. He's angry, Dean thought. Please don't be angry. I didn't mean to hurt her.

'Come on,' Father O'Ryan said. He went over to the box.

Dean started to follow him. What if it isn't true? he thought. What if you do something really bad, and you say about it?

Father O'Ryan went inside.

Dean thought, I have to tell him. He's in the box. I'm in the box. He can't tell. But he might. He might.

Dean thought about sitting in the darkness, telling Father about Joanne. He thought about being locked away by the police, in the dark, listening to the rats scuttle and run.

He licked his lips. He wanted to go in the box with Father. But he couldn't. He turned and ran out of the church, listening to the sound of his trainers pound first on the wooden boards, and then on the grass, and then on the pavement.

Beck would never let it show in front of Harriman, but he was pig sick of waiting for this sicko Saunders to show up. The reason he'd never let it show was that patience was a prime virtue of the good detective, and he reckoned that he owed it to Harriman to set a good example.

So they just had to wait it out, without even the radio on or a quick look at the afternoon's horses to relieve the tedium of –

'There he is,' Harriman yelled, pointing.

Damn, Beck thought. He caught a glimpse of Saunders's jacket as he ran through the gap in the gate to his building. Then he was out of the car – just ahead of Harriman, so that was OK – and was diving after Saunders. The overgrown bushes at the side of the wall whipped at his face. He ignored them.

Saunders was already inside by the time they rounded the wall. Beck's feet crunched on gravel. He banged the door open. Saunders was at the top of the stairs, and again Beck only got a glimpse of his back as he turned the corner.

He was fast, but Beck would be faster. *Would be faster*. And in any case, there wasn't anywhere for Saunders to go.

The last flight of stairs. Saunders turned, and Beck got a fleeting impression of a beaky, red-blotched face. Then he was gone.

Beck was right behind him. He got to the third floor just in time to see Saunders's door slamming shut. He pitched himself at it, but it was too late. He shoulder-rammed it, but it didn't give. Bloody thing, he thought, glancing at Harriman. He braced himself, one hand on the door jamb, the other on the wall, and booted the door. It sprang open.

The recoil sent him sprawling back, just long enough to let Harriman get in first.

So it was Beck who was able to go in slow – past Harriman who had, quite correctly, grabbed Saunders – and take a good look round.

And it was Beck who first realised they'd got their man, because the whole room – all four walls – were daubed in exactly the kind of obscene crap that had decorated Joanne Barnes's body.

Christ, he muttered, confronting the black shape of a man – or maybe a girl – that the pervert had drawn. He'd surrounded it with squiggles and lines – yes, there was a sunburst, and there was a clock, and a spiral of circles – just like Joanne Barnes.

Harriman had Saunders in a headlock. Good man, Harriman. Pointless to take chances.

Beck grinned wolfishly at Saunders. 'Gotcha,' he said.

TWENTY-FOUR

Fitz was at it again, and if Penhaligon wasn't exactly bored, she wasn't in the mood to play mind games with him. She had just parked her car up outside Kenneth and Virginia Trant's house, and Fitz was staring at it thoughtfully.

It was a neat suburban semi, just like many others Penhaligon had visited in the course of her duties. Some of them had belonged to witnesses, some to victims and some to suspects – or criminals. It would have been useful if Fitz had produced some insights about the people who might live in this particular house.

But no, he was talking about letterboxes, though being Fitz it was as much an excuse to talk about himself as anything else.

'Theirs will definitely be furry,' he said. Penhaligon sighed. She was supposed to ask how he could be sure, or what it might mean. He would tell her, then turn it around so it was something about her. Probably, something salacious about her, or nearly so. Well, she wasn't playing today. He'd have to find another game. She looked out the window. It didn't stop him. He just went on as if she were fascinated. 'I had this vacation job once when I was a student. Postman. It's amazing the different kinds of letterbox you'd meet.' Here we go, Penhaligon thought. Doctor Edward Fitzgerald's general theory of personality types as demonstrated by choice of letterbox. 'Big, open, generous ones, welcoming enough for the kids to get their arms through so they could take the key and never need to carry one. Mean little snappers you could hardly get a postcard through.' This is it, Panhandle thought: the Freudian analysis. Any minute now

157

he'll ask me what kind of letterbox I have at home – as if he
didn't know, considering he's shouted through it often
enough when he's been drunk – and then tell me What It
Means. And whatever I say, he'll put a spin on it. She pulled
a sour face. But he didn't. 'Vertical ones, high up. Vertical
ones low down, that just about do your back in. And then
they had these ones with furry brushes inside.' He held out
his hands in front of him and made a disgusted face. 'When
you put your hands in, it was all squidgy, like you were
being disinfected –'

Wrong again, Penhaligon thought. Obscurely disappointed, she said, 'Come on, Fitz –'

She got out of the car and led the way to the Trants'
house. The front lawn was clipped to within a millimetre of
baldness, the roses decently this side of overblown. Disinfected, Penhaligon thought. Yeah, right.

The door was pristine white, inset with expensive-looking
leaded stained glass. Penhaligon pressed the doorbell, and it
rang out with a discreet two-toned chime. There was a
vertical letterbox set at a convenient height. Fitz spotted her
looking at it, and grinned.

He stuck his hand into it and his smile changed to a look
of disgust. He withdrew his fingers. 'Furry,' he mouthed at
her.

Penhaligon found that she was laughing despite her best
intentions. She slapped Fitz lightly on the chest just as the
door opened.

Virginia Trant stood there. Penhaligon composed herself.
She held out her ID card. 'Mrs Trant?' she said.

The woman stared at them as if they were monsters. Her
hair was a bit of a mess, and she had a slightly crumpled
look about her that was a world away from what Penhaligon
had been led to expect.

'About Joanne Barnes,' Penhaligon prompted, when it
became clear that Mrs Trant was not going to respond.

'Oh. Yes.' The word hissed out of her. Her eyes, already
as wide as a rabbit's in headlights, widened further. She

158

started to bring her hands together in front of her, then visibly forced them to her sides.

'Could we speak to your husband, please?'

Virginia Trant played with her wedding ring. She licked her lips. 'One moment, please,' she said, for all the world like a switchboard operator.

Kenneth Trant had her well trained, if nothing else, Penhaligon thought. She'd been right first time. The man was a piece of slime.

He appeared in the hall, hastily folding his paper. 'Hello again,' he said as he came to the door. 'Do come in, please.' He waved a hand in the direction of the living room. 'If you'd like to go through –'

Penhaligon went in, with Fitz right behind her. Kenneth shut the door, and as she heard it click shut, she thought, this is what the fly felt like, as it accepted the spider's invitation to go into its parlour.

Kenneth Trant's living room was like the rest of his home, relentlessly middle-class: nothing too trendy or ostentatious, nothing too old-fashioned, certainly nothing cheap. Very nice if you liked that kind of thing, Fitz thought. He didn't, much.

Kenneth was talking quietly to Virginia in the hallway. Fitz would have given much to overhear that conversation, but since he couldn't, he used the time to explore Kenneth's bookshelves. He pulled out a well-thumbed copy of *A Brief History of Time* by Stephen Hawking, from where it nestled next to *Chaos* by James Gleick and *In Search of the Edge of Time* by John Gribbin.

The Planck Wall. A boiling mass of chaotic energy that existed before the universe as we know it organised itself into existence.

Joanne Barnes's body, scrawled with equations and symbolic representations of the heat death of the universe.

Oh yes, Fitz thought. I think I have a fair idea now who might have done that.

'Doing some research, doctor?' Kenneth asked.

Fitz turned, startled out of his reverie. 'You make any sense of this?' he asked. He held the book up so Kenneth could see it.

'Couldn't make head nor tail of it,' Kenneth said, perhaps too smoothly.

Fitz put the book back. 'You interested in that sort of thing?'

'No,' Kenneth said. 'It was a Christmas present.' He waved Fitz to a seat on the sofa. 'How about you? Have you read it?'

Fitz grinned ruefully. 'I gave up halfway.' He sat down on the sofa, with Panhandle next to him. 'Bit of a letdown,' he said. 'I thought I was going to find all the answers in there.' Kenneth took what appeared to be his customary chair. Virginia stood by, uncertainly. Fear came off her like sweat. Unless, Fitz told himself, I only think that because I've just seen those books: it was hardly good scientific method to force the evidence to fit his theory.

Kenneth smiled and picked up a Bible from the coffee table. 'You're looking at the wrong book,' he said.

'You think I'd find all the answers in there?' Fitz said.

'Well,' Kenneth said easily, 'the answers are there but whether you find them depends on you.' He smiled. 'Do you believe in God, doctor?'

'I can never catch him in,' Fitz said drily.

'Don't worry, I'm not going to try and convert you.' Kenneth matched his tone.

Virginia shifted from foot to foot. Was she unhappy with the talk of religion, or with the idea of Kenneth converting people? Fitz didn't have enough information to tell. Yet.

'Why not?' he demanded.

'You expect me to?' Kenneth said, apparently eager for the joust.

'You do proselytise for your faith, don't you?'

'Proselytise?' Kenneth said, as if the word were new to him.

160

'You have recruited several of your pupils for your church.'

There was the tiniest of whimpering sounds, so quiet he could hardly be sure he'd heard it. But Panhandle glanced sharply at Virginia.

'I would hardly say "recruited –"' Kenneth objected.

'That's why I said proselytise: to convert someone from one faith to another –'

'I know the meaning of the word, doctor.'

He's being deliberately bolshie to distract me from Virginia, Fitz thought. He wished he could have asked Panhandle to concentrate on her, but as it was all he could do was try to split his attention between the two of them.

'But you don't like it.' Fitz glanced from Kenneth to Virginia. She looked just like a frightened rabbit, he thought – all big eyes, turned-up nose and front teeth. But he had to get what he could from Kenneth. 'And you won't have "recruit". What then? Draft? Enlist?'

'Are you here to debate semantics with me?' Kenneth sounded as if he were having difficulty keeping his voice level.

Virginia rubbed her hands together. Her fingers caught at her wedding ring, and she twisted it round.

Interesting, Fitz thought. He snapped at Kenneth. 'No. I'm here to talk about Joanne Barnes.' Time to be done with word games.

Virginia chose that moment to speak. 'Can I offer you some tea?' she asked Fitz.

'No,' he said.

Kenneth glared at her. But she turned to Panhandle. 'Coffee?'

'No thank you.' Panhandle smiled.

Virginia licked her lips. Kenneth smiled up at Virginia, then turned back to Fitz. 'Well, I don't think I can add anything to what you learned from young Sarah at the school.'

Fitz shifted his bulk back against the sofa. 'Oh, you know what she told us?' Well of course you do, he thought. You probably rehearsed every word with her until she could lip synch.

'Yes, of course,' Kenneth said. 'She reported it to me later.' Somehow, Fitz didn't think he meant a casual enquiry. 'She said that Joanne was lonely, and that she was having problems with her parents.'

'When did you last see Joanne?' Fitz said quickly.

Kenneth appeared to give that some thought. 'On Sunday night at our church.' Odd how he emphasised that, Fitz thought. The way Virginia looked at him when he said it was even odder – as if she were frightened she might say the wrong thing and make him angry.

'Your church?' Panhandle said. It was a normal part of the double act they did so well: she kept quiet, then took them off guard.

'Yes.' He met Panhandle's gaze. She simply stared back at him until he added, 'Well, surely you must know that Joanne was a member of our church?'

'Why must we?' Panhandle's tone was mild. Fitz knew just how deceptive that tone could be. The voice of an angel and a mind like a steel trap, his Panhandle.

It worked. Kenneth said uncertainly, 'Her parents would have mentioned it.' He raised his clasped hands as though he longed to fidget with them, but knew better. 'After all, she was there every Sunday night, and sometimes during the week as well –'

'Why didn't you mention this at the school?' Her voice was harder now, and her eyes never left Kenneth's.

'Hardly seemed relevant to your enquiries,' he said after a moment. He shifted in his chair. 'I mean, after all, she didn't go missing that night. She was at school the next day, as usual.'

Too fast, Fitz thought. Too fast, and too glib. 'How did she seem that Sunday night?' he asked.

'No different from usual.' Kenneth seemed lost for something to say. 'She read a verse – her usual self –' He glanced at Virginia. She rubbed at something in her eye as she smiled and nodded. It could be genuine of course. There was always, Fitz told himself, that most minute of possibilities. Then again, maybe she couldn't look her husband in the eye because of something else . . . something he couldn't name yet, but which they would much prefer he didn't find out about.

'Are you a member of the church, Mrs Trant?' Fitz asked.

Virginia gaped at him. She clutched her hands together, but she didn't speak. Again, she made that almost inaudible whimpering sound. Her mouth began to tremble. Eventually, Kenneth reached out and took her hand, drawing her closer to his chair.

'Yes,' he said, when it became clear that Virginia wasn't going to answer. 'My wife is a member.'

Virginia let out a low moan. She covered her face with her free hand, and began to sob.

Kenneth got up quickly. He put his arm round Virginia, as solicitous as you could imagine a man being, Fitz thought. Or perhaps just as quick as he could be to shut her up. 'I hope you'll excuse us. Virginia hasn't slept since this happened,' he said. He propelled her towards the door. 'It's left everyone at school feeling shattered – and at the Fellowship.' Fitz and Panhandle followed him. 'That poor young girl. Such a dreadful waste of a life –'

'Yes, I know,' Fitz said. He sighed. 'That's why we want to catch the maniac that did it.'

Kenneth froze, just for a second, then moved on.

Virginia sobbed.

'Well, that was good value,' Fitz said, as he and Panhandle walked back to the car.

'You think he did it.' It wasn't a question.

'Maybe. I certainly think he knows more than he's letting on.' He wondered what she'd do if he tried to kiss her now – right now, in front of the Trants' house and for all the world to see.

Slap his face and leave him to walk home, no doubt.

Bilborough had said he'd put Fitz in traction if he hurt Panhandle again: last time he'd succumbed to her charms he'd stood her up at the airport, leaving her with a massive bill for a holiday he'd lost the nerve to take.

But Bilborough was dead and Judith had left him, probably for good. And they had a case to solve.

'What say we really put the wind up him,' he asked. He cocked his head at the house.

Panhandle grinned and raised her eyebrows.

'Go back and ask him for a list of everyone in his Fellowship. That should upset him.' It was Fitz's turn to smile. 'Who knows,' he said. 'We may even need it.'

TWENTY-FIVE

So they had the pervie little shite, and this time there wasn't going to be any mistake about it. No letting him out on the street to kill again. Not if Jimmy Beck had anything to do with it, no sir.

But it had to be said there was a certain lack of hard physical evidence to go with all the circumstantial – the motive, the opportunity, above all, all that crap Saunders had written on the walls of his flat. So what they needed was a confession.

And Beck was going to make sure they got it. He faced the little bastard across the interview room table.

'Just tell us what happened,' he said.

Saunders raised his hands in that freako sign he liked to make.

Beck had had enough of it. More than enough. 'Do that one more bloody time I'll chop them off.' He jabbed his index finger at Saunders, who slowly lowered his hands.

'Before you're cautioned; before you see a solicitor; before my boss starts interviewing you, you've got a chance,' Beck said. Saunders started to tremble. Christ any minute now, the kid would be in tears. Good. He couldn't wallop the little pervert – not with Harriman standing there behind him, straight up from Hendon and full of space cadet idealism – but he could certainly put the fear of God up him. 'One chance Dean, to come clean. Do you understand?' He leaned on the table, with his face right up close to the little shit. Either his breath stank, or his clothes did: most likely, both.

Saunders just stared at him out of those huge kick-me

puppy dog eyes. Beck could see he wasn't getting through. Maybe nothing ever had.

'Can I have some water please?'

Beck could have spit. Understand? Maybe the little queer did. Maybe it was all just a wind-up. Still, there was an opportunity in everything, if you had the balls to grab it. He nodded to Harriman, who went out to get the water.

Beck stood up. He moved back a bit, where Saunders could get a good look at what he was facing. He shoved his hands in his pockets, and said, 'I know everything, Dean. I just want you to tell me.' Nothing. Just those big, staring eyes and the trembling lips. It made Beck want to hit something. The little bastard needed some more encouragement. 'I've been to your flat. I've seen.'

That would get him: even he should be able to figure out that the things he'd scrawled on the walls were the same as he'd written on Joanne.

But he said, 'We see through a glass darkly, then face to face.' He was smiling, as if he were telling Beck good news. In fact, he really seemed excited.

What the fucking hell was that supposed to mean? Time to get down to business, to really give him something to worry about.

'Face to face,' Beck said. He came back to the table and leaned on it. 'Me. You. Now,' he paused for effect. Dean made fists of his hands on the table. The knuckles were white, even compared to his pallid skin. 'I talked with Joanne. Before she died she told me everything about you, the disgusting things you did. What you did to her,' Beck said. He couldn't help it. He thought about the photographs, about all that creamy skin, firm young breasts daubed with pen – buttocks, thighs, belly, all marked with signs – about how young she was. What would Dean Saunders have made of that? Beck was betting he hadn't made anything much of it at all. Not in the end. Not after he'd done whatever he had to do to feed his twisted little perversion. Not like a real man would have. 'How you hurt her –' Oh yes, Beck could imagine that all right: and from the blind panic on Saunders's face, so could he. '– those things you wrote, the things you said.' Beck was almost whispering now. He licked his lips. 'Joanne told me everything you little scumbag, and I'm nailing you.'

Saunders was obviously having trouble holding back the tears. Good, Beck thought: very good. He wanted to see him cry, the way he imagined Joanne would have cried as Saunders dug deep into her firm flesh with that pen of his. . . .

Beck stood up. He walked slowly round the table, until he was standing close to Saunders's right side. He bent down till his head almost touched Saunders's hair. 'Confess. Confess now, Dean, or I'm throwing you to the wolves.'

Beck moved round until he was standing behind Saunders. Speaking to him from here would disorient him. It was a technique Beck had picked up from some of his reading.

Saunders put his hands up in that sign of his. Time to prove it couldn't protect him at all, Beck decided.

'Lovely girl like that,' he said. 'You touching her, defiling her . . .' He wished he could see the look on Saunders's face, so he could tell if he were hitting home. He crouched down, so that he was whispering directly into the pervert's ear. 'The dirty, disgusting things you did will be done to you twice over,' he whispered. It wasn't any use. Subtlety had no place in dealing with a turd like Saunders. He let the anger he'd been repressing find its way into his voice. 'Confess or you're in trouble, Saunders –' he was roaring now ' – I swear.'

Just then, Harriman came in with the water. Beck stood up – no need to hurry – and patted Saunders on the shoulder, as if they'd just been having a good old chinwag. He wandered back round the table and leaned against the wall.

Saunders's gaze never left him.

I've got you now, you bastard, Beck thought. I've got you.

TWENTY-SIX

They weren't going to get anywhere with Kenneth Trant. Fitz could feel it in his water, and he said as much to Panhandle.

They radioed in to Anson Road, only to be told that Dean Saunders had confessed. Wise wanted them to get down to Michael Trant's packaging factory, and let him know what was going on.

'Suits me,' Fitz said as Panhandle broke the connection.

She raised her eyebrows at him.

'There has to be a weak link in the chain. All we have to do is find it.' He sucked his cheek.

'You don't think Dean did it, then?' she said wrily. They both knew how much a confession was worth. She stared at him, with that level assessing gaze that let him know she understood him better than he was comfortable with.

There had been a time when he'd been obsessed with finding a pure motive: not an unmixed one, but one that was totally good-hearted. Well, Nigel Cassidy was banged up for killing Timothy Lang, a murder he almost certainly hadn't committed. That was at Fitz's door: since then, he'd decided the pure motive could go to hell. He'd settle for the truth – if he could get it.

'Do you?' he asked. She'd seen Dean Saunders's flat, with its parody of the graffiti from Joanne's body scrawled all over its walls, just as he had.

She smiled sardonically at him. She knew it wasn't over yet, the same as he did.

● ● ●

Michael Trant was a much smaller man than his brother Kenneth, Fitz mused. The difference wasn't so much physical as a matter of presence. Put Kenneth Trant in a room full of strangers, and he would be the centre of attention in a matter of minutes. Put Michael in the same room, and he'd be lucky if anyone even remembered he'd been there.

He had looked terrified when Panhandle introduced herself and Fitz. Now that she had told him that Dean was at Anson Road, he looked like the world had fallen away from beneath his feet.

The weak link in the chain. Maybe.

'He's in custody, then?' Michael Trant said. His voice sounded thin and panicky, and he blinked a lot.

'He's helping us with our enquiries,' Penhaligon said.

Fitz didn't let him have the time to think that through. 'Do you know anything about his family?' he asked, making sure he kept his manner light, almost teasing. He paced round behind Trant.

'Never mentions them,' Michael said. Fitz raised his eyebrows expectantly. 'All I know is that his mother died. . . .' Michael's voice trailed off. Fitz stared at him, sucking his teeth, letting his expression say, *Are you sure that's the truth? It isn't what I heard.* Eventually Michael said, 'Or . . . or ran away.' Fitz stared at him. The bugger was hiding something. Something specifically about Dean. 'I'd no idea . . .' Michael said.

'You'd no idea of what?' Fitz cut in sharply. 'That his mind was so deranged?'

'Yes,' Michael said. He blinked rapidly and his head bobbed up and down like a noddy dog in the back of a car. 'Yes.' He sounded relieved, like he'd figured out the answer to a particularly tough exam question.

Sorry to disappoint you, Fitz thought. He smiled. 'See, there I have to disagree with you.' He turned to Panhandle, but looked at Michael out of the corner of his eye, an effect he knew would disturb the man. 'I don't think what we saw in Dean's flat this morning is the work of a disordered mind.' He began to pace again. He had Michael's complete attention now – like a cobra staring at a mongoose. 'I think that it's the work of a classically tutored intelligence; a knowing, ordered, considered brain.' He paused. Michael seemed to have passed through panic and got to the stage of numb terror remarkably quickly. Time to put the pressure on. Time to demand a response. 'Not the way most people would think of Dean, wouldn't you say?'

He glanced at Panhandle. She was watching intently, waiting for that moment when a change of pace or voice would crack Michael Trant open like a cold chisel slipping into a fracture in a slab of granite. They were good together, Fitz and Panhandle, a double act that rarely failed.

'What's Dean's background?' Fitz asked, in a tone that made it obvious he already knew the answer. 'Special school. Bullied. Poor attendance. Metalwork. Art.'

'Dean's . . .' Michael's voice trailed off. He tried again. He blinked a couple of times. 'He . . .' He gave up. 'Yes. That kind of – what you said.'

Oh yes. Definitely something up between Michael Trant and Dean Saunders. Could Michael be the killer? Fitz doubted it. Whoever killed Joanne Barnes had been brutal and calculating in equal measure: and murder itself required a great deal of initiative. Fitz didn't think Michael Trant had enough to start an affair in the first place.

But he needn't know that. Time to up the ante. 'What about yourself?' he asked. 'Poly?'

'University.' Michael looked suitably rattled.

'Leicester?' Fitz machine-gunned the question. He didn't want Michael to have time to think.

'Hull.'

'Engineering.'

Michael smiled weakly, as if he were the one relieved to have got an answer right. 'Correct.'

Poor Michael Trant, Fitz thought, though he didn't really feel all that sorry for the man. He must have lived his entire life in the shadow of his smarter, better-looking older

170

brother, saying thank you to life when it kicked him, and feeling like he should apologise on those rare occasions when he did get a right answer.

Fitz glanced at Panhandle. She grinned. One up to me, he thought, even as he said, 'Then marriage, suburbia and working in daddy's factory.' He made statements of it, not questions.

'Yes.' Again, the weak smile.

'Yeah.' Fitz grinned, keeping his manner just this side of obvious contempt. 'The sixties really passed you by, didn't they, Michael?'

He turned to leave, letting Panhandle say their goodbyes.

She didn't say anything until they were back in the car. 'What was that all about?' she asked.

'Just yanking his chain to see if it would break,' he said.

She grinned and drove off. The late sun gilded her coppery hair, and he couldn't help noticing the delicacy of her pale hands on the steering wheel.

Now where the hell did that come from? he wondered. He'd thought they were long past the unrequited love stage, and well back into being reluctant friends.

A couple of months without sex, and he was anybody's, he thought. Not that his sex-life with Judith had been likely to make the front page of the *News of the Screw*, but at least he'd always known the possibility was there: it had made all the difference.

'Penny for them?' Penhaligon said.

'Pounds couldn't buy them,' he said, thinking I don't dare tell you. I just don't dare.

TWENTY-SEVEN

So the little perv had cracked, Beck thought. Made his confession for the tape recorder *with* his brief present, *no* problem.

That had to be worth a toast in any language. He pulled his private supply out of his desk drawer. None of your bloody Scotch, either, but good Irish whiskey. He poured generous ones for himself, and for Harriman and a couple of the others who happened to be hanging around the incident room. A day like this when he'd made a collar and seen the man put down, he deserved it.

'Cheers!' he and Harriman said together as they clinked glasses, and they all grinned. Down in one, and Beck poured another.

Penhaligon and Fitz came in. She had that determined look on her face that meant there was trouble ahead. As for him, he had a gob on him like a butcher's slab. They went straight to Wise's door, and Penhaligon knocked on it. Probably thought they had some hot information. Too bad. Fitz turned round and scowled at Beck.

'What's the gob on you for?' Beck demanded. Ghost at the bloody party. That was Fitz all over. 'We're putting a man down. Join the party –' He held the bottle out.

Fitz came over. 'I think you're making a mistake.' Just for once, he didn't sound like he was trying to pick a fight, but Beck didn't give a damn to hell either way.

'I don't,' he said. Chew on that, you fat bastard, he thought.

Fitz grinned. 'You're a bit like a doctor, really, aren't you?'

172

Now what the bloody hell was that supposed to mean? Beck paused, hoping Fitz would explain it; when he didn't, Beck was forced to say, 'You've lost me.'

Fitz wasn't grinning any more. 'You tend to bury your mistakes.' He turned and followed Penhaligon into Wise's office.

Beck turned back to Harriman. He slammed the bottle down on the table so hard it made the glasses jump. The bastard, he thought. He was never going to let what had happened to Bilborough go. He'd never let Beck be free of it. He poured himself another one – a double – and this time he didn't hand the bottle around.

Wise was just as bone-headed as Fitz expected. He had hoped for better, but then he'd always known what hope did: waited at the airport while its boat was coming in.

He glared at Wise, who lounged back in his chair. 'He's innocent.' Fitz wasn't shouting – but not by much.

The same was true of Wise, who was obviously prepared to give as good as he got. 'Then why did he confess?' Light glinted on his spectacle lenses, and made his face unreadable.

Fitz snorted, not bothering to hide his derision. He turned to Panhandle. 'Wise by name, thick by nature,' he whispered, loud enough so Wise couldn't miss hearing. She shot a worried glance at her boss, but Fitz didn't have time to decide why: she might have been worried that Wise would get pissed off with him, and her by association; or she might have been concerned that Wise would go with Dean's confession.

'Look,' Fitz said, fumbling in his jacket pocket. 'Here's a list of Dean's Bible-thumping buddies.'

Wise leaned forward and took the piece of paper.

'Everyone on it should be treated as a suspect, sir,' Panhandle said. She was doing a better job of keeping a level temper than Fitz had. Then again, she wasn't haunted by the spectre of a probably-innocent Nigel Cassidy banged up for twenty years.

173

It had happened once, and it was mostly Fitz's fault. He damn well wasn't going to let it happen again.

'Reading the Bible's not a crime –' Wise said.

'Particularly the Trants,' Fitz said, as if it were a direct response to Wise's statement.

Wise was dubious. 'These all look –'

'Respectable, solid citizens?' Penhaligon said drily.

'Yeah.' Wise made the word a challenge.

'Dean's just a scapegoat, sir.' Penhaligon was intense.

She's just as committed to this as I am, Fitz thought. And she's got more to lose than me. A hell of a lot more. 'Let me question him,' he said.

Wise looked through the window behind Fitz. 'Now that'd go down well with Beck, wouldn't it?'

Fuck Beck, Fitz thought. Since when were his feelings more important than the truth? He'd thought Wise was too old and too tough to have to play the kind of games Bilborough had so often indulged in. It seemed he was wrong. But saying it wouldn't get him anywhere.

He decided to play on Wise's self-interest instead. 'If he retracts his confession, what have you got?'

'Not a lot,' Wise admitted reluctantly.

Suddenly Fitz had had enough of all the head games and office politics. Stuff Beck's feelings, and stuff Wise too. 'I just want a chance to get at the truth, if that's not too radical,' he snapped.

Maybe Wise appreciated the honesty. 'Look, the confession's being typed up.' He stood up and headed towards the door. As he passed Fitz he said, 'If you want to talk to him in the meantime, that's OK by me.'

Fitz and Panhandle grinned at each other. Fitz got the impression it was all she could do to stop herself from punching the air.

Wise opened the door for them. As they went out, he said, 'By the way, Fitz, are they all your own teeth?' He put his arm on Fitz's arm.

'Yeah?' Now Fitz reckoned he knew how Beck must feel

most of the time – lost.

'Look after them,' Wise said. He wasn't that much smaller than Fitz. 'Floss them. Brush them. And don't call me thick ever again.'

Fitz scowled. One up to Wise, he thought. Then he remembered that he'd got permission to talk to Dean. More like one all, he decided. And the game was far from over.

They had put Dean in a little, little room with a window up high so not much light came in. Then after a while they came and took him to a bigger room, where there were some men police and lady police and another lady who said she was a solicitor.

Tell us what you did to Joanne, they had said, and he had told them, nothing, nothing, nothing.

But they didn't believe him. When was the last time you saw her, they asked him. They weren't angry, they didn't shout, but they kept on asking him and asking him. What was she wearing? He wanted to say, she was wearing the sheet, I didn't see anything. Nothing bad, nothing I shouldn't have seen.

I wanted to touch her but she didn't like it.

Maybe he'd said that. Maybe he had, because the one who had been angry with him before, the one with the moustache, he got angry with Dean again.

You gave her drink, he said. Like, a cup of tea, like after a prayer meeting, Dean thought. Maybe he had one time.

Tell us, they said. Tell us, tell us, tell us.

So he had told them, and he thought that meant they would let him go back to his room. His own room, with his own things.

But they put him back in the little room with the high window, and told him he would have to stay there.

And now here they were again, saying he would have to come and answer more questions.

Dean put his hands up in his special sign, to stop them. But it was no good. They made him go with them.

TWENTY-EIGHT

Dean Saunders had huge, slate-coloured eyes, a too-big mouth with oddly mobile lips and a bad haircut. Fitz paused at the interview room door, assessing him. He would be the butt of every joke, the scapegoat for every error, every mishap, every misfortune that happened, anywhere he went.

Just as he was now.

Fitz went into the room, with Penhaligon close behind him. As soon as he started moving, Dean's hands came up in front of his face. The index fingers and thumbs of each hand made L shapes, and the tips of the thumbs were pressed together. Dean stared through the half-rectangle his hands made.

Fitz sat down. Penhaligon took up a position behind him, near the wall. Neither Dean's hands nor his staring eyes wavered.

Fitz wondered what Dean could be doing. Warding off evil spirits – the devil, demons, whatever terrible thing Dean's theology made the world contain? Or the world, which to Dean would be inexplicable? That seemed more likely, but how? A camera lens? Too sophisticated. A television? Maybe. Either would distance you from the world, put a layer of unreality between you and it. There was only one way to be sure.

'What do you see, Dean?' he asked.

'Me.'

Fitz frowned. It wasn't the response he'd expected. He made an identical shape with his own fingers. 'What am I doing, Dean?'

'Mirror.'

Aah, he thought. It explained so much. If the world is a terrible place, don't look at it. Look at yourself instead. You may still see terrible things, but at least they'll be familiar.

'Tell me,' he said. He kept his voice low, non-judgemental. Scare Dean now and he'd be off like a frightened deer.

'Crying.' Dean's mouth worked. 'Mum gone away. Kids pushing. Kicking. Calling names.' He was almost shaking. 'Don't like fighting.'

It was hard for him, having to talk about it when he'd probably never spoken about it before. But letting him retreat from it would do him no good: you cannot vanquish demons by running from them. And in any case, Fitz needed to know – to know for sure, not just by his instincts – that Dean hadn't killed Joanne Barnes. Because if he hadn't, the killer was still out there somewhere. Most likely sitting in Kenneth Trant's house.

'School bell rings, you stay behind,' Fitz said, building a fantasy for Dean to live in.

'Yes.' The lad's face had a dreamy, almost hypnotised look to it.

'Hide under the desk until the caretaker kicks you out.'

'Dark,' Dean said. 'Cold.'

Slowly, Fitz lowered his hands. 'They'll still be waiting.'

'Run through the fields, through the bushes.'

'Clothes torn. Muddy.' They were colluding now, building up a picture of a time that was no time, but all times from Dean's past, not a specific instant but a sample of all the horrible times he had had. 'No-one to notice – to ask after you –' Of course not. He would have grown up in a home. He would have received expert affection from committed carers far too professional to let themselves get involved with their charges.

'Cold in bed,' Dean said. He was seeing a nightmare.

'Keep your clothes on.' Dean nodded. 'What did they call you?'

'The Smell.'

'Every time you walk in the classroom – "What's that

177

terrible smell?" "Can we open the windows please, Miss?" '
Oh yes, Fitz thought. Schooldays. Best days of your life.
Like hell. If the teachers didn't get you, the other kids
would. 'Bring in cans of air freshener, spray you.' Dean
nodded, almost imperceptibly. He seemed to be in pain
beyond words. Fitz continued, 'But there was one teacher
who looked after you – treated you right –'

Dean grinned, suddenly as happy as he had been hurting
before. 'Miss Morgan.'

'What did she teach?'

'Art.' He almost whispered the word, like it was too
important to say out loud.

'You were good at drawing.' It wasn't a question.

'Drawing. Copying.'

Fitz heard a sharp intake of breath from behind him that
could only have come from Panhandle.

'Like that writing on your walls.'

'Yes. Copied. Copied Joanne. And me.' His face was
haunted. Not unhappy. As if he were remembering the only
time in his life when he had been happy.

Of course, Fitz thought. He'd copied himself – that had
been the blocked-in man-shape in the centre of the wall; and
all around it a distorted version of the graffiti from Joanne's
body.

Dean had brought them together the only way he could.

Norma Trant had married an idiot. She had always suspected
it, and now she was sure of it. She watched him pace up and
down Kenneth's conservatory, growing closer and closer to
panic. It was embarrassing, especially with Virginia watching. Any minute now, Kenneth would arrive. She only
hoped Michael would have pulled himself together by then.

'He'd covered the wall of his flat with writing like on
Joanne!' he said. He waved his hands around like some
ludicrous puppet. 'Kenneth's equations – all that! That's
why they arrested him –' For God's sake, Norma thought. It
was almost as if he were blaming Kenneth for what had

happened – for writing on Joanne like that. True, she didn't quite understand it, but she was sure that whatever Kenneth's reasons were, they were good ones. She was also sure that a man as weak as her husband had no place criticising someone as powerful as Kenneth. 'They'll break him down,' Michael said. He'd reached the end of the conservatory, and he turned, making this awful floppy fringe bounce. 'They'll get it out of him –'

Kenneth came out of the living room. 'They'll get what out of him?' he demanded. His presence seemed to fill the conservatory. Norma felt herself filled with the conviction that they would be safe. Kenneth would think what they should do, and the police wouldn't be able to touch them.

He'd put it down to God's will, but Norma knew better. It would simply be down to the fact that Kenneth was a superior type of man, far more intelligent than anyone you would find in the police force.

Michael, on the other hand, was still whimpering and snivelling like a beaten puppy. 'They know he didn't dream all that up himself. The psychologist – he said it was the work of a classically tutored mind, a clever brain –' his voice rose to a squeak. He put his hand to his face. He was actually crying. Norma felt her mouth curl in disgust, and for once she didn't bother to hide it.

'Oh Kenneth –' Virginia said. At least she had reason to panic. If it hadn't been for her – for her hysteria when she'd been confronted with the evidence of what Kenneth had been up to with that little minx – all of this could have been avoided.

It should have been otherwise. It should have gone the way Norma had planned it when she had taken the photographs: Virginia outraged, Kenneth distraught and looking for comfort – and finding it in Norma's arms.

'They'll be on to us,' Michael said to Kenneth. 'They'll be coming for us next –'

'Michael!' Norma snapped. 'Sit down!'

Michael sank into the chair next to her, obedient as a

child. Kenneth would never simply do as I told him, she thought contemptuously.

'Is there any chance that you could talk to Dean?' she asked. She glanced at Kenneth, hoping he would realise that she, at least, was still thinking. 'He trusts you. If you could get to talk to him, you might be able –'

'You mean go to the police station?' Michael said. He sounded terrified.

'Yes,' Norma said. They could say he was the closest thing Dean had to next of kin –

'No,' Kenneth snapped.

Norma frowned, disappointed. She had desperately hoped that Kenneth would be impressed with her idea.

'But –' Virginia murmured. 'What if . . . what if he tells them about Joanne?'

Kenneth turned to her, all solicitous. 'What can he tell them? He saw nothing.' His voice was gentle. In that moment, Norma remembered all over again that she hated Virginia in equal measure to her love. She was weak, she wasn't bright, and Kenneth forgave her for it. He loved her for it, not despite it. In comparison, all Norma could hope for was his respect – and that was a very cold thing indeed.

'Virginia,' Kenneth went on, 'you heard me tell the police that the last time I saw Joanne was at the prayer meeting on Sunday night.'

'Yes . . .' Virginia said. She sounded panicky.

'When did you last see her?'

'When we all –'

Norma sighed. Virginia was stupid, stupid.

Kenneth stared at her. 'Think, Virginia. When did you last see Joanne.'

'At the last prayer meeting.' She sounded doubtful.

Kenneth turned. 'Norma?'

'At the last prayer meeting,' Norma said promptly. If respect was the best she could have, she would settle for that.

'Michael?'

It was hopeless. Michael was still panicking. 'They won't believe it, they'll –'

'When did you last see Joanne?' Kenneth thundered.

'At – the prayer meeting . . .' Michael muttered reluctantly.

'That's all we have to say. What matters is that we all say it. Then we're safe.' That was clear enough to Norma. She only wished that she could be sure Virginia and Michael were as certain of it. She listened to Kenneth, longing to take him in her arms and rub the tension out of his shoulders. Such a responsibility, saving all of them, when Michael and Virginia were so weak. 'Dean is deranged,' Kenneth went on. 'He should have been put away years ago. You think they'll take his word against ours?' Well, that was true enough, she thought. She'd been against Michael taking him on from the start: and if they all said it loud enough, it would become the truth. 'The boy is guilty. He'll have to pay the price for his sin.' Doubt flickered across Norma's mind just for the merest instant. Kenneth couldn't really believe that, could he? He couldn't somehow have forgotten that strange moment in the basement, when they had prayed for Joanne's soul while giving her the gin and pills, could he?

It was a ridiculous idea, and Norma pushed it away from her as soon as she had thought it.

Kenneth sat down. 'Let us pray,' he said. He took one of Virginia's hands, and Norma took the other. She wished she was sitting next to him. It would be a comfort to feel the strength of his hand in this hard time. Instead, she had to make do with Virginia. Michael took her other hand reluctantly. His was cold and clammy.

Norma shut her eyes. But she didn't pray. There didn't seem much point.

Mr Fitz made Dean put his hands up in the mirror sign. No-one else had ever done that. Most people didn't like it when Dean did his sign.

'What can you see?' Mr Fitz asked.

'Man on fire.'

'What else?'

No time to think. Answer the question or Mr Fitz might be angry. 'Woman bleeding.' Mum. A man. A man's fist. Daddy?

'What else?'

'Flying glass.' Going back from school. A bottle slamming into a tree trunk.

'What else?'

'Postman Pat.' Warm. Cosy. A lady's lap.

'What else?'

'Flowers.' A stone cross.

'What else?'

'Space.' The final frontier. These are the voyages –

'What else?'

'Baby crying.' I'm crying. No-one comes.

'What else?'

'Joanne.' Joanne in the dark, with the sheet wrapped round her.

No-one said anything for a long time. Dean wondered if Mr Fitz wanted him to say something. But his head was full of Joanne, and things he didn't want to talk about.

'Where is she?' Mr Fitz said at last.

In heaven, Dean thought. 'Through the mirror,' he said. We see through a glass darkly, then face to face.

'Describe her,' Mr Fitz said.

Crying in the dark with the sheet wrapped round her and her skin marked all over, and her eyes crying and Dean wanted to touch her, but she didn't want him to touch her. He hadn't touched her. He wanted to, but he hadn't. It was like he'd forgotten that part, but he remembered it now. But if he told them, they would be angry. Mr Fitz would. Miss Jane would. 'All flesh is grass,' he said instead. It meant she was dead, was gone to Jesus, through the mirror.

Mr Fitz looked disappointed. Dean liked Mr Fitz. He didn't shout, or make Dean put his hands down. He'd known about Miss Morgan. Dean wanted to please Mr Fitz, but not enough to say about Joanne in the dark.

'Did you give her tablets, Dean?'

'No,' Dean said. They would be angry now. He had lied when the others had asked him. He had said yes, because he thought they might let him go home.

'Did you give her drink?'

'No.' He could hardly look at them. He had lied. He was bad.

'Why did you confess?'

He didn't really know. 'They said.' They'd said it would make him feel better, but it hadn't.

Miss Jane came forward then. She was ever so pretty, but not as pretty as Joanne had been, and she had reddish hair instead of bright shining gold.

'Dean,' she said. 'You've made a statement that you helped Joanne to die. Is that true?'

She sounded kind. She didn't sound as if she would get angry if he told her he lied before. He stared at her. Then he looked away. 'No,' he muttered.

'You wouldn't do that?'

'No!' He was nearly shouting, but he wasn't supposed to shout. Shouting was wrong. He tried to explain. 'I –' There was a word. He knew the word, but he couldn't say it. 'L –' he tried. His mouth felt frozen, and his throat had gone all tight. He could barely breathe.

'Why can't you say it, that word?' Mr Fitz said. He sounded sort of sad. 'Have you never said it to anyone? Has no-one ever said it back to you?'

Dean stared at Mr Fitz. Say the word. That word? It was for other people, not for him. He felt his heart hammering at his ribs. He shook his head.

'It's just a word Dean.' Mr Fitz was almost laughing, like that word was nothing at all. 'Say it.' He was smiling, smiling at Dean.

Dean looked away. He wanted to be good. He wanted to please Mr Fitz, because Mr Fitz had been kind to him, and because then maybe he could go home. But how could he say that. If he said that, it would be true. He tried to say the words, but he couldn't make his teeth part to let them through. What came out was somewhere between a moan and a sigh.

'Joanne?'

'Love her,' Dean managed at last. He had thought something terrible would happen if he said it; but all it meant was that Mr Fitz seemed pleased with him. 'Love her,' he said again. 'I love her.'

TWENTY-NINE

They had taken Dean back to the little room again. He stared at the door.

'I love her,' he said. It was like a blossom of fire burning in his brain, in his gut. 'I love her I love her I love her,' he said to the walls.

But no-one answered. And he remembered now. Joanne was with Jesus. She was beyond the mirror. He had wanted to touch her, when he should have said the words Mr Fitz had set free in him.

And now it was too late. She couldn't answer him. She couldn't smile at him, or come to him.

'I love you,' Dean said again. He wanted to go to her. To be with her. In heaven.

Wise wasn't so much thick by nature as a bloody-minded moron, Fitz decided. Wise, Bilborough, Beck: they were all the same – more concerned with their clear-up rate and giving each other a good old boy pat on the back than anything so irrelevant as truth or natural justice.

Well, Fitz might have fallen for that once, but he wasn't going to make it twice. He slammed his hand down on Wise's desk.

'Stefan Siszko spent sixteen years of his life banged up for a crime he couldn't possibly have committed – looks odd, sounds odd: he must be the killer,' he said. He was having a hard time not shouting, but he knew from the washed-out over-the-edge look of Wise that if he started ranting now he'd lose whatever chance he had of pulling Dean Saunders back from the edge of disaster. He pushed his face closer to Wise's. 'And do you know what finally sent him down?' He raised an eyebrow, gave Wise time to remember that glorious episode in the history of British policing. 'A hastily sought and eagerly accepted confession that he only made because he was confused and frightened and just wanted to go home to his mammy.'

Wise leaned back in his seat, hands clasped at the back of his neck. He'd taken his tie off, and his collar was undone. What he wanted was to go home, Fitz was sure. So Fitz had to make him realise that the quickest way to make that happen was to co-operate. 'Dean's confession was –'

'– was got under pressure.' The hell with not shouting. The hell with everything except making sure he got his way. He was the good guy this time, after all. 'You can't afford to make a mistake on this one –'

Too far. Wise had had enough. 'Are you infallible?'

Well, so had Fitz. He rolled his eyes to heaven and grinned entirely without humour. 'Yes. The other guy's an impostor.' Wise glared at him. Fitz was losing him, and he knew it. He took a deep breath and said more quietly, 'All I ask is that you talk to him, with me, for five minutes. Or just listen.'

Wise took his glasses off. He rubbed the bridge of his nose. 'All right, Fitz,' he said. 'But you'd better make this good.'

Good? Fitz thought. I'll make it the best goddamned performance of my career.

He followed Wise out the door and down to the holding cells. They didn't speak. Fitz knew that he was right on the line with Wise. Anything he said might push the man over.

'Open cell three, please,' Wise said as they passed the Duty Sergeant. He didn't wait for a response. They went through the security door into the holding cell corridor. 'Ten minutes, no more, all right, Fitz?' Wise said.

Ten minutes? Fitz grinned. It was twice what he'd asked for, three times what he'd need.

They approached the green metal doors of the holding

cells, each with its closed hatch. The place had that smell of cheap disinfectant over urine that Fitz loathed: nothing you could do about it, he supposed. After a while it must seep into the tiles and the lino.

Wise got to Dean's cell first. He flipped down the hatch and peered through it. 'Jesus!' he cried.

Fitz couldn't see what the fuss was about.

'Key!' Wise screamed. He turned away from the door. 'Key! Key!' he shouted again.

Fitz peered through the hatch.

Dean had hanged himself.

His body dangled unmoving in the harsh light of the cell.

'My God,' Fitz murmured.

Up at the duty desk, all hell began to break loose.

THIRTY

Fitz's head felt fit to explode. He stared at himself in the bathroom mirror. Barf-room, he thought. Never had a place been more aptly named.

He'd got through three-quarters of a bottle of Scotch before he'd passed out on the sofa. The nightmares he'd had – Dean Saunders's dangling body fading and reforming as Timothy Lang's younger one, hanging in the woods where he'd been found; Dean's face, transforming into Nigel Cassidy's, bullied into confessing then retracting but refusing to make the retraction official: and binding them all together, Joanne Barnes lying on the mortuary slab, her body clothed only in the symbols of science, begging him with her eyes and her silence and her tormented ravings to find the man who'd harmed her.

All in all, Fitz thought, it would be a good morning for a hair of the dog. He glanced at his watch. Morning? It was closer to mid-day. Well, whatever time it was, he had to go in and face Wise, and make sure the man wasn't going to give in to Jimmy Beck's idiot blatherings and close the case. So, he made do with some noxious chemical crap that was supposed to deal with his headache.

After that, he headed downstairs to make some coffee; but as he went to the stairs, he passed Mark's room. The door was standing open. The curtains were drawn and sunlight was streaming into the room, but Mark was sprawled on his bed asleep, only half covered by his duvet. For reasons he didn't bother to fathom, Fitz went in. Get the lad some coffee: it would make a change.

But Mark was soundo, with his white limbs and long

black hair splayed across the bed. Underestimated you, that's what I've done. He glanced around Mark's bedroom. It was the cleanest, tidiest room in the house. And hadn't Mark been the one – the only one – to understand the graffiti on Joanne's body. He'd given Fitz the key to the whole case.

If he'd died . . . like Joanne had died, like Dean had died, and Timothy Lang too. It gripped Fitz's heart even to think of the idea. You don't really hate me, do you, son? Fitz wondered. In a fit of unexpected tenderness he twitched the quilt back over Mark's exposed shoulders.

He wandered back out of the bedroom and downstairs, pondering the fact that he'd never had such a rush of feeling towards Mark while the lad was awake. Not since he'd been able to talk, anyway.

So Fitz had got it wrong again, Jimmy Beck thought. They were going to shut the case on Joanne Barnes regardless of what the obnoxious bastard thought: she'd got herself knocked up by that perverted moron Saunders, and topped herself trying to get rid of the brat. All that was left was the paperwork.

Plain as the nose on anyone's face except Fitz's.

And here he came now, marching in like he owned the joint when all he ever really did was cause trouble. He went straight to the boss's door, with never so much as a good morning for Beck.

Well sod you, Beck thought. I've got better things to do with my time.

Maybe Fitz caught his thought. He turned round, stumped across the room and loomed over Beck. Give him his due, he looked like death only slightly warmed over. By the looks of him he'd killed a bottle or two thinking about Saunders. Not that he needed an excuse, by all accounts.

'You think I'm to blame for Dean's death?' His tone was surprisingly mild. Must be the lack of sleep, Beck thought.

Well, lying about it wouldn't make things any better. You

took a kid like Saunders, locked him up, made him face things better left hidden – terrible things, twisted things – you dragged all that out, kicking and screaming into the daylight – of course there were going to be consequences. But it was never the likes of the *Doctor* Fitzgeralds of this world that had to pay them. 'Yeah,' Beck said.

'I'm not,' Fitz answered. Oh sure, you can tell yourself that, Beck thought: shout it as loud as you like and it still won't be true. But Fitz was going on, and now there was an edge of bitter triumph in his voice. 'But if I were, I'd expect a bit of sympathy from you, Jimmy. You know exactly how it feels.'

Now what the hell did – Beck suddenly couldn't breathe. His collar was tightening round his throat, and he felt himself flushing.

Bilborough. He had to mean Bilborough. One simple mistake Beck had made. A mistake anyone could have made. He'd been lied to by Albie Kinsella and believed him. Albie Kinsella the murderer. Beck had let him go, out of compassion because he believed the man when he lied that he had cancer. And Albie Kinsella had gone on to murder David Bilborough. Beck's best friend. The finest copper he'd ever known.

'You bastard,' he muttered at Fitz's retreating back. 'You fucking bastard.'

He stumbled out of the incident room towards the toilets. He banged past someone but didn't stop to apologise.

He had nothing to apologise for. Nothing.

Nothing.

Wise was still failing to live up to his name. Fitz realised it as soon as he walked into the office. Panhandle was already there. By the look of it, Wise had already had a go at her – she was standing in front of the desk like a naughty schoolgirl. Now there was a thought. Down boy, Fitz told himself. He couldn't let himself get distracted now.

Wise walked past him and shut the door. As he went by he

said, 'You know what I'm going to say, but I am going to say it anyway.'

Fitz grinned at Panhandle, and slid his hand into hers. She shook him off impatiently, but she was smiling.

Wise came back to the desk. 'Right?' he said. He glared at them.

'Right,' Fitz said. Maybe he should volunteer to go and get the tawse now.

'If you hadn't poked your nose in,' Wise said. 'That lad would still be alive. Joanne's death would be solved. Everything would have been boxed off.'

'Boxed off,' Fitz repeated. It was the worst euphemism for a miscarriage of justice he'd ever heard.

Panhandle glanced from Wise to Fitz, then backed off a step or two. It was the first time Fitz had ever seen her look scared.

'Boxed off,' Wise said firmly, like he'd just invented the phrase. 'Dean killed himself. Joanne died trying to terminate a pregnancy. Case closed.'

Case closed. Clear-up rate one, justice nil. Fitz had tried being reasonable. He'd tried it with Bilborough, and it had ended up with Cassidy banged up. He'd tried it last night with Wise and it had taken so long Dean had managed to kill himself in the meantime.

Well, Fitz had had it with being reasonable. 'Dean killed himself because Joanne was murdered.' He didn't bother to stop himself from shouting. Wise sat down and started leafing through some documents. Bloody paper pusher. 'There's more reason than ever for keeping the case open.' No response. Fitz turned to Panhandle. 'Pontius bloody Pilate had more sense of social respons–'

Wise looked up. He was ready to explode.

'Fitz –' Panhandle cut in before either of them could speak.

Wise went back to his papers.

Fitz sighed. Time to change the subject. 'I haven't been paid yet.'

'I need an invoice.' It was as good as a dismissal.

'Any chance of a sub?' He had to try, if only to prove they couldn't quite walk all over them. Besides, he was down to his last fiver. Again.

'No chance.'

Wise would have been at home with the tawse, Fitz thought. He scowled and headed for the door. Panhandle followed him.

Beck's snotty little sidekick, Harriman, was sitting on a desk just outside. He grinned as he saw Fitz coming out.

Fitz turned back to Wise. 'You're wrong. Joanne was murdered and I'll prove it.'

Now all he had to do was work out how.

In the toilets, Beck splashed water on his face from one of the sinks in the central block. Got to calm down, he told himself. Got to think. Got to breathe.

But he couldn't think, couldn't breathe.

'You all right?' someone said.

Beck looked up. A uniformed constable was staring at him. What was his name, now? Christ, you'd think it would be easy enough to remember. There were only half a dozen black coppers in the station, tops – Skelton, that was it.

'Are you all right?' Skelton said. There was a Brummie twang to his voice.

Beck splashed more water onto his face before he answered. 'You haven't seen me like this.' he said. 'Right?' Bastard would agree if he knew what was good for him.

'Right.'

Beck kept throwing water on his face, wishing the plod would go away, but Skelton just kept staring.

'What's up,' Skelton said after a bit.

Fuck *off*, Beck thought. But he said, 'Bilborough was a mate of mine. It gets to me now and again.'

He'd expected sympathy, maybe for Skelton to say that he missed Bilborough too. Everyone did. But what he said was, 'No-one's blaming you.'

The words were like a rabbit punch. His head came up. There was a pressure in his chest so he could hardly breathe.

Blaming me, he thought. Blaming me . . . 'Why should they?' he said. And then it occurred to him: Skelton knew. They must all know. He walked round the sinks to Skelton. 'What do you know?' he said. He got up close to Skelton, let the bloke stare him in the eyes. 'What have you heard?' His voice was low. He knew it was dangerous.

'Kinsella gave you a load of bullshit. You let him go. He killed Bilborough.'

Canteen gossip, Beck thought. It's just canteen gossip to him, good for a bit of a laugh. A bit of a laugh at my expense. And someone had started it.

That bastard Fitz. And Penhaligon, the bitch.

Well, he'd show them. He'd show them.

He didn't know what his face must look like, but whatever his expression, Skelton was surely terrified of it.

Well let him be. Let them all fucking be.

He had to do something. He couldn't breathe. He wanted to hit something. Fitz maybe. Penhaligon. He saw his fist coming down on a face – his, hers, he didn't care – saw the blood and jelly spurting out of a popped eye ball, heard bone crunch as he brought his hand down again.

He realised he was snarling. Skelton was really worried now.

Beck turned away. He braced himself between the sinks and the wall, consumed by the need to do damage, to hurt something if not someone. He booted open the door. It slammed against the wall and bounced, filling the room with the sound of metal on plaster.

'No-one's blaming you –' Skelton said.

'Piss off,' Beck screamed, and realised he was crying.

He went into the cubicle and waited for Skelton to go. What would he tell his cronies? Beck was snivelling like a baby in the bogs? Something like that. Well let him. Let him.

193

When he was sure Skelton had gone, he went out and cleaned himself up. He didn't hold with all this New Man crap, but sometimes it did no harm to let it out.

He'd kill any man who said different.

But anyway, it was time to put it behind him and get back to work.

Then, in the hall, he saw Fitz and Penhaligon coming towards him. They were grinning at each other like schoolkids, not like people who'd had a richly deserved roasting from the boss.

Well, if Wise couldn't wipe the grins off their faces, he would. There wasn't anyone else who could have been spreading stinking lies about him, now was there?

He went straight up to them. 'So, you told everyone.' No point making a meal of it.

'Told them what?' Fitz said, like he really didn't know. Lying devious *scum*.

'Bilborough's death was down to me.' Even saying it made the blood thunder in his ears.

'I didn't.' Yeah, sunshine, Beck thought, and there are fairies at the bottom of your garden. 'I didn't.' He had the bloody nerve to sound offended.

Well all right then, they could play it that way if they wanted. He turned to Penhaligon. 'Then it was you.'

'Wrong,' she said, in that prissy-missy schoolmarm tone of voice she had.

Ball-breaking bitch, he thought. You'll get yours one day, I swear. I swear. 'You're lying.' He hissed the words out like a stream of venom.

She looked at him like he was something she'd found dead in the road. After what she'd done, she dared look at him like that. And then she walked off before he could tell her what he thought about it.

But not Fitz. Oh no, he had to have his say. 'Look, if you want to talk to somebody about this –'

'Ahh, Christ,' Beck said. He would as soon have talked to Satan himself.

THIRTY-ONE

She was a fool and she knew it, Penhaligon thought. That was her trouble.

She slid her card into the cash machine and punched in her PIN number. Fitz had protested all the way to the bank, but she'd ignored him. It had rained earlier. She pushed a damp-flattened curl back off her face and pretended to reconsider what she was about to do.

Well, he had started to pay her back for the holiday. And it quite suited her to have him in her debt.

'This isn't necessary, you know,' Fitz started again. 'I was just winding Wise up.' Penhaligon ignored him. He put on a martyred voice. 'I'll manage, always have and always will do. I do not need charity.' Yeah, yeah, yeah, Penhaligon thought. She beeped her way through the machine's instructions. 'I've just got to get on with life, pay the bills –' his voice turned suddenly serious. Penhaligon swivelled round to face him ' -and keep the guilt monster locked up in the cellar until I'm strong enough to grapple with it.'

It was the nearest thing to an admission of weakness as she had ever heard from Fitz. He was so damn good at analysing others – and, she had to admit, at helping them – that sometimes it took her breath away. Yet he understood so little about himself that sometimes he made her want to scream. 'And when will that be?' she asked. 'How many beasts are locked up down there?' she slapped him lightly on his ample belly. 'How long before they break down the door and tear you apart?'

The machine churred and spat the money out. She turned to get it as he said, 'No that's me talking. I'm the doctor,

195

you're the policewoman.' He sounded mildly pissed off, but it was his best defence and anyway, she knew he was faking. 'Do you see me directing traffic? No. You know why?' He didn't give her a chance to answer. 'That's not my speciality. Don't try talking nuts to a monkey.'

'Then stop talking shit to a Panhandle,' Penhaligon said. She rarely used the nickname he'd given her – she didn't like to encourage him. He stared glumly at his toes. Maybe, she decided, this was all a bit more serious than she'd thought. 'I'm your friend aren't I?' she said. There had been a time, a while back, when that had been in doubt. When he'd failed to turn up for their holiday, she'd been so spitting mad at him she'd sworn never to get close to him again. But then Bilborough had died, and it had put a lot of things in perspective. She made a despairing little sighing noise. Sometimes you just had to hang on to what you had, because it was the best you could have. 'Believe me, charity doesn't come into it,' she said. She waved the wad of notes at him. 'Two hundred and fifty enough?' He sighed, but didn't take it. She pushed it at him. 'You can give it back when our lot pay you.'

Finally, he took it. 'Thanks,' he muttered. 'Look, I know it's a bit early, but –'

She grinned. 'I know. I could do with a drink as well.'

She slipped her arm through his, and together they wandered off through the rain-slicked streets. It was almost worth getting bollocked by Wise for this, she thought. But only almost.

Virginia laid a reassuring hand on Michael's shoulder. All four of them were in Michael and Norma's living room, trying to work out what to do for the best.

Virginia was terrified. Every time the doorbell rang, the thought flashed through her mind that it was the police, or that dreadful psychologist fellow, Fitzgerald, come to ask more horrible questions – or even to arrest them. And when she tried to sleep she saw Joanne, lying in the cellar with those peculiar marks that Kenneth had made on her – she hadn't asked him about the marks, there were some things it was better not to know – while the candlelight made her seem almost ghostly.

All in all, Virginia thought she was probably in a pretty bad way, though the good Lord knew she was trying to disguise it for Kenneth's sake. But she wasn't as badly off as Michael. The poor man was almost in tears: a terrible thing, a man crying.

'I keep seeing him there,' he said. He was sitting next to Virginia, on the white Chesterfield she had helped Norma to choose. Kenneth, who was leaning on the false mantelpiece, glared at him. 'In that cell,' Michael said. His voice was close to breaking. 'Alone. What he must have felt.'

'Michael, what's done is done,' Norma said. Her voice was firm. Virginia envied Norma her courage and certainty, and the faith that bred it. She only wished that she could share it.

But she did feel sorry for Michael. It did seem he was failing the terrible test God had set for them.

'I should never have involved him,' Michael said. At least, Virginia thought, he wasn't trying to make them responsible for his folly.

But when she looked at his face, and saw he was punishing himself, her heart went out to him. All of this trouble – all of it – went back to that little slut Joanna. If she hadn't lied and deceived and trapped Kenneth, none of this would have happened. 'You mustn't blame yourself,' she said. 'It isn't your fault –'

'Oh but it is,' Kenneth said. He turned to face them. His voice was low and calm, but it was obvious that he was furious. 'If Michael had done what he was supposed to do, the boy would never have been arrested and we wouldn't be in this mess.' He turned away, so that he was staring out of the window, and gnawed gently on the knuckle of his thumb.

'Kenneth's right, Michael,' Norma said. She was a good

friend, Virginia thought – always ready to support Kenneth in his work. Sometimes she felt that Norma and Kenneth held them all together, while she and Michael dragged along, bringing them down.

They would fail. She could see it now. Between them, her and Michael, they would do something wrong, say the wrong thing to the police, and fail the terrible test God had set them. Fail Norma. Fail Kenneth.

All shall be well, and all shall be well and all things shall be well, she said to try and calm herself down. All things shall be well: that knowledge had done for Julian of Norwich in the fourteenth century. It would do for Virginia now – all she had to remember was to do exactly as Kenneth told her.

And it was true, because Kenneth was turning to them. 'However, as he died in police custody, my instinct tells me they'll be eager to close the case.'

He seemed so certain that Virginia could not be less so. 'Oh Kenneth,' she said. 'Do you think so?'

'I'm sure of it,' he said, turning to them again. 'I just wish I could be as sure of Doctor Fitzgerald.' He stepped forward, to a position where he commanded all their attention. 'Remember what we agreed,' he said. 'We speak as a group, with one voice.' Oh, yes, Kenneth, Virginia thought. She looked at the others. They seemed stronger and more united already. 'As long as we are a group we are invulnerable.'

Yes, Virginia thought: Kenneth made it all so simple. With his help and encouragement, they would stand together, and neither the police nor Doctor Fitzgerald would break them down.

They were being really bad, Penhaligon thought: sagging off in the middle of the day first for a long pub lunch and now to shop.

Well, to hell with it. What Wise didn't know couldn't make him angry. She'd think of something to cover the time. After all, she hadn't been pulled off the Barnes case yet. Not officially.

For now, she was quite happy wandering around Sainsbury's with Fitz, helping him fill his larder with her money: a lot of tinned and frozen stuff, and no fresh fruit or veg at all. Now he was pushing the trolley slowly along the wine shelves. Somehow it didn't surprise her.

'I haven't done this in ages,' she said. 'Not with someone.' It was true. The last time would have been with Peter, long before he'd moved out – and he'd left because of the holiday she'd planned with Fitz. More or less.

'Neither have I,' Fitz said, seeming to pay more attention to the French reds than what he was saying.

Penhaligon couldn't resist it. 'Not with Judith?' she said as she ambled along beside him, relishing his bulk and the feeling of togetherness.

'Can't remember the last time,' he said. They were in the Spanish wines now, the whites. 'We always used to. Then some time we just stopped.' He brought the trolley to a halt and took a bottle off the shelf. 'Eighty-five,' he said. For a second she was startled – that was a bloody long time for a marriage to be in decline. 'The Rioja,' he explained, but by that time she'd realised he was looking at the label on the bottle. He put the wine in the trolley. 'I think it's over. Me and Judith.' He straightened up and they moved on. Penhaligon thrust her hands into the pockets of her jacket. She had to, to keep from punching the air. 'Really, this time,' he said. 'Over.'

He stopped to choose another bottle of wine.

Penhaligon wandered on down the aisle. Grinning.

THIRTY-TWO

Fitz led the way up the path to his house. Panhandle followed, picking her way carefully through the rubbish – bottles, take-away wrappers, tins – strewn all over the once pristine lawn. The goddamn dustbinmen hadn't been to collect the rubbish, and a cat must have got into the bags.

Of course, it could have happened days ago. Fitz had had other things on his mind.

Never mind, they were on the porch now. He unlocked the door, but before he could open it, Panhandle said, 'Are you sure this is all right?'

Fitz stuck his fingers in the letterbox. 'A big, wide, generous letterbox.' He grinned. So did she. 'I rest my case.'

They went in. There was an awful smell of cigarettes and stale booze. Fitz toed an empty beer can into the corner of the hallway, hoping Panhandle wouldn't notice. She did. He grinned. Well, what had she expected?

In the kitchen, he started unpacking the carrier bags on to the kitchen table. Panhandle twisted round. Fitz felt vaguely uneasy, suddenly. Once, this bright yellow room had been the warm heart of the home he had made with Judith. It had never felt the same since she left – since the marriage had fallen into trouble, really. Having Panhandle there should have felt like a betrayal; and yet, oddly, he felt more at ease now than he had at any time since Judith moved out.

'I think I should go, don't you?' Panhandle said. She seemed uncomfortable.

For one awful instant, Fitz saw the kitchen through her eyes – the dishes stacked to a precarious height in the bowl, the overflowing rubbish bin, the piles of take-away cartons on the worktop.

Of course she could go. Anyone sane would go. If she went, he didn't think he could take another night of Jack Daniels and staring at the four walls of the living room, even with Ray Charles for company.

'No,' he said, and started putting things away. Soda and white wine in the fridge, pizza in the microwave. How long? Oh to hell with it. He twisted the dial to five minutes and hoped for the best.

'There's so much going on for you, Fitz,' she said. Christ, he thought. A classic – no, a clichéd – brush-off line. He'd thought better of her, he really had. Even as he thought it she was continuing, 'I'm not sure I –'

'I need you,' he said, over the top of her words. He had his back to her. Lucky. He couldn't have said it if she could have seen his face.

He could feel her staring at him. After a long moment – the longest moment – she said, 'I'll back you, Fitz; with Jimmy, with Wise, with anyone.'

He couldn't see her face, either. Was she deliberately misunderstanding?

Reluctantly, he turned round. 'Not that way,' he said.

'How?' She sounded vaguely impatient. She wasn't usually so slow . . . so she wanted him to say it.

And he couldn't. Wouldn't. Probably shouldn't. 'You know,' he said.

'I don't.' He'd heard her lie to suspects in exactly the same tone, when she knew it would help get information out of them.

He had a very good goddamn idea why, too – and he couldn't say he blamed her, not after what he'd done to her last time.

But he needed her. He didn't think he would hurt her again. He had to try. Sod it, he knew he'd do anything it took.

So it was time for dirty tricks. He said, 'Already anticipating failure, the retreat.' Panhandle started pacing up and down. She shook her head, and her mane of hair, redder than usual in the bright light of the kitchen, bounced. If she went now . . . if he lost her. . . . And yet he had to continue. 'Make me say everything, then you can abdicate yourself from any responsibility –'

'Please don't, Fitz.'

She was genuinely upset.

He had to make her understand why they were doing this to each other. If she understood, she might not need to go: if only she would stay long enough to listen. 'All right, I'll do it to me,' he said. He thought of the washing up in the sink, the beer can under the hall stand. 'I bring you into my home, having taken every precaution to ensure that it's as inhospitable as it could be.' He was well into it now, as if Panhandle were a whole lecture hall full of undergrads. 'What message am I sending there? I've given you every chance, every opportunity for an escape route – which means, of course, that then I can blame it all on you – "I tried. I tried. She led me along but couldn't stay the distance." ' He paused for breath, suddenly exhausted and a little sick with the trick he'd played on her: she'd have to have a heart of granite to go now. He had to be more honest than that if they were going to make it work: but he didn't have the energy for honesty, or for dealing with her. 'Look, I'm still covered in bruises from last time and the mistakes I made.' He couldn't face her, so he stared at a beer stain on the floor. Dammit, it sounded like a guilt trip, and now he couldn't even work out if that was what he'd intended. Well, there was one way to sort that out, and make sure that even if he was confused, she wasn't. He said, 'So just make my life easy and go away, will you?' He started to turn round, and saw that she was leaving. Shit, he thought. How could she think he'd meant it? 'I think I love you,' he muttered quickly.

She swung round to face him, fury etched on her face. He couldn't face her.

The microwave rescued him by pinging. Gratefully he turned his back on Panhandle and took the pizza out.

The damn plate was hot. He turned back and put it on the table. 'One nine-inch Margarita with anchovies,' he said, as if nothing unusual had happened.

'You bastard,' Panhandle screamed at him.

'What?' Fitz asked. Playing innocent seemed the only possible defence.

'You've got the cheek to say a thing like that.' Her cheeks flamed with fury.

He wondered if saying, 'Gee but you're beautiful when you're angry' in a fake American accent would earn him a slapped face.

He decided not to risk it. 'Nine-inch Margarita with anchovies?'

'I don't like anchovies!'

Shit, Fitz thought. I didn't even think to ask her.

THIRTY-THREE

Fitz poured Penhaligon another glass of wine. Her third. Or fourth. She wondered if he thought he needed to get her drunk.

He was wrong.

It was a terrible thing to fear sleep, Virginia thought. She had told Kenneth she was going to bed long ago, but when it came to it she couldn't bear the thought of lying alone in the dark, with Joanne's face staring at her every time she shut her eyes. Instead, she had switched on the bedside lamp, and now she sat up in bed reading the Holy Bible – where else would she find solace in these difficult times?

If only it could have been different. If only she had seen that Kenneth was drifting away from her – if only she had been good enough for him to love forever. She knew she must have failed him greatly for him to have turned to Joanne.

She would not make that mistake again.

Kenneth came in. The golden glow of the bedside lamp softened the tired lines of his face. He looked so worried. She knew he was trying to think of ways of protecting them all from the police.

Her heart went out to him. She had doubted him. There had been a moment, before . . . when she had confronted Joanne with the photographs, when she had really thought he had betrayed her.

She knew better now. His betrayal had only been of the body, not of the heart.

He came and sat on the edge of the bed next to her. He took her hand. His own was warm and strong. She wanted to tell him that it was all right, that whatever he'd done – whatever awful things he thought he'd done – she forgave him.

But when she opened her mouth to speak, what came out was, 'Kenneth, do you really think they might leave us alone now?'

'I'm sure they will. It'll soon be over, this whole nightmarish thing.' He put his free hand on top of hers. 'Darling, I'm sorry, I'm so deeply sorry. . . .' His voice trailed off. He wouldn't look at her. 'I was weak, and I fell. . . .' His pain was a terrible thing for her to see. She caressed his cheek, then moved her hand quickly to his mouth to stop him saying such terrible things. As if she blamed him, after all he'd been through!

He squeezed her hand, then moved it gently away from her face. 'I'm not worthy of you, Virginia,' he said, 'but I will never make that mistake again.'

'I know –' She was almost crying for his pain.

'I do love you. I love you so much. . . .' His voice trailed off as he turned her hand over and brought it up to his mouth. He kissed the delicate place on the inside of her wrist, just as he used to do when they were teenagers.

She reached for him. She had won him back. Now she must make sure she never lost him again.

Kissing Panhandle was everything Fitz had fantasized about. She tasted of wine and . . . strawberries, and her hair was unexpectedly wiry under his hands. She ran her tongue over his lips.

Much more of this, and he would have to move on.

His hands started to drift downwards.

He pulled away and took a long shuddering breath. Her eyes were sapphire in the soft light. His hand hovered, then rested on the delicate juncture of shoulder and neck.

'Are you sure?' he asked. He owed her that much.

'No.'

Before he had time to be disappointed, her hands swept under his jacket and pushed it off, then came forward and pulled him towards her.

And then there was no more time for talking.

Norma stared at the bedside clock. It was nearly one. Michael still hadn't come to bed.

She got up, threw on her bathrobe and went downstairs.

The light was on in the kitchen. Michael was sitting at the kitchen table. He had a mug of coffee clasped in his hands, but he was just staring at the wall.

For a second, Norma felt sorry for him. But then she remembered Kenneth's anger at him, and it sparked her own again.

She had married a fool. And he might yet destroy them all.

Penhaligon lay next to Fitz, nestled against his great bulk. His hand was inside her blouse, covering her breast. She slid her thigh up and over his leg.

'Are you sure?' she asked him.

'No,' he said, and kissed her again.

Kenneth lay unsleeping in the darkness. His back was to Virginia.

He loved her, he told himself, told God. He did love her. It was a failure of the flesh, not of the heart. He had wanted a sign: had told himself that if God were still on his side, he would be able to be a man with her. This one time.

But it was the same as it always was: a failure of the flesh, not the heart.

The same failure that had led him to Joanne . . . and others.

Dear Father, he thought, I have tried to serve you. Why hast thou forsaken me?

THIRTY-FOUR

Fitz sat on the edge of the spare bed, staring uneasily at the pictures of Joanne Barnes.

It was that or look at Panhandle, who was still asleep. He didn't dare. It would be too easy to romanticise that mane of coppery hair, those alabaster limbs . . . or to climb back into bed with her and forget the whole sordid world of police work.

And to forget that he still had a wife, a family, bills to pay.

Never mind anything Bilborough had said. If he hurt Panhandle again, he'd put *himself* in traction.

Sunlight shafted into the room. Birds sang. He hadn't felt so wonderful – so young – in years. You want to add a few more clichés to that list? he asked himself. Oh to hell with it. Just for this one morning, he'd had enough of cynicism. He felt good. He decided to revel in it.

He turned to stare at her, to marvel at the faint blue tracery of veins on her upturned wrist, the almost invisible frizz of sun-gilded curls around her temples. He leaned across to kiss her awake.

The door banged open. Mark stood there, coffee cup in one hand, paper in the other, and a look of outrage stamped across his face.

He flapped the paper helplessly at Panhandle, who pulled the duvet closer round herself and stared at something on the floor.

'We never had that chat, did we?' Fitz said. As jokes went, it was pretty feeble, but it was all he could think of.

Mark made a disgusted noise and left.

Panhandle sat up. Her flush went all the way down to where she clutched the duvet round her: Fitz would like to have speculated how much further it might go, but he knew he had to talk to Mark.

He found the lad in the bathroom. He was washing his hands, as if he thought the sight of what he'd just seen had tainted him.

'Look, I'm sorry,' Fitz said to his son's back, wishing he sounded more sincere; but all he really felt was embarrassed.

'Does Mum know?' He didn't bother to turn round, but in the mirror his face was flushed with anger.

'Not yet,' Fitz said. He hadn't even considered that. Christ, it wasn't as if he'd planned any of this. But he had to concede that Mark had a point. Yet the habit of argument died hard, and one good conversation about the state of the universe wasn't enough to kill it off. 'Your mother left me, Mark.'

Mark turned. The line of beads he'd woven into his long hair glittered in the sun. His face was alight with anger. 'She didn't leave, you drove her away. Because –' he paused, as if he were trying to work out what came next. Or gathering his courage. ''cos you're a dickhead.'

Fitz stared at his fingers. Thoughts of drunken nights and sober rows flashed through his mind. Thoughts of money lost on the horses, the dogs, cards. Thoughts of Judith's tears, and too-rare smiles. 'Yes, well that's a fair summary of the facts, probably.'

'I'm older than her,' Mark shouted. He still wasn't quite as tall as Fitz, though he'd turned nineteen in the spring.

Nothing like the moral outrage of near-children to make you feel old, Fitz thought. He pushed the door till it clicked shut. 'Hardly,' he said. He made a deliberate effort to lower his voice. 'Look, what did you expect me to do? Spend the rest of my life like Cliff bloody Richard?'

Mark snorted derisively and left the room. Fitz followed him, just in time to see Panhandle coming out of the bedroom. She was wearing the bamboo-patterned kimono

208

Fitz had bought for Judith two Christmases ago.

Mark glared at her 'That's my mother's,' he snapped, and pushed past to get to the stairs.

Panhandle went to Fitz and hugged him, but nothing could restore the feeling of wonder he'd woken up with.

Penhaligon walked into Anson Road with Fitz, feeling like she was fifteen again, and had just managed to bluff her way into an eighteen-rated movie.

She'd thought about asking Fitz to get out and walk the last block or two, but it seemed a bit silly. After all, she'd regularly picked him up on the way to work.

But that was before she'd found out about the mole on his bum, and traced the length of his appendix scar with her finger . . . she found herself grinning.

'I have to go and type up my report,' he said.

'Yeah,' she said. 'See you later.' She smiled up at him – God, he was *big* – and resisted the temptation to kiss him. Just as well, she thought, when she turned and saw Harriman and Beck watching her through the window of the duty room.

She went inside. Harriman whispered something to Beck, and they both sniggered. It hadn't been this bad since she'd first transferred to the Anson Road CID, and Beck had made her prove herself every day. At least then there had been Giggsy to calm him down. In fact, she thought, he'd been a lot worse since Giggs died. Maybe it was because he'd been killed by a woman . . . but she couldn't think such gloomy thoughts. Not on the morning after this particular night before.

She dumped her bag and jacket, thinking of the smoothness of Fitz's chest, the rolls of fat she found so unexpectedly arousing. 'Where are we keeping the pile of cuttings found in Dean's bed?' she asked.

'In the filing cabinet,' Beck said. Something in his voice let her know she'd said the wrong thing, but she couldn't figure out what it was.

To hell with it. She pulled out the folder she needed and started going through it.

'Only they were found in his wardrobe,' Beck said.

There was one particular drawing Fitz wanted: one that was actually a picture of a postman's van, when you looked at it up close, not any of the symbols that had been written on Joanne. She couldn't find it. 'Yeah,' she said belatedly. What the hell was that all about?

'You said "in his bed".'

She still couldn't find the drawing. 'No,' she said distractedly. 'No, I didn't.'

'Yes you did,' Beck said. He turned to Harriman. 'Didn't she?'

Harriman waved his coffee mug. ' "Dean's bed", you said.'

Penhaligon gave up on finding the drawing. She re-ran her words in her mind: *Where are we keeping the pile of cuttings found in Dean's bed?* Oh bloody hell, she thought at herself. You stupid cow –

There was only one defence now. She turned to Beck and Harriman. 'What are you trying to say?'

Beck took a long drag on his cigarette. 'You're doing the talking.'

Bastard, Penhaligon thought at him. She picked up the folder and held it in front of herself, like a shield, then went over to them. 'No,' she said. 'Come on lads. Spit it out.'

But she knew. She knew. They'd been waiting for this. Beck had, anyway.

He took another drag on his cigarette and watched the smoke wreathe the air before he replied. 'Who was on top?' he asked, as if it were a side-splitting joke.

I ought to ask him which time he means, Penhaligon thought. I ought to tell him to go fuck himself, since no-one else is ever likely to want to.

But the moment was past and the room was full of voices laughing at her.

What really hurt was that at least one of them was a woman's voice.

Fitz realised that Wise was still stinging from the argument over Dean Saunders, as soon as he walked into the office. Not that the DCI would see it like that: he'd think he'd given Fitz and Penhaligon a dressing down that they'd chosen to ignore.

Panhandle was already there. She looked pretty pissed off, and Fitz wondered if Wise had had another go at her. He felt an anachronistic rush of protectiveness towards her – found himself thinking 'Go and pick on someone your own size' at Wise. It was pretty Neanderthal: he'd screwed her, so he owned her, or at least had a duty to protect her.

Yes, well he knew what she'd say to that.

A nine-inch Margarita, with or without anchovies, wouldn't begin to make up for it.

So, instead of doing any of that – instead of taking her hand and giving it a quick squeeze, like he had yesterday – he handed Wise his invoice.

'That's my fees to date,' he said.

Wise glanced at it quickly. 'No problems there,' he said. Yes there bloody is, Fitz thought. It's not half as much as I'd like it to be. 'I expect you'd prefer cash,' Wise continued.

Sarcastic bastard, Fitz thought.

Wise turned and leaned on the desk to initial the invoice. Fitz caught Panhandle's eye, then jerked his head towards Wise.

'Fitz would like another week on Joanne Barnes,' she said to his back.

'No chance,' Wise said. He straightened up. 'She's with the Coroner tomorrow.'

'Well, give me until then.' Fitz realised, to his disgust, that he was almost pleading. There was something about Joanne's fragility and Dean's helplessness that had got under his skin. He knew it connected up with Mark, with the fact that because of this case they'd had a really good talk for the first time in ages. But it was to do with Panhandle too: he hadn't gone on holiday with her in the end, because he was scared that having screwed up the Tim Lang case, he'd also fail with her. Now that he'd finally begun with her, he didn't dare mess up the Joanne Barnes case – it might just rub off on the relationship.

Or something. He didn't have time to analyse it. All he knew was that he had to have time to talk to the Trants and break down the armour of pious bloody righteousness that surrounded them.

'Beck's winding it up, now.' Wise went and sat down. It was a dismissal, but neither Fitz nor Panhandle made a move towards the door.

They moved up to Wise's desk. 'Two people have died, boss,' Panhandle said. Fitz hoped Wise wouldn't realise that Panhandle was trying to butter him up by deferring to him; in fact, he doubted that she herself did. She continued, 'They both belonged to the same religious sect which includes Kenneth Trant who was Joanne's headmaster and Michael Trant who was Dean's boss.' Wise looked up. She'd caught his attention, at least. 'Fitz would like to interview all four Trants and I think we should agree to that.'

'You're asking me to gamble police time and money,' Wise said.

Yeah, Fitz thought. Let's play five-card stud with the judicial system: police time and money in the pot with tainted confessions the wild card and truth and justice only win with four aces.

See you and raise you four hundred quid.

He stuck his cigarette in his mouth, reached over and plucked his invoice off the desk. 'Double or quits I get a confession.' He tore the document in half and half again.

Wise took a long sip of tea. He put the mug down slowly, and said, 'OK. I'll give you till tomorrow.'

Double or quits, Fitz thought. 'And Penhaligon,' he said.

'Take Beck.' His manner had thawed. Maybe he thought he couldn't lose, or maybe he was impressed with the

212

importance Fitz was placing on this.

Bloody hell, Fitz thought. I might as well give him two aces and a queen. 'Beck's no use to me,' he said. 'Panhandle understands the way I work.' Wise still needed convincing. You had to give Wise that – he'd change his mind if you could prove something to him. The only trouble was, most times you had to bury him neck deep in it before he could see it at all. 'Beck's too old school, too Starsky and Hutch. He's only got one tune.' He was pleading again, but he didn't care. 'I can't do it without her,' he said, and thought, Jesus – what am I saying? What can't I do without her? But Wise hadn't noticed. He just stared at Fitz, completely unimpressed. One last chance, Fitz thought. 'I'll give you odds,' he said. 'Four to six.'

'One to two,' Wise came back immediately.

Trust a Scouser to know the odds for everything. 'You're windier than Ladbrokes,' Fitz said.

'One to two you get a confession.' Wise took another swig of tea.

'Done,' Fitz said.

Sometimes you just had to take the best odds you could get.

213

THIRTY-FIVE

Virginia was close to panic. Doctor Fitzgerald and DS Penhaligon had come back, and Kenneth was not there to protect her. They sat on chairs to either side of the sofa where she perched, pinned between their stares. It made her feel like some kind of . . . of criminal or something.

But I am, she thought. I helped to kill Joanne. She refused the thought. The girl was a sinner. Virginia had simply done what Kenneth told her and helped to send Joanne to be judged by God.

It might not be in accordance with the laws of man, but it was God's will.

DS Penhaligon clinked her spoon against the side of Virginia's Spode teacup.

As if it were a signal, Doctor Fitzgerald asked, 'You knew Joanne was a Catholic?'

A Catholic? Virginia wondered. She hardly considered them Christians at all: all those saints and painted effigies, all that Mary worship. Besides, it hardly seemed relevant – but in that case, what was he getting at? 'No,' she said.

'A very devout Catholic, according to her parish priest,' Doctor Fitzgerald said. His vast frame almost obscured the chair he was sitting on. His stubby fingers, fat as sausages, fiddled with the cord edging on the arm of his chair. Virginia noted with distaste that they were stained yellow with nicotine. His voice was gentle, almost hypnotic: but Virginia wasn't fooled by it. Not for one minute. 'She belonged to the Legion of Mary,' he continued. 'Attended regularly for Benediction and confession, never missed Sunday Mass – until last Christmas. . . .' his voice trailed off uncertainly, as if he were unsure, and he raised his eyebrows at the sergeant.

Virginia whipped round to look at the other woman. What were they doing? Had she given something away? The man was a psychologist. The sweet Lord only knew what he might read into anything she did or said. But Penhaligon simply smiled her agreement, then took another sip of tea.

I ought to say something, Virginia thought. But what could she say? Anything she said might go against her. She might let Kenneth down, let the others down. She felt a pulse beating too rapidly in her throat.

Then it was too late to say anything at all, because Doctor Fitzgerald was speaking again, in that soft, relentless, terrifying voice of his. 'Whoever drew her to your church must have had a tremendous attraction for her.'

Now Virginia saw it. They were trying to imply that Kenneth had snared Joanne into the Fellowship just so he could – the word was hateful – seduce her. They thought they could use it to lever her away from Kenneth, perhaps get her to betray him.

They were wrong. She knew that Joanne was a sinful little bitch who had seduced Kenneth, not the other way around. Kenneth loved her, and her alone. As long as they spoke with one voice, they were invulnerable.

It was God's will, just as Joanne coming to the Fellowship had been.

'I'm sure He did . . .' Virginia said. Doctor Fitzgerald looked startled; it took a moment for her to work out why: he thought she had already betrayed her Kenneth. 'God, Doctor Fitzgerald.'

'Working through your husband?' Doctor Fitzgerald smiled, as if he'd said something particularly clever.

The man was impossible, Virginia thought. He couldn't see what was put plainly before him. 'Yes,' she said patiently. 'Drawing her to the Bible.'

'You don't think it's possible that it wasn't the Bible that attracted her, but your husband?'

215

The memory of those disgusting photographs flashed through Virginia's mind. Kenneth touching Joanne, kissing her . . . doing other things. She wanted to scream, of course it's possible. That's why she joined the Fellowship: so she could seduce him, corrupt him, take him away from me. But they wouldn't understand. She blinked rapidly, and laughed because she had to do something to relieve the tension that was building up inside her. 'Doctor Fitzgerald. She was a seventeen-year-old girl, and my husband is a –'

'– A forty-six-year-old pin-up,' he finished for her.

It was a ridiculous idea, wasn't it? It wasn't. 'Kenneth? A pin-up!' Virginia said to Doctor Fitzgerald. She laughed, then turned to Penhaligon and laughed again. Terror made her laugh: she hoped they would think it was disbelief.

Penhaligon smiled, as if they were teenagers sharing a secret about a boyfriend. 'I had a crush on my music master at her age, and he was no spring chicken,' she said. Her voice was slightly husky. She smiled, not at Virginia but at the doctor. 'You know what girls are like at that age.'

She's flirting with him, Virginia thought. It was infuriating. They were scaring her this much, and they were flirting!

'I don't. I never found out,' Doctor Fitzgerald said. A wealth of depraved possibilities were implied in his tone.

Virginia smiled, embarrassed, and stared at her tea-cup. She'd let it go cold. A pity. Drinking it would have given her something to do with her hands.

'Mrs Trant, your husband is a very attractive man,' Penhaligon said. Virginia smiled, pleased by the compliment in spite of herself. 'I suppose it is just possible that Joanne might have – well, fancied him a bit?'

Oh, it was so crass, so vulgar, Virginia thought. And Penhaligon wasn't the least bit embarrassed to be saying such things, sitting there with her hands clasped casually in front of her as if they were discussing the price of apples.

'I never noticed anything to suggest that,' she said, and then more confidently, 'and I'm sure Kenneth didn't.' She was talking too fast. Norma always said that when she was upset she talked too fast. She hoped they wouldn't notice; but then she was smiling – a fixed, too-wide grin that had nothing to do with pleasure.

'He did say she was a shy, withdrawn sort of girl – not the sort of girl to flaunt her feelings.'

That was Doctor Fitzgerald again, challenging her, poking at her with his theories and refusing to take her word for everything. 'Maybe. But that doesn't prove any –'

He wouldn't even let her finish. 'Mrs Trant. We're not trying to prove anything.' He sounded impatient. He had the nerve to sit in her living room and accept her hospitality, and speak to her like that. 'We can't ask Joanne what she felt, so we're asking you. We're just thinking aloud.' He was obviously on the edge of losing his temper, Virginia realised. She realised she didn't mind. So was she. 'I'm just wondering if there's a possibility – the remotest possibility – that Joanne fancied your husband, even though he wasn't aware of it?'

Virginia took a deep breath. She had to keep calm. If she got angry, she might say anything at all. 'It seems very unlikely –'

'So it's possible?' Fitzgerald said.

'I didn't say that.' Now Virginia really was getting very cross indeed.

'So you're saying it's absolutely impossible?'

He wouldn't stop. He twisted everything she said, when he must know very well what she meant. 'I didn't say that –' she said, and realised that she was talking very fast, but she couldn't slow down and she couldn't stop. 'I didn't say it was absolutely impossible.'

'I think there are a number of things you're not saying,' Doctor Fitzgerald said. There was iron in his voice. 'Can you live with those things?'

'I haven't done anything wrong –' Virginia said automatically. She had been a good child, a good teenager, a good wife. She had never felt guilty about anything. *You should now*, said a small dark voice at the back of her mind. *You killed Joanne Barnes because you were afraid she'd take your husband away from you.* But she mustn't listen to it. She must speak with Kenneth's voice, the voice of the righteous who had done God's will. If she faltered, they would all be lost.

'Somebody has. And you know who,' said Doctor Fitzgerald. His hands were quite still now, and his gaze never wavered from her face. 'Don't you think it's your duty to tell us?'

Duty? He dared to speak to her of duty? 'I know where my duty lies, Doctor,' she said, and thought: to Kenneth, to God and to the others, and then, guiltily, but not necessarily in that order. But she couldn't say that, so she said the other thing, the thing that bore her up whenever she felt the weight of the world oppressing her. 'I have always tried to live a decent –'

'Joanne Barnes is lying stiff on a slab –' Doctor Fitzgerald cut in.

'– Christian life.' Surely that would stop him? But no.

'She had marks all over her body left by some sick demented soul –'

He was talking about Kenneth. Her Kenneth. 'Please –' He, with his sick perverted mind dared say such things about her husband. 'I don't want to hear this –' she said determinedly.

'Her parents are banging the floor with grief, "A good girl, Joanne", they kept saying that –'

She wasn't a good girl, she was a wicked corrupting little tart, Virginia wanted to scream at him. But she couldn't and his words just kept coming, kept beating at her. She turned to Penhaligon in desperation. 'Can't you stop him?'

But Penhaligon just stared at her with an insolent, why-should-I expression on her face, and Fitzgerald's words just kept breaking over her. 'Saying who's the evil bastard that's responsible for this good girl's death?' Virginia put the back of her hand to her mouth to stop herself from screaming. All shall be well and all shall be well and all things shall be well,

218

she told herself, but still the awful words kept coming. 'Joanne is dead. Dean is dead. What does it amount to, this decency of yours?'

Virginia was suddenly furious. They had come here, drunk her tea, eaten her cakes, slandered her husband and all but called her a liar to her face. And neither of them had done a tenth of the good works in their entire lives that she had done in the last year.

'Thirty-seven thousand, six hundred and forty-two pounds. In the present financial year,' she said. Let them challenge that. Let them say that was nothing.

'That much?' Fitzgerald said, in a voice thick with contempt.

It meant nothing to him, she realised. All her hard work, her love of God and the Holy Bible, the fact that she'd lived out her forty-four years and never broken a single commandment – *except*, said the small voice at the back of her brain, *Thou Shalt Not Kill*; but she put it away from her, because, after all, they had not killed Joanne but sent her cleansed to God – all of that was nothing compared with one evil, seducing little minx.

'Eighteen thousand four hundred – Cancer Research,' Virginia said. She knew the figures by heart. Now she chanted them like a litany, to force silence on Doctor Fitzgerald and his filthy-minded lies. 'Six thousand nine hundred and four Cerebral Palsy; two thousand and five pounds twenty-three pence to Help the Aged; eleven hundred and sixteen pounds the Church Restoration; a round thousand to Cystic Fibrosis, Guide Dogs for the Blind, Children in Need –' she turned to Penhaligon, 'and the Police Widows and Orphans.' The younger woman had the good grace to look abashed. Now it was Virginia's turn to keep talking when they would rather she were quiet. 'Along with smaller cash payments to the local old, infirm and needy.' She stood up and got the collecting box from where it sat on the mantelpiece, next to the majolica bowl. 'I'm currently collecting for Cerebral Palsy,' she said. She rattled the box under Doctor Fitzgerald's nose with a practised swing of her wrist. 'Perhaps a donation might be in order?'

She had done it. She had actually made him feel as embarrassed as she had been. 'You've caught me a bit short at the moment,' he said.

Penhaligon fumbled in her purse and eventually drew out a fifty pence piece, which she pushed into the box. After that, it was much easier for Virginia to take control, and a few minutes later she suggested, quite calmly, that perhaps they ought to go.

It was only after she had seen them to the door and watched them drive away in the car that she sat down on the sofa and began to sob. She would have called Kenneth at school, but she was sure he would think she was being silly.

The car smelled of hot vinyl and strawberries. Or maybe he was imagining the strawberries, Fitz decided. Or remembering them. He'd certainly tasted them last night: and that thought led him to another, of Panhandle's skin turned to gold and shadows by the soft lamplight; and then to thoughts of all those hidden places, places of secret delights that were no longer secret –'

'She's lying,' Panhandle said suddenly, practical as ever.

'She's loyal,' Fitz said, startled.

Panhandle glanced at him, while outside the suburban landscape of widely-spaced houses and neat lawns rolled by. She obviously knew his mind wasn't on the Trants. Perhaps she'd even guessed where it was; but all she said was, 'Next stop Norma?'

'No,' Fitz said, thinking fast. 'Next stop Sarah.'

That would worry Kenneth far more than talking to his wife.

THIRTY-SIX

Penhaligon and Fitz waited outside William Street High School for the lad they had bribed to fetch Sarah. Penhaligon felt vaguely uneasy about that – not the bribe, but the fact that they hadn't told the school authorities they wanted to talk to her. She was sure it was against guidelines, but Fitz had said it was imperative that Kenneth Trant not find out what they were up to.

To hell with it. It was a beautiful day, and it wasn't as if they were likely to use the tape they planned to make as evidence.

She'd find a way to cover it. She always did.

She grinned, thinking about the way she'd covered certain other things last night. She suppressed the smile quickly, and made sure she was standing just so – neither too close nor too distant, not with her body turned completely towards him nor completely away – in case Kenneth Trant should happen by and see them and guess that there was something different between them. Once was enough for one day.

The small boy they had used as a messenger appeared next to them, all blond hair, loose tie and wide-eyed innocence.

'She's coming,' he said. 'One pound.'

'You said 50p,' Fitz said, aggrieved.

'Each way,' said the boy, equally aggrieved.

Here we go again, Penhaligon thought; but she found that affection had replaced the irritation she normally felt at Fitz's money troubles. She fished in her pocket for the money, but to her surprise Fitz slapped a pound coin into the boy's hand without further argument.

A few students came out of the school, Sarah among them. She said goodbye to a friend, then stared round nervously till she caught sight of them.

She hesitated, then started across the tarmac to them.

'Thanks for talking to us again, Sarah,' Penhaligon said.

The girl smiled. She was terribly nervous: she kept tugging her skirt, and her gaze flicked here and there.

'Is there somewhere we can talk?' Fitz asked. Sarah glanced at the school. 'Oh, not in there,' Fitz said. 'Let's get a breath of fresh air –'

'OK,' Sarah said. She led them round the side of the building. They were suddenly confronted by an expanse of grass covered with children – could you call them that at their age? Penhaligon wondered – in the middle of a sports lesson.

'Fourth Years,' Sarah said, by way of explanation.

Any minute now they'd be challenged, Penhaligon thought. She said as much to Fitz.

'Nah. It's the purloined letter syndrome. You're the detective – you should know: the best place to hide something is in plain view.'

Oh sure, Penhaligon thought, cocking her head up at him. I'm sure you're very inconspicuous.

They walked down a path towards some benches on the far side of the playing fields. Around them, some of the fourth years practised hurdling and ball skills while others stood around in groups, watching. They were, Penhaligon thought, remarkably well behaved. As far as she could see, no-one was about to sneak off, or talking about last night's television, or eyeing up a member of the opposite sex. If it were true that the atmosphere in a school was down to the head teacher's leadership, Kenneth Trant must be an outstanding principal.

Which didn't stop him being a murderer.

'Mr Trant seems to get on well with the kids,' Fitz said. Sarah nodded vigorously. While the girl's attention was on Fitz, Penhaligon flicked the switch on the dictating machine she was carrying in her shoulder-bag.

222

She was so young and innocent, Penhaligon thought, feeling old. That made her feel peculiar, because next to Fitz – now that they were together – she felt like a child. Just for a second, she wondered if he saw her like that. It had never occurred to her before.

'The only time our teachers ever spoke to us was to threaten us with hellfire,' Fitz said. 'Or detention, which was slightly worse.'

Sarah laughed. 'Mr Trant's not like that.'

No, Penhaligon thought, I don't suppose he is. If what Fitz suspected were true, his relationship with Sarah was far from teacherly.

A small ball thudded at her feet. She picked it up and hurled it back to a lad who stood grinning at her some way off. He caught it and moved away, and Penhaligon saw that Kenneth Trant was deep in conversation with a couple of people on the far side of the playing field. Penhaligon didn't think he had seen them.

'You're lucky,' Fitz said. 'You find you can talk to him, do you?' There was nothing hard about Fitz now, nothing bullying or tough. 'I mean, he doesn't mind you coming to him with your troubles?'

'Oh no,' Sarah said. Too fast, Penhaligon thought. Sure enough, the girl pulled back almost immediately. 'I mean, he doesn't mind. He likes to know what's going on.' She paused. 'He likes you to go and talk to him.'

I'll bet, Penhaligon thought. She supposed that the attraction a teacher like Kenneth Trant could exert over an innocent young girl like Sarah – or Joanne – might be pretty much like that exerted by . . . well, by a fat, middle-aged, hard-living psychologist over an ambitious young police sergeant.

'Mr Grogan,' Fitz said. Sarah looked puzzled. Penhaligon knew it was just the start of one of Fitz's rambling, only apparently pointless, anecdotes. 'My history teacher. They all said "It's exams, it's a tough time. Don't suffer. It only takes a minute to go in and see the principal".' He grinned wrily. 'Yeah, and three hours to get out. We called him Taphead 'cos someone said he had water on the brain.' He rolled his eyes. 'Barking.' Sarah grinned.

Penhaligon grinned too, but her attention was on Kenneth Trant. The teacher he was talking to moved aside. He stared straight at her. Damn, she thought. If he tells us to get out we won't have a leg to stand on. But if he does that, it's as good as a confession of guilt.

Sure enough, Trant contented himself with glaring at her. He nodded curtly at her, and then walked off. They were almost at the benches. Fitz was still holding forth, and Sarah seemed entranced by him. 'Grogan was different. He seemed to know what you were going through without the subject arising,' he said. He waved his hand around as if he had a cigarette in it, the way he usually would. Sarah smiled attentively. I wonder if I look like that when I'm with him, Penhaligon thought – if that's what Beck sees that makes him want to take the piss all the time. Fitz said, 'He'd make you a cup of tea in his cubbyhole and get the ashtray out. You know? He just made you feel human.' Sarah nodded. Penhaligon suddenly found that she was jealous. She laughed at herself silently. It was one way of dealing with it. 'That's what I call a teacher,' Fitz said.

They settled down on the bench, with Sarah between the two of them.

'Is that how Mr Trant makes you feel,' Penhaligon said.

'Oh, yes,' the girl answered. 'He's always got time for you – he makes you feel like you're the only person in the world.' She suddenly seemed much younger than sixteen, and Penhaligon wasn't at all proud of the fact that she was about to betray her.

In Penhaligon's bag, the dictating machine whirred on.

224

THIRTY-SEVEN

The police interview room was just the way Norma had imagined it would be: small and chilly, with discoloured grouting between the tiles on the walls, and black marks on the floor where cigarettes had been stubbed out.

The coffee was terrible too, thin and bitter with an aftertaste from the long-life milk in it. She wrapped her hands round the plastic cup and stared out of the window. She could barely see through it, because it was made of small panes of extremely thick glass, as if they thought you would try to throw yourself through anything less tough.

Well, she thought, it could be an extremely scary place to be – if you were weak. But she wasn't weak, and she'd come here to prove that, by facing down this psychologist, Fitzgerald, who'd so scared Michael and Virginia. Not that scaring either of them was difficult.

The door clicked open behind her. She turned. The shambling hulk of a man who came in could only be Doctor Fitzgerald. The young woman behind him had a mane of wild red hair and determined expression. She was almost certainly Penhaligon – she certainly fitted Virginia's tearful description.

Fitzgerald smiled, tight and hard, while Penhaligon stood off to one side, near the far wall.

They've done this before, Norma thought; and it occurred to her that this was just a job to them, nothing out of the ordinary at all. That worried her. Who knew what tricks they'd worked out during the time they'd worked together? I have to take control of the situation, she thought. Take the initiative. After all, that was why she had volunteered to come here when they had phoned to say they wanted to speak to her.

She took a sip of coffee and looked at Fitz over the rim of the cup. She knew men found it attractive. She was dressed up – earrings in, nails painted, enough but not too much make-up. Well, it couldn't hurt, could it?

She lowered the cup slowly, and said, 'Doctor Fitzgerald, I presume? I've heard a lot about you.'

She'd intended it to sound witty, but from his unimpressed expression, it was clear he heard only the cliché.

'I'm surprised you preferred to talk to us here,' he said.

'Why? It's fascinating.' She stared around the room as if it were the most beautiful piece of architecture in the world. 'It's a new experience for me.' She took another sip of coffee, and again gazed over her coffee cup at him.

She wondered how much it would take to get him to forget whatever it was that made him suspect her and the others. An intriguing thought: he wasn't conventionally attractive by any means, but she could see why – for instance – Penhaligon's gaze was as much on him as on Norma.

She'd thought he would make some comment about that – a joke, an anecdote, something to put her at her ease, but he didn't.

He just launched an immediate attack. 'Virginia Trant told us she thought it possible that Joanne fancied her husband a bit. What d'you think?'

So they knew. ' "Fancied him?" ' she said immediately, managing to sound shocked. 'Did Ginny say that?' Norma knew she hadn't – it just wasn't the kind of word Virginia would use. But that didn't necessarily mean they were lying.

Be careful, she thought. Be very, very, careful.

'What do you reckon,' Fitz said. He was smiling now, as

if they were sharing a bit of gossip.

Norma made a derisive sound, and said, 'Bit of a giggle!' She grinned, as if the idea were ludicrous.

'I'm not sure,' Penhaligon said, 'but I think she was a bit upset about it.'

I'll bet, Norma thought. But she knew it was up to her to stop this whole idea taking root in their minds. 'Upset?' she said to Penhaligon, sounding properly incredulous.

'Uhuh,' the policewoman said. Her gaze was level, assessing. She was, Norma realised, every bit as dangerous as Fitzgerald.

'About a schoolgirl taking a shine to Kenneth?' Norma dropped her cup into the bin and sat down at the table. So did Fitz. 'She'd have had to be pretty insecure to feel upset about that,' she said as she settled herself.

Penhaligon sat down too, but on a chair near the wall. She crossed her legs, so that her already short skirt rode up even further, revealing what looked like about five yards of leg.

That's for Fitzgerald's benefit, Norma thought, but she didn't have time to consider it, because the psychologist was asking her another question.

'Was she?' he said. 'Insecure?'

Yes of course she was, Norma thought: and was long before Kenneth gave her cause to be. She meant to say something bland, something about him being a perfect husband; but what came out was, 'Ohh, you've met Kenneth. Any woman married to him might feel a bit insecure.' A wistful thought of him against that tree with Joanne brushed across her mind and was gone. She reached out a finger but didn't quite touch Fitz's arm as she added quickly, 'But he never gave her any cause.' Damn him.

'How do you know?' Fitz asked.

Because I tried hard enough to give her cause and failed she thought, and I was just as shocked as she was when I realised. 'Well,' she said, trying to think of something convincing. 'Well, Ginny would have told me.'

'Don't you think that Kenneth might have been flattered by Joanne's pash?' Fitzgerald asked. Norma allowed a dismissive smile to spread across her mouth. She found, to her surprise, that she was enjoying this: she liked the feeling of power her deception gave her, but more than that, she liked the attention; it was better than the way Michael tiptoed round her, anyway. But Fitzgerald was still talking, and she knew she had to concentrate on him.

'– might even have encouraged her?' he said. Oh yes, Norma thought: all of that and more. 'A middle-aged man getting the eye by a sixteen-year-old girl – a pretty girl? Don't you think he might have got a kick out of that? I know I would.'

I'm sure you would, Norma thought, and was proud of the fact that her gaze didn't flicker across to Penhaligon, even for a second. 'He didn't notice,' Norma said. She shook her head. 'And he didn't need those kicks.'

'So who got Joanne pregnant?' Fitzgerald asked.

For a second, Norma didn't know what to say. The baldness of that casual statement appalled her, but not as much as the way Fitzgerald just kept doggedly on with his single idea. 'If not Kenneth, you mean?' she asked at last.

'If not Kenneth.' He smiled, but there wasn't any humour in it.

If they'd been alone, she might have been more direct. As it was, all she could do was suggest . . . after all, he had her phone number, for afterwards. If she could make him want her sufficiently.

She leaned across the table, wishing her blouse were lower cut. 'For a psychologist you're a pretty poor judge of character.'

'I'm better with women,' he said. There was a closeness there, a warmth from him that made her think she was winning; but then, to Norma's disappointment, he turned to Penhaligon and said, 'Aren't I?'

The policewoman took a sip of coffee and turned away

with an expression that was only half amused. They were more than colleagues, Norma was sure.

Not that it mattered. She might have failed with Kenneth, but this Fitzgerald wasn't half the man.

To her delight, he pulled out a packet of cigarettes and handed her one. As she took it, Norma glanced at Penhaligon and saw that same look of amused disgust on her face.

We'll see, she thought, as Fitz flicked open his lighter. He touched the flame to her cigarette, and she cupped her hands over his, keeping it there for far longer than was necessary. They stared at each other for the space of a heartbeat or two.

He wanted her. He couldn't hide it.

You're mine, she thought at him. Mine. And Kenneth will thank me for it.

She leaned back and breathed out smoke. It wreathed the air between them. She noted with part of her attention that Penhaligon seemed a little annoyed. Good. It confirmed Norma's feeling that she was winning.

'Dean killed Joanne,' she said, emphasising each word as she thought at Fitzgerald: just believe me, or pretend to believe me, and you can have me.

Fitzgerald took a long drag on his cigarette. His gaze flickered from Norma to Penhaligon and back again.

'He was sweet on her,' Norma said. She suddenly remembered that she would have to convince Penhaligon as well as Fitzgerald. She turned to the younger woman. 'You should have seen him at the meetings. He couldn't take his eyes off her.' And then back to Fitzgerald: 'Always pointing at her. He was crazy about her.' She leaned a little closer. 'You knew that, didn't you?' she asked, as if she were doing him a kindness by pointing out something terribly complicated that he might have missed.

'Oh yes, crazy about her,' Fitzgerald said. 'Crazy for her, maybe. But crazy in his head. All in his head.' It was what you would expect from a psychologist, Norma thought: ignore common sense and work out some ridiculous theory.

The really irritating thing was that he was right. And now he was lecturing her: 'Classic hopeless romantic passion. He idealised her. But he never laid a finger on her.' Fitzgerald took another long drag on his cigarette. He watched the smoke disperse before he said, 'Dean didn't have a proper relationship with Joanne.'

He was earnest, dogmatic and totally lost to her, Norma realised. Well, she thought, God helps those who help themselves. She had one more trick to try, one she'd thought of during the journey over.

'He came to the house one weekend when Michael was away,' she said. 'Dean knew he was away, of course. Anyway, he pushed past me, down the hallway, into the sitting room. Sat on my sofa.' She'd thought the next part out carefully, knowing that detail would make the story seem more realistic. 'He had grease on his trousers – I wondered if it would wash off the sofa. He had his eyes closed and he was chanting from the Bible.' That was likely enough: you only had to speak a bit sharply to Dean and you got a lot of nonsense about the Four Horsemen of the Apocalypse. 'I didn't pay it much attention.' Fitzgerald looked surprised, which was exactly what she'd intended: if she was prepared to admit to that, why would she be unreasonably loyal about anything else; especially when they would know she would have worked out that they might very well mention it to Michael. Or Kenneth. 'To be honest it doesn't mean that much to me,' she said for emphasis. 'I'm not sure I believe at all.'

She took a quick puff of her cigarette, for effect, then, not wanting to give them time to change the subject, hurried on. 'I made a mistake. I got too close. He touched me. I didn't like it. I told him. Still, his hands . . .' she allowed her voice to trail off, as if she were reluctant to think about it; but she couldn't help wondering what it would be like if Kenneth were touching her like that, saying those things. Or even Fitzgerald. Things no-one had ever really said to her: certainly that mouse Michael never had. With him, it was

230

strictly missionary position only, and in the dark – and not too much of that, even.

She took another drag on her cigarette. Her hands were shaking, but that was all right. 'I pushed him away,' she said. 'He came back. He wouldn't let go. He was hurting.' A little shiver went down her neck at the thought of it, of Kenneth's hands. 'And all the time this Bible stuff. And then the words changed. To personal things. About my body . . . You know . . .' She glanced at Penhaligon, who nodded agreement. 'Crude, crass words for things –' Words Kenneth had used with Joanne? she wondered. She forced herself to concentrate. 'I walked out of the room, out of the house, into the town. Came home in the evening and nothing was missing. Dean was never a thief,' she said. That was good. It made her seem non-vindictive, and it got her out of explaining why she hadn't reported him to the police. 'No sign he'd ever been there,' she concluded, and then remembered she'd said his trousers were greasy. 'Well, save for the stain on the sofa.'

She dragged at her cigarette again. Fitzgerald just watched her. She knew she had convinced him.

'And Michael – what did he say?' he said at last. It wasn't what Norma had expected him to say. Who cared about Michael? What did Fitzgerald think the Mighty Mouse would have done anyway? Beaten Dean to death with a cream puff?

'You did tell him?' Fitzgerald prompted.

'No!' Norma exclaimed. 'I didn't want to get Dean into trouble.' It was reasonable enough, she thought. She was always reading newspaper stories about how women fail to report sex attacks.

'Kind,' Fitzgerald said, but it was clear he meant nothing of the sort.

'You don't believe me, do you?' She looked at Penhaligon; surely a woman would understand. 'Why should I make it up?'

'To divert attention from Kenneth,' Fitzgerald said, in a

tone that made it obvious he thought Norma was an idiot. He tapped the ash from the end of his cigarette. 'Did you meet him through Virginia?'

'Yes.' What was he trying to get at? Had she given something away? Norma felt herself starting to panic. 'We were at school together. We met then.'

'Ah . . . she saw him first,' Fitz said. He held her gaze for an instant.

So that was it . . . the dirty-minded – 'There was never anything between Kenneth and me,' Norma said, and stubbed her cigarette out to emphasise her fury. She was angry at herself for being so transparent. Angry that she had failed to get Fitzgerald on her side. And absolutely incandescently angry that it was true: there had never been anything between her and Kenneth. She had always thought he was besotted with Virginia, that no other woman could ever hope to attract him. So she'd never tried, because a rejection from Kenneth was the worst thing in the world she could imagine. And then she'd found out that he was playing around with that little tart, and knew she could have had it all.

'Nothing fulfilled.' Fitzgerald measured her with his eyes the way another man might have undressed her. 'Would you have married him?'

'He didn't ask me, he asked Virginia.' Damn him, she thought, and wasn't sure whether she meant Fitzgerald or Kenneth.

'And Michael asked you. That wasn't the question.' Fitzgerald took a deep breath. 'You're obviously very attracted to Kenneth. Did you ever think what it would be like if you'd married him . . .'

Of course I thought about it! Norma thought. She wanted to scream it at him. She wanted to slap his face and refuse to answer any more pathetic, hurtful questions. But all she had left was dignity.

She made a derisive noise. 'No point in thinking . . .' She realised what she'd said, and after that she couldn't face

Fitzgerald, so she sat staring at the long red nails she'd painted specially for the occasion.

It didn't make any difference. Fitzgerald's voice just kept coming at her. 'Let's take it as read, then, that Kenneth Trant may have harboured thoughts about Joanne.' She glanced at him. He was stroking his chin with the side of his thumb. He looked at her from under hooded lids; she realised that he was hurting her quite deliberately, leaving her no place to hide from the fact that Kenneth had cheated on Virginia with a beautiful young girl, when he wouldn't cheat with her. 'She's a young girl, he saw a lot of her – who could blame him for having those thoughts?' I could, Norma thought. I bloody well do. Fitzgerald leaned back in his chair as he continued. 'The question – the life with a minimum of twenty years recommendation – question, is: did he act on them?'

Fury shot through Norma again, but this time she was ready for it. She stared at the ceiling for a moment, to give herself time to think. You want to damage me? she thought. I'll show you damage! I'll pull your sordid cradle-snatching little affair apart, and then we'll see what I can think of next.

'Tell me, doctor,' she said. She turned to Fitzgerald and leaned across the table towards him. 'Is a man happier who acts on his instincts, or who represses them?' He smiled. She had his interest now. She kept her voice low, as if they were the only people in the room. 'When you lit my cigarette . . . I know that look.' His smile broadened into a grin, and she realised he was laughing at her.

Condescending bastard!

Penhaligon started to speak. 'I don't think this has got anything to do –'

Norma turned on her. She stabbed at her with her finger. 'And you knew it too. And you were jealous as hell because he lit my cigarette.' She was triumphant. Surely now they realised she'd seen through their little affair, they'd leave her alone. If not – well, it might even be a sackable offence –

'I'm sure I've got nothing to teach you about jealousy,' Penhaligon said. She smiled, a secretive little smile that said she was completely happy with whatever was going on.

You little cat, Norma thought.

'Could I have another cigarette, please?' she asked Fitzgerald, to cover herself.

He held out the packet. As she took one, he murmured, 'You love him, don't you?'

Taken off guard, Norma could only ask, 'Who?'

'Kenneth.'

'Kenneth!' Dear God, she thought. Am I really so transparent?

'Kenneth,' Fitz confirmed, as if it were the most obvious thing in the world. 'You love him. You've always loved him.'

She peered at him across the table, as if she would find out he was saying something different by reading his lips.

But the words stayed the same.

'You've always loved him.'

Now Norma really couldn't face him. She turned sideways in her seat and clutched her cigarette with shaking fingers. Fitzgerald's voice kept coming at her, and there was nothing she could do to stop it.

'Ever since that first dance. At the church hall. What was it? Mungo Jerry? David Essex? You remember.'

It wasn't, she thought. It was the Beatles: the DJ had just played *Penny Lane*, and Kenneth requested *Love Me Do*, even though it was old. He came over to us, smiling – it was the smile that did it, and his shoulders, and that confident way of his – and I thought he was coming to ask me to dance. But he asked Virginia; and I had to stand there watching them until, in the end, Michael took pity on me.

'You fell for him then. You fell in love with him and you've loved him ever since –'

'No,' Norma whispered, and then again, 'No. No!' Her face burned.

234

'– but he married Virginia. Idiot! Think how much happier he would have been if he'd married you . . .'

He wouldn't have cheated on me, Norma thought. I'd have been everything he needed. 'Kenneth and Virginia have a very happy marriage,' she said. She glared at Fitzgerald through the haze of his cigarette smoke, and tried to pretend that it was that, and not tears, that made her eyes sting.

'Did Kenneth Trant have sex with Joanne Barnes?' He was shouting at her.

'No!' she shouted back.

'Cross your heart and hope to die?' He was testing her.

There was a trap here but she just didn't care. 'I'm beginning to think that you're jealous of Kenneth.' Well, Fitzgerald would be, wouldn't he? A great big lump of a man like that? He was hardly likely to find himself fending off beautiful young women – even that Penhaligon was almost certainly just leading him on. 'He's just not that sort of a man,' she said; and then she realised with a jolt that for the moment of time it took to say it, she had actually believed it, even though she'd watched Kenneth doing it with Joanne in broad daylight. She spat out, 'He has never been unfaithful to Virginia.'

What had Kenneth said? *As long as we speak with one voice, we are invulnerable.* Well, Fitzgerald could play silly games all he liked. He could stir up old memories, old hurts for as long as he wanted, but he'd never make her betray Kenneth.

Her Kenneth.

She turned away from the table and stared at her hands, pretending boredom. At least, she hoped that was what it looked like.

'Or another girl?'

It was desperation, surely. Ridiculous in any event. Norma threw her hands in the air. 'Any girl! Any woman!' Suddenly she couldn't control her anger. She threw her unlit cigarette on the table. 'You can keep it, thanks.'

235

She leaned her head on her hand. If she couldn't convince him, couldn't even get him to shut up, at least she didn't need to look at him.

'Do you know Sarah Jennings?'

Now what, Norma wondered. 'Sarah . . .?'

'Schoolfriend of Joanne's.' Fitzgerald's voice was too quiet.

Trap! Norma thought. This is it, this is what I've been expecting. She got ready to defend Kenneth again, to think of some defence for whatever small-minded piece of nastiness he was going to spew out next.

But Fitzgerald didn't say anything. He reached into his jacket and pulled out a dictating machine. He laid it on the table.

Norma stared at it. She knew what it had to be.

Dear God, she thought. Please not. It was the most sincere prayer she'd made in years.

It didn't help. Fitzgerald pressed the play button. The tape hissed for a moment, and then a young girl spoke.

'Out of all the girls at school, he chose me.' It wasn't Joanne, so it must be this Sarah. Norma felt herself flushing again, and her heart hammered in her chest. 'He's always wanted a child, and she could never have them.' Norma placed the voice then. It belonged to a girl she'd spoken to a few times at the Fellowship – speaking about Virginia like she was some kind of second-class citizen. 'As soon as I leave school we're going to live together . . .' Norma stared at Fitzgerald, then glanced at Penhaligon. Both of them wore the same expression: pity. She couldn't stand it. He wouldn't do this – but he had, with Joanne. And now with this Sarah. How many more were there? And none of them her. The voice, the terrible voice, spoke on. 'He's a wonderful man. I feel special when he's there.' And then Norma realised the little tart could be talking about anyone. Anyone! Yet her heart still raced, the muscle in her throat still jumped. And Fitzgerald and Penhaligon were still looking at her with those horrible, pitying expressions. 'He loves me more than anything. I'll never want anyone else. 'Oh, Kenneth's wonderful –'

Norma couldn't stand it. She jumped up, knocking the chair over as she did so. She was at the door before either of them could stop her.

THIRTY-EIGHT

Michael Trant pressed the button that started the baling machine. Doctor Fitzgerald and DS Penhaligon were standing next to him, and they stared at the machine in fascination.

He'd hoped they wouldn't be back, but the last thing he'd expected was that they'd come and ask to be shown how the baling machine worked.

Fitzgerald pointed at the machine, where the whirling blades were tearing a batch of paper to pieces. 'Right, so, the paper's shredded and drops down,' he said.

Yes, Michael thought; but in his mind he saw gobbets of meat and strips of skin, all oozing red with blood. And he thought that in the shriek of the blades he heard Joanne scream her terror and agony as they first sliced into her. Drugged or not she would have woken up; theadrenaline surge would do it. Woken to darkness and pain and death.

'– and then the hydraulic ram compresses it.'

Michael thought he heard the crack of bones grinding together, and the squelch of organs bursting. But most of all he heard that scream of pain and terror.

'It comes out as a block. What happens then?'

A question. Michael was glad of the distraction. 'It goes for recycling.'

He wandered off, making a show of studying his clipboard. He half hoped that they might get bored and go away, but they tagged along behind.

'We saw your wife this morning. She dropped into the station for a chat,' Fitz said. That sounded ominous to Michael. He turned to Fitz, hoping he didn't look worried.

'She was dressing the church hall earlier, she was telling us,' the big man said. 'She had pollen all over her fingers.'

That didn't sound much like Norma. Virginia usually had to persuade her to help out. Still, with all this worry, maybe she'd wanted the company.

He led them down to where the bales of waste stood ready for shipment. They might be waste, but they brought a good price so it was worth keeping their records up to date. No point not getting on with something while he waited . . . he realised that the end of that thought was, *for the police to catch up with them*, but he put it out of his mind.

Fitzgerald followed him, and Penhaligon brought up the rear, which seemed to be her particular role. Bit like me and Kenneth, Michael thought.

'What's the appeal of all these new religious groups?' Fitzgerald asked. They wandered between vast stacks of white waste paper. 'Rock combos singing for Jesus. One World Weirdoes. Bible thumpers –'

Michael supposed he ought to be offended, but he didn't have the energy.

'I'm a Left-footer myself – lapsed,' Fitzgerald said, as if he thought Michael would care. Maybe he wanted to get into a theological debate, like the one Kenneth said he'd tried to start.

'We didn't read the Old Testament,' Fitzgerald went on.

Well more fool you, Michael thought: as far as he was concerned, a Christian who didn't know the Old Testament was like a child who had never met its grandparents: cut off from its history, it could know only the present, and without a context to set it in that meant nothing.

'Do you believe all those old Hebrew stories are true?' Fitzgerald asked. He was cleaning out his ear with his finger.

Virginia was right, Michael thought: the man was not only a bit of a bully, he was vulgar with it.

'I mean, literally true – every word?'

Michael turned to him. 'Yes,' he said shortly, hoping that this time he would give up.

One of the lads came up with a dispatch docket to be signed. Michael hardly looked at it as he scrawled his name on the bottom.

'Your wife thinks it's a load of rubbish,' Fitz said, as if it were a revelation. 'Says she only goes for the company – see friends, see Kenneth – like other people go to the pub, she said.'

That was probably putting it a bit strongly, Michael thought; but he'd known for a long time that Norma's commitment to Jesus wasn't as firm as it could be. He had always hoped he would be able to help her find the true path. He was about to explain that – at least, he would if Fitzgerald would let him say more than two words without interrupting him – when the psychologist continued.

'Do you go to the pub, Michael?' Then added quickly, 'You don't mind me calling you Michael?'

'No,' Michael whispered, wishing they would both just go away.

Doctor Fitzgerald pulled out a pack of cigarettes. 'Smoke?' He proffered the pack to Michael.

Michael shook his head. Fitzgerald lit up.

I should tell him smoking's not allowed. The insurance. The fire risk. But he knew Fitzgerald would think he was being stupid. After all, everyone else did.

'Don't smoke, don't drink, don't gamble – what do you do, Michael?' Fitzgerald asked. He sucked at his cigarette.

Michael tried to think of a reply. I work. I read the Bible. On Saturdays I drive into the country for a walk.

'Sex? That your scene?' Fitzgerald asked.

Michael felt himself flush. Could you call a couple of times a month with an oh-so-dutiful wife your scene? For a moment, he was tempted to tell Fitzgerald about the stack of *Knaves* he kept under the refuse sacks in the garden shed. Maybe that would take the look of quiet contempt off his face. But it would also mean that Fitzgerald had won. Not over Joanne. Michael was quite sure that Fitzgerald would win that battle sooner or later, and wasn't even sure that would be a bad thing. But that had been one thing, one lapse in an otherwise good life. He didn't want Fitzgerald taking that away from him.

'Oh, come on, Michael,' Fitzgerald said. 'A sly wank in front of *Baywatch* on a Saturday evening is hardly a mortal sin. I mean, what did God create *Baywatch* for?'

He thought that was funny. Michael couldn't even look him in the eye.

'You go to church, it's like going to the launderette. There's no point in going unless you've got some stains you need to wash away.'

There had to be an answer to that; but it sounded so very much like the things that Kenneth sometimes said, and Michael had never been able to win an argument with him, either.

'But you're the one who believes in whiter than white. Me, I'm a firm backer of dishcloth grey as pretty much the colour of everything.'

He sounded proud of himself – proud of his blasphemy and his casual immorality. Just listening to him turned Michael's stomach. And yet, he thought, dishcloth grey people don't murder young girls. They don't drug them and package them up to be torn to pieces in a machine. They don't leave innocent people – people much weaker than themselves – to take the blame.

Perhaps Fitzgerald read Michael's thoughts; perhaps he saw into his soul. He said, 'You're not a good man, Michael – but you're not a bad one.'

You're wrong, Michael thought. I'm as bad as it's possible for me to be, and the only reason I'm not worse is because everything I do is so middling.

'You're in between, just like the rest of us. Go on. Admit it. Admit to the chocolate bar under your pillow. Admit to taking the change when you were undercharged.' Suddenly his tone changed from slightly amused to fierce. 'Admit to envy, lust and covetousness. I do.' He spat the last couple of words out.

Michael stared at him, suddenly afraid. He does know, he thought. He knows and he's going to keep coming back and back until I give in and admit it to him. That's what I want, isn't it? he asked himself. To get it over with; but it wasn't. Not this way. Not when it meant he'd been bullied into it, and betrayed his brother. What I want is to be forgiven by God. That's the only forgiveness that counts.

'You have to admit to these things, Michael,' Fitzgerald went on, still furious, 'before you can admit to what you did to Joanne.'

There, Michael thought. He's said it. Now he's told us that he knows. He knew that if Fitzgerald asked again, he would tell him. And he must not. Kenneth had said they must speak with one voice. Michael's need to explain himself was nothing next to that. 'Carry on with your soliloquy,' he said. 'I've got two men's work to do.'

He walked away. It was really that simple. They couldn't force him to speak. He went past the baling machine on the way to the makeshift office he had set up to replace the one wrecked by the fire. The blades churned and the ram slammed down on to the waste, but he ignored the sounds. He sat down at his desk, and stared at the drifts of paper that covered it. She died anyway, he thought. I didn't save her. Another bale of waste went into the machine; he could hear the whizzing of blades even from his desk. But I did save her dying like that, he thought.

He prayed God it was enough: if not to make him a good man, at least to make him – what had Fitzgerald called it? – dishcloth grey.

He settled down with the ledgers, but he couldn't concentrate. He wasn't dishcloth grey, no matter what Fitzgerald said: his soul was black, black with the stain of Joanne's death. All he could do now was keep his silence, because the alternative was to compound his sin with treachery.

He heard footsteps: two sets, one heavier, one lighter. Fitzgerald and Penhaligon. He might have known he

242

wouldn't get rid of them so easily. He didn't look up. It was a victory, of sorts.

'How long have you been a member of the church, Michael?' Fitzgerald said, settling down on the far side of the desk, while Penhaligon walked round to stand next to Michael's shoulder.

'Ten years,' Michael muttered, feeling as if he were making an admission of guilt.

Fitzgerald puffed on his cigarette. 'Who introduced you?' Before Michael could even begin to formulate his answer, Fitzgerald rushed on, 'No, don't tell me. Kenneth. Big brother. He joined, so you had to join.'

Michael smiled uncertainly. He ought to say something, but what was the point? They knew everything, anyway. Penhaligon sat down. He had to move his head slightly to see her, and if he did that, he couldn't keep all his attention on Fitzgerald and his questions. It worried him.

'You always do what he does?' Fitzgerald asked. Again, he hurried on. 'Correction. You always try to do what he does. But you can't, can you – don't have the charm.' He emphasised the last word, giving Michael plenty of time to think about it. 'What was it like, competing in the sex market with a man like Kenneth? God, I ache for you, it must have been murder.'

Competing in the sex market? Michael thought. It sounded so sordid; and anyway, it hadn't been like that, had it? It had been so long ago, before Norma, and he had no clear memory of it: there was just the lingering feeling of having missed out, of the ghost of the other life he could be living if things had been different.

'Always second-best, always second choice. Even to the woman you married –' Fitzgerald paused.

He's trying to hurt me, Michael thought. Trying to drive a wedge between me and Norma, me and Kenneth. But what I already know can't hurt me. It doesn't! he told himself fiercely, though there was a part of him that ached.

Fitzgerald was watching him intently. Michael couldn't

match his gaze. 'Course, you and Norma were well matched,' the psychologist said. He paused to take a drag at his cigarette. 'She was always second-choice too,' he said, letting smoke leak out of his mouth. 'To Virginia. Her best pal. Virginia, the belle of the ball. Virginia introduced Norma to Kenneth. He swept her off her feet. She fell head over heels madly in love with him.'

I know, Michael thought. I know, I know, I know. He'd thought he was immune to the hurt, after all this time. And yet he couldn't stop the muscle that jumped under his right eye. He wanted to leave, but he knew they'd only pursue him, and so he endured their pitying gazes while Fitzgerald held forth.

'And the years have not altered her. She still burns for him, still longs to touch him. She's still as obsessed with him now as she was when she first met him.' Fitzgerald's tone changed, became deliberately hurtful. 'She admits it. She brags about it,' he said. He turned to Penhaligon. 'She told us this morning, didn't she?'

'Yes. I had to feel sorry for her.'

She's as bad as he is, Michael thought. Trying to break me down. They expect me to get upset, to start calling them liars. But I won't; I won't give them that. He didn't speak. What could he say? He wished he could have laughed it off, but they'd dragged all the old pain to the surface, and he knew it was written on his face.

'How does it feel, Michael?' Fitzgerald demanded, in that bullying way of his. 'Your wife loves another man – always had done –'

'I know,' Michael muttered. He couldn't meet their eyes. He stared at the papers on his desk. They were what his life amounted to: that and watching Norma as she looked at him with contempt because he was not Kenneth.

He'd thought he'd grown used to it. He was wrong. He'd just grown numb.

'You know –' Fitzgerald was properly shocked.

And for some reason, Michael found that he could meet

the big man's gaze at last. 'I knew when I married her,' he said after a long moment.

They looked at him as if he'd admitted to child abuse or murder. And then he knew why he could look them in the eye again: they'd thought they could use it as a weapon to tear him away from Norma and Kenneth. He'd deprived them of that weapon.

He felt like he was dying inside, but at least he'd finally done something right. 'If you'll excuse me, I have to see to the waste collection.'

He got up and left, and this time they let him go. I love you, Norma, he thought. I've always loved you.

Not that it made any difference.

'What next?' Penhaligon asked. 'We haven't got that much time left . . .'

They were back at Anson Road, in the duty room. Fitz lounged against the window. He chewed his lip. 'Time to give Kenneth a call,' he said.

Penhaligon dialled the school's number, watching Fitz as she did so. All day, she'd had to make a huge effort not to look at him, not to touch him. Any minute, Beck or Harriman might walk in, but for now they were alone and she could indulge herself.

Fitz pulled his cigarette packet out of his pocket. Empty. He screwed it up and chucked it at the waste paper bin. It bounced off the wall and landed on the floor.

Penhaligon got through to the school. To her surprise, Kenneth Trant agreed to talk to her: she had expected to be fobbed off with his secretary. To her even greater surprise, he volunteered to come to Anson Road and talk to them.

She put the hand-set down and told Fitz.

'He's sending messages,' Fitz said.

'You mean he's letting us know he's not scared of us?'

'No,' Fitz said. 'That's just what he wants us to think. But what he's really letting us know is that he wants this over with.' He patted his pockets. 'You think anyone around here would have a fag?' he asked.

Penhaligon shrugged. 'Do you think we'll get a result?'

'Maybe. He'll want us to – he won't know it but he will.' Her eyebrows went up. 'Think about it: he believes in Christianity, and all that. Penance, Repentance. Hellfire. He can't escape that unless he confesses. Besides, if he doesn't get caught now, he'll spend the rest of his life waiting for it to happen, waiting for Virginia or Michael to break.'

'Not Norma?'

'No. She'd rather have her heart ripped out than betray him.' He grinned. 'It's the power of love, Panhandle. The power of love.'

A life spent loving the wrong person, Fitz mused as he strolled toward his house. How did you do that? He supposed the days turned into weeks that slid into months and rolled into years: and then it was too late, you had too much invested in the situation to leave; maybe you thought you were too old to start again, or too frightened to try.

But, God, what a waste Michael Trant's life looked from the outside.

He went through his garden gate and was halfway up the path before he registered that the estate agent's board had been replaced.

Sometimes starting again was a mistake, of course.

He went back and grabbed the board. It took some doing, but eventually he managed to yank it out of the ground. He hurled it across the road as if it were a javelin. It bounced once, then skittered to a halt on the tarmac.

Fitz grinned, and went inside.

The place looked a bit tidier than he remembered it. There was a faint smell in the air: strawberries. It triggered a memory of Panhandle – her lips, her hair, her hands wandering over his body.

Then again, maybe Mark had been squirting air freshener around the place again.

The light on the answering machine was blinking. Fitz hit

the button. The message was from Judith, and she wasn't happy.

'You're pathetic, Fitz – spending your days like this. You should know better – you attack my car, frighten my daughter's friends –'

Fitz walked away, leaving the tape running. Let her rant. When he told her about Panhandle, she'd really have something to rant about.

Sometimes it wasn't time to change your life. But sometimes it was.

He glanced at his watch. A whole hour to kill before Kenneth Trant was due at the station. Anyone sensible would have made lunch, taken some time to unwind. But Fitz didn't feel sensible, he felt confused.

'You think you can do anything you want,' Judith's furious voice said. '– live like an animal, demand more than anyone can give – and I'll still be there. Well maybe I won't –'

He poured a couple of fingers of whisky into an almost clean tumbler, then sat down at the piano. How did it go again? He picked out the first few chords, then began to play more confidently, as Judith continued to berate him from the answering machine.

It had been one of Judith's favourites. Sometimes all you could do was lose yourself.

The answering machine suddenly cut off. Mark walked in.

'You haven't played that one for years,' he said. He hooked his thumbs in the belt loops at the back of his jeans.

He sounded pissed off, but at least he was talking. It was more than Fitz had really expected after the morning.

'Well, your mother liked it,' he said, as both reason and excuse.

'Yeah. I've just left her.' He ambled off without waiting for Fitz to answer.

It took a second for that to register. Fitz chased after him. 'Have you? Where? When?' And then he thought: my God,

247

if he told her about this morning. 'When?' he demanded. As he followed Mark into the kitchen, he said, 'You're not too big for a skelped arse –'

'Yes I am,' Mark said, sounding bored.

'Yes, you probably are,' Fitz agreed. He swiped at his face with the back of his hand. 'I've never hit you, anyway.'

Mark opened the fridge. He wrinkled his nose in disgust. 'That time.'

Well, he wasn't the only one who could get pissed off. 'Oh, yes. Once in my life. A gentle slap, if I remember.' He gazed around the kitchen, suddenly hungry.

'You hurt me.' Mark turned round.

'You'd been bad,' Fitz said, reasonably.

Mark wasn't having it. 'I was a kid. Kids don't know anything.' He stuck his head back in the fridge.

Yeah, thought Fitz, and some of them still don't.

'Where's your mum and Katie?' he asked as Mark rummaged in the fridge.

'Who's asking – you or your girlfriend?'

Bloody little whelp, Fitz thought. Skelped arse wasn't in it, not compared with what he'd like to do. He bit down on his anger, though. There was that one question that needed answering. 'Did you tell her?'

Mark emerged from the refrigerator with a can in his hand. 'These beans have got mould in them. How can you live like this?' he demanded. He dumped them in the bin, then headed towards the door.

'I said –' Fitz started.

'No,' Mark said over his shoulder. He started sorting through a pile of tee shirts.

'Where are you going now?' Fitz asked.

Mark turned round. 'Listen,' he said. 'If you cared you'd have asked me before now.' He scowled. 'Don't wait up.'

Where did he ever learn that much cynicism? Fitz wondered. Once again, he found himself chasing after Mark. 'Well look, at least –' My God, he thought, how much smaller can my ambitions get? 'At least get Katie to give me a phone or keep in touch or something.' Mark paused by the door, and Fitz caught up with him. 'Will you?' he demanded.

Mark shook his head, making his pony tail bounce. He slammed out of the house. The door banged shut behind him.

Damn, Fitz thought. Damn damn damn.

He went back to the piano and started playing again. The blues. What else?

Michael Trant stood by the baling machine with the switch in his hand. He stared down at it, at the thin band of gold on his ring finger, the band that had defined his life. He squeezed the switch, and the blades slid out and started to whirr.

Norma's never loved me. I've always known it.

He squeezed the switch again. The blades stopped. She burns for Kenneth. My life's a wasteland.

Squeeze, and the blades whirled on. Joanne would have died in agony, cut to gobbets of meat and bone, crushed to bits of bone and blood.

Squeeze. The whirring stopped. But she died anyway. Dean died. I'm a traitor.

Squeeze, and the machine ground on, whirring and slicing and slamming. She never loved me. Everyone knows. I'm just Norma's buffoon, Kenneth's fool. Joanne's murderer.

He squeezed the switch one last time, and the machine stopped. He stared at it for a moment, then wandered off towards his makeshift office. It was all he could do.

THIRTY-NINE

Penhaligon stretched out her hands and beckoned to Fitz. As he came closer, she brought her leg up and laid it on the desk next to him, so that it rubbed against his thigh.

They were alone in the duty room, which was just as well since she was wearing a pair of standard-issue handcuffs.

'Manhandle in manacles,' Fitz murmured. He ran his hand along her leg, without letting his gaze leave her face.

'I'll let you get away with calling me that just this once,' she said. She licked her lips. Slowly. 'But try it again, and –'

Detective Chief Inspector Wise came in. He thumped some files down on a desk. Penhaligon swivelled round and scrambled to her feet. Her cheeks flamed. She yanked at the handcuffs and hid them behind her back. Meanwhile, Fitz was failing to look innocent.

Wise stared at them. He looked more bemused than angry, but Penhaligon knew that could change in an instant.

Say something, Penhaligon told herself desperately. But what? Sorry, sir; just our little game, sir, won't happen again? 'Kenneth Trant is coming in for questioning,' she said eventually.

'Willingly?' He sounded dubious. He slid his overcoat off.

Fitz took a couple of steps forward. Penhaligon watched the two big men square off at each other. 'Very willingly,' Fitz said. She couldn't see his expression, but she could imagine it: he'd lost that edge of anger, and she knew that meant he was getting desperate. 'Smarmy bastard. He's guilty as hell. We've gone right to the edge with the rest

of that family. But they all drew the line at Kenneth.'
He paused. His shoulders slumped just a little. 'Totally
obedient.' His head came back up. 'But I can crack him. I
know I can.'

Wise wasn't impressed. He picked up his paper and
folded it. 'Cocky, aren't we?' he said. He went into his
office. As he shut the door behind him, he turned and glared
at them.

Penhaligon stared at Fitz as he came back to her. He had
such a lot riding on this. All that male ego, all that pride. But
he was good, and Wise knew it.

He grinned. She saw that he was looking at the cuffs,
which were still in her hands. Mustn't laugh, she thought.
Mustn't giggle. Wise is watching: she could see him through
the window of his office. But she allowed herself a smile.
That was safe enough.

Kenneth Trant stared at Doctor Edward Fitzgerald and
Detective Sergeant Jane Penhaligon. He felt calm, totally in
control of the situation, and completely in command of his
responses. He knew, for instance, that the police would not
keep this investigation open indefinitely. Not with so little
hard evidence, and not when there was a perfectly good
suspect lying conveniently dead in the mortuary and unable
to defend himself.

It followed that to proceed, the police needed a confession. Kenneth knew he had to resist them. More, he knew
this was a test – perhaps the greatest test God had set for
him. Fail, and he would slide down into the darkness, into
the chaos that waited beyond the edge of the universe. But
he knew that with God's help, he would not fail. He wished
he could be as certain of Norma, Virginia and Michael, but
that was in God's safe keeping.

For now he must put up with sitting in this small, rather
shabby room, with smoke from Fitzgerald's cigarette stinging his throat. He must appear totally concerned, totally
earnest.

251

'You know,' he said, 'I worked out the other day that in my years at the school, between thirty and forty thousand pupils have been through my hands.' He allowed his voice to grow regretful. 'There have been tragedies along the way. Leukaemia. A car crash. A climbing accident on a school trip.' He tapped the table with his finger. 'And now this. You don't always know the pupils very well – you can't know them all. You always feel it anyway – like one of your own.'

'Mmm.' Sympathy from Fitzgerald? It seemed unlikely. So this was just a ploy. Sure enough, the psychologist said, 'But it was different in this case. In this case you did know the student.' His cigarette burned down, unsmoked.

'As I have explained –' It was the first test: he must not forget what he had already said or allow them to make him angry.

'Yeah,' Fitz said. 'You must have known her better than most of the students, since she was in your Fellowship.

He could hardly dispute that. 'I dare say,' he said. Surely that wasn't giving them too much? His gaze flickered from Fitzgerald to Penhaligon, trying to gauge their response; but their faces were as unreadable as those of serpents. Thus must Adam have felt in the Garden, he thought; but Adam had not fallen. Not to the snake. Eve had been his downfall, just as Joanne had brought Kenneth low. But the police were hardly God, to see into his soul.

'She must have spoken to you?' Another easy, tricksy question from Fitzgerald.

'Of course,' Kenneth said. He would allow them to lead him so far, no further.

'What about?'

That required more thought: just as it might if he had not been close to her at all, and had forgotten their conversations. 'Ahh,' he said to buy time. 'Usually matters affecting the church, Bible studies –'

Fitzgerald puffed at his cigarette. A weak man, Fitzgerald, Kenneth thought: prey to the sins of the flesh – certainly drugs and food and alcohol, and probably others.

Cigarette smoke hung in the air between them.

'But not about school, or her home?' the psychologist asked.

'No, not really.'

'Not even when you drove her home?'

Aah, Kenneth thought. Here we have it: Fitzgerald's little trap, out in the open for all to see. 'Drove her home?' he said, all innocence.

'Are you saying you never drove her home?' Fitzgerald smiled, but not with any warmth.

Did they know the places he had taken her? The times she'd visited his house when Virginia was out collecting for charity? The place in the woods? The flat in Harold Street? Kenneth leaned forward. 'From the church?' He feigned puzzlement, while he tried to see the dimensions of the pit Fitzgerald was digging. If he denied it, they'd think he was at best a liar, at worst uncaring. But if he admitted it – well, that might be to bring the sides of the pit in on himself.

'Where else?' Again, that coy little smile. The cigarette smoke wreathed around Fitzgerald's head as if he himself was burning. Which, Kenneth thought, he undoubtedly would do one day.

'I thought for a moment you meant from the school,' he said, hoping he'd masked his relief adequately. 'Of course, I drove her home from church, once in a while –' Suddenly, his collar seemed too tight. He resisted the urge to loosen his tie.

'Dark nights?' Fitzgerald said it as if they had finally found common ground.

'Precisely.' He must never make the mistake of thinking they were on his side, that they would understand one iota of what he had done, or why. They didn't know God. They weren't capable.

Fitzgerald glanced at a notebook. Kenneth suspected that he didn't really need it. 'You introduced her to the group at Christmas?'

'Yes.'

'So there'd be a lot of dark nights?'

'Yes.' Another trap, Kenneth realised. Was there no end to the snares and delusions of the devil?

'So you must have driven her home quite a few times?'

It seemed to Kenneth that the room was inexplicably a fraction darker. He knew what it was – the darkness that waits where God is not, come for him because he had been weak and failed to see Fitzgerald's trap in time. Only by his strength could he push that darkness back.

'Yes,' he said. Fitzgerald's eyes, hooded as the snake's, regarded him. Kenneth turned to Penhaligon. 'Come to think of it, quite often.' It sounded dreadful, the worst kind of bluster. 'As you say,' he added. 'After all, I introduced her –' Worse, he was making it worse '– and being her headmaster –'

' Yes,' Fitzgerald cut in.

'– felt responsible . . .' he let his voice trail off. If God thought him worthy, there would be a respite now.

But there wasn't. 'Did she talk in the car?' Fitz said.

What to say? What to say? He let his gaze drop to the table top, then looked up and said, 'She was a very quiet child.'

'How old was she?' Fitz said.

The change of subject startled Kenneth, but at least it gave him a chance to recover lost ground. 'You don't know her age?' A little aggressive, perhaps, but at least it would give them fair warning that he wasn't beaten yet.

'You called her a child,' Fitzgerald said, as if it were on the statute book as a criminal offence.

'She was seventeen,' Kenneth said. She had been so irresistibly fresh and young, so innocent. 'She had her GCSEs.'

Penhaligon sighed. She stared down at the ground, looking immeasurably bored. It was the first reaction he'd got from her.

'A young woman I'd say,' Fitzgerald said. 'Wouldn't you?'

'Yes,' Kenneth said. He didn't understand where this was going. If she were a young woman, rather than a child, surely his . . . affair with her was more understandable, less blameworthy? Yet he couldn't believe they were trying to lessen his guilt.

Penhaligon spoke. The sound of her voice shocked Kenneth. It was so young, and yet it held such a wealth of experience. 'When I was seventeen I would have been most offended for you to think of me as a child.'

'Well of course, girls mature more quickly than boys.' It wasn't relevant, but it was better than silence.

'I should think she welcomed the chance to talk with an older man,' Penhaligon said. She smiled, and her face turned from merely pretty to beautiful. 'I mean, fathers are no good, and boys your own age are worse than useless.'

Kenneth couldn't really see what she was getting at, but he smiled anyway. She probably welcomed the chance to say something: he imagined that Fitzgerald had her completely overawed. 'Well, that may be, but . . .' he realised he had to make sure they understood that he hadn't got close to her. 'She didn't say much.'

Penhaligon bit her lower lip. It made her seem quite childlike, especially with the sun picking out the highlights in her red hair and turning her pale skin creamy. 'I was desperate for someone like that – a sort of uncle.'

Of course, she was nowhere near the truth. His relationship with Joanne had been far from avuncular. Her skin had been pale, too, but with a golden tinge to the cream; and that soft golden hair that haloed round her head. And those soft dark places of her, paler than the rest because they never saw sunlight . . .

'So why no kids yourself?' Fitzgerald's voice shocked Kenneth back to the present. Much more of this and they would have him in that devil's snare of theirs.

'I've had forty thousand children,' he said sharply.

Penhaligon laughed indulgently. Her gaze flicked from Kenneth to Fitzgerald and back again almost immediately, but it was enough to let Kenneth know that there was something between the two. He wondered if he would be able to use it to his advantage.

'Not like having one of your own,' Fitzgerald said. His tone was only marginally less amiable, but Kenneth knew his respite was over.

No, he thought. No it's not. He couldn't quite meet their eyes. 'I've had a full – and fulfilling – life,' he said. It was only partly untrue. In the circumstances, he was sure God would forgive him.

'And your wife?' That was Penhaligon, and now she wasn't playing the little girl at all.

My wife is as barren as Elizabeth and as pious as the Blessed Virgin. If she had, at times, seemed as cold as charity, perhaps that was only to be expected. 'She's had a busy life – lots of voluntary work –'

'You miss out though,' Penhaligon said. Her head was tilted to the side, and she sounded wistful. Perhaps she was already regretting that she'd chosen a career over a family – for all these young women said they could have it all, Kenneth knew they were fooling themselves – or perhaps she knew there was no future in this relationship she seemed to be having with Doctor Fitzgerald. She could not be unaware of the wedding band he wore.

'No,' Kenneth said, too loud, too fast, too defensive. 'I would say no, not really.' It didn't sound convincing to him, let alone to them.

Penhaligon seemed to consider this for a second. Strange how she had taken over the conversation; then again, they were talking about children, so perhaps it was only natural. 'No,' she said. 'I suppose you can get quite . . . close to some of your kids.'

The insinuation was obvious. Kenneth rather wished they would just come straight out with it. 'Not in that way,' he said levelly. He knew that now, above all times, he must not appear too angry, or he would seem as guilty as sin to them.

'What way?' Fitzgerald asked.

256

It was truly ridiculous, Kenneth thought. They must know what it had sounded like. He wouldn't have been surprised if they hadn't planned it all. 'Sorry?' he said.

'That way?' Fitzgerald said. 'What way?'

Very well, he'd play their childish games, just for now. 'There was an insinuation . . .' he let his voice trail off as he nodded towards Penhaligon.

'What were you insinuating, DS Penhaligon?' Fitzgerald turned to her.

I was right, Kenneth thought. They've planned this. They must do this all the time. Trapping people. Bringing them down, like the devil.

'Like an uncle,' she said shaking her head so that the sun glinted off the golden highlights in her red mane. She made it sound so innocent, but her eyes told him that he'd taken her bait.

Liar, Kenneth thought at her.

For a moment, no-one spoke. Nothing moved in the room except for the smoke curling up from the cigarette that hung, almost forgotten, from Fitzgerald's fingers.

I mustn't say anything, Kenneth told himself. Anything I say now will be wrong. It would send him spinning off the edge of the world into that formless void he so feared.

And so he let the silence continue, until Fitzgerald said, 'Joanne spoke to me before she died.'

No, Kenneth thought. It wasn't possible. The drink, the drugs, the exposure – she couldn't possibly have been coherent: except that this was God's test for him, and so He might have made it so; how else to ensure Kenneth's faith was tested to the limit?

'She wouldn't talk to her parents.' Fitzgerald shook his head. His face was set like stone. 'Couldn't face them – too ashamed.'

'Ashamed of what?' Kenneth asked. Suddenly, he wanted it done with: the words spoken, the charges laid. God knew what was in his heart – that he had killed Joanne to be rid of the knowledge of the chaos that lay at the heart of creation, the knowledge that ate at his faith.

She was, after all, sent to him by the devil: his failure had not been in killing her, but much earlier, when he had failed to recognise her for what she was.

'Are you going to tell me, or am I going to tell you?'

Kenneth stared into space. 'I can't tell you what she was ashamed of,' Kenneth said. It was true: how could anyone know another person's heart, especially when that person was a tool of damnation. 'If she was ashamed –' He heard the sound of papers being slapped down on the table, and looked round.

Penhaligon was putting photographs out. Joanne's body, all inscribed with his markings. The geometry of the universe, its life and death in mathematical equations. Everything chaotic, unGodly, that existed: the boiling anarchy beyond the edge of space, before and after time, and Joanne, girl-flesh, damnation in the form of woman. He stared, horrified, at what he had done. In daylight it looked so different.

And yet, God had willed it. Kenneth was a child of the Creator. However it looked to these unbelievers, he knew that he had been doing God's work.

She was gone. The chaos was gone. And soon order would be restored to his life. All he had to do was be strong for a little while longer.

He prepared himself to face their questions. But there were no questions.

'You notice her at a distance at first,' Fitzgerald said. 'Coming through the school gates in the morning, lining up in the dinner queue, gazing up at you in assembly.'

Kenneth knew what the man was trying to do – draw him in, until he was taking part in the fantasy, so that he would agree with something – or disagree, it didn't matter – and betray himself that way. Well, he wouldn't be caught. Yet he couldn't help remembering that first time he'd noticed her: he was covering her English class for a sick teacher. She'd read out the 'Quality of Mercy' speech from the *Merchant*. Such a beautiful voice, he'd thought.

258

Fitzgerald's voice rolled on, breaking over him as implacable as ocean waves. 'She's slightly different from the other girls – doesn't seem to have a gang. There's something vulnerable about her. Perhaps she's being bullied. Then one day you see her in the corridor. She's crying. She should be in lessons.'

No, Kenneth thought. She was wandering at the edge of the playing fields. They'd been teasing her about going to church.

'You ask her what's wrong. You tell her to come and see you after school. So far, nothing strange, unusual, untoward. You're doing your job – more than your job – concerning yourself with the pastoral care of your pupils. She's there for an hour, in your study.'

That was right, at least. It had been a Wednesday. She'd worried about missing Benediction, and they'd talked about the Bible.

'A long chat: the pressures at home, not fitting in at school. There are tears, but smiles too.'

Oh yes, Kenneth thought. That smile, that devil's device that had brought him to his knees . . . just as this little chat of Doctor Fitzgerald's was in danger of doing. Well, no more.

'Your heart goes out to her. You comfort her. A friendly arm around the shoulder; a friendly grasp of the hand; a friendly pat on the knee –'

'I get your drift, doctor –' Kenneth snapped. This had gone far enough. He banished all thoughts of Joanne.

'Good.' Fitzgerald's voice was hard, now; there was nothing seductive in it.

'You're sick.' Kenneth let his disgust at this whole tawdry charade come through in his voice. He had done what he had to do – what God had told him to do. But Fitzgerald – Fitzgerald was revelling in it.

As if to prove it, he smiled. 'As sick as the next man, Mr Trant.' Their gazes locked. Then Fitzgerald went on, 'I spent a day in Joanne's company; I'm not immune to her dependence, her softness, her fragility.'

259

'I refuse to participate in this,' Kenneth said. He started to get up.

Fitzgerald motioned to Penhaligon. She took a dictating machine out of her bag and placed it on the table. She pressed the play button.

Sarah's voice blared out at him. Sarah who he had trusted to help him.

'He's a wonderful man. I feel special when he's there,' she said through the hissing of the tape.

'This is preposterous,' Kenneth said.

'He loves me more than anything. I'll never want anyone else. Oh, Kenneth's wonderful –'

Penhaligon turned the tape off. 'Well, Mr Trant?' she said.

There was only one defence, and that was attack. 'I don't know how you bribed or bullied that poor child into perjuring herself,' he said, 'but you can expect a formal complaint –'

Fitzgerald laughed. 'Well, that's one way of taking it,' he said. Then he made a face as if his mouth were full of lemon juice. 'Another would be to admit that Sarah, like Joanne Barnes, is a victim of your manipulation, your lechery, and your lies.'

Kenneth took a deep breath. 'Let us assume for one moment, doctor, that this absurd allegation has some truth in it.' He glared at Penhaligon, hoping to intimidate her, but she just stared back at him. 'It doesn't, but just for now I'll indulge you. Let us assume that I have had an affair with Sarah. Just how is this supposed to link me to Joanne?' He scattered the photographs and the dictating machine with a sweep of his hand. 'No, doctor. You should admit that what you have is a farrago of lies and a mishmash of circumstantial evidence that bears no relation whatsoever to the truth.' Fitzgerald scowled. He was right, and the doctor knew it. He got to his feet. 'I refuse to participate in this nonsense any further.'

'Go now and we'll think the worst,' Fitzgerald said.

'We will,' Penhaligon agreed.

'Then by all means think just that,' Kenneth said.

He left the room, being careful not to let the door slam behind him. They would never leave him alone now, never. But everything he had done, he had done because it was the will of God. He would only fail if he lacked faith.

'My God, I believe,' his whispered as he got into his car. 'Help me in my unbelief.'

Jimmy Beck knocked back his second pint of the afternoon, and never mind the time. He banged his glass down on the counter, and wondered if Harriman was going to get another round in. Bit slow at times, Harriman. That or he had short arms and deep pockets.

Who cared? That damned fat bastard had lost, and Beck was going to get his collar after all.

That little pervert Saunders, he'd done it. Who cared if he was dead already? He'd have been dead sure enough after a month or two inside Parkhurst or wherever.

Very right-thinking blokes, some of your criminal scum.

Harriman got a round in – cheap round, just the three of them: him, Harriman, and the boss. Bit surprised to see the boss here, mind; but when it came to it Scousers were the salt of the earth and a celebration was a celebration in any accent.

Just as he was thinking he might suggest they go and grab some seats before the place got crowded out, Harriman whooped and pointed to the door.

Fitz and that cow Penhaligon had just walked in. Beck thumped his glass on the bar, and joined in with Harriman's shouting.

'Thanks, by the way, Fitz,' the boss shouted over the noise.

'What for?' Fitz snapped.

'For the drink,' Beck said. He raised his glass.

Wise tapped his watch. 'One to two, you lost your bet,' he said. 'Come and help me spend my winnings.'

261

'No hard feelings,' Beck said, 'but we started spending it yesterday.'

That raised a good laugh, especially from the boss. For all his crap and his education, Fitz was never going to know what it felt like to really be part of a bunch of the right blokes.

Fitz glared at them. He pretended to laugh along with them for a minute, but when they weren't fooled and just kept on laughing, he stormed out. Penhaligon turned and followed him. She would.

'Walkies!' Beck called after here. 'Here girl!'

She turned just as she got to the door and gave them the finger. Now what kind of behaviour was that for a girl?

'Aw, Janie,' Harriman shouted to her, in a baby voice.

'Leave it out,' Wise said. 'Leave it out. He's fair game, but not her.'

Bloody typical, that's what she is, Beck thought. Wants to be one of the lads and then can't take a joke.

FORTY

Fitz clambered out of Panhandle's car. He stared at the church where Kenneth Trant's Fellowship of Souls met. It was an unimpressive building, a box built of red brick and glass, like a thousand others.

Only a thousand others weren't run by a manipulative, murdering bastard, he thought as he started towards it. Panhandle hurried to catch up with him.

The sound of singing drifted across to them on the warm evening air. *Praise Him in glad adoration*, indeed, Fitz thought. The trouble was, only half the people in that hall were singing about God. The other half were singing about Kenneth Trant.

We'll see, Fitz thought. We'll just bloody well see.

He hurried up the steps, then paused on the covered porchway.

'You have got the tape, haven't you?' he asked Panhandle.

She nodded and patted her jacket pocket. 'Do you really think it'll do any good?' she asked.

Fitz chewed his lip. 'Maybe. At the very least it'll give his flock something to think about.' He pulled open the door. The singing got louder. 'Anyway, it's our best shot,' he said.

They went in. The foyer was almost clinical, softened only by the sunlight that barred white walls, and the poster pinned to an easel in the corner. It bore what Fitz first assumed was the message of the day. Beneath a picture of a stained glass window, it said, '*Dust thou art, and unto dust shalt thou return.*

263

Not the message of the day at all, Fitz thought. Just the message, period. Fear death. That was the whole substance of Kenneth Trant's message. What had Dean Saunders said? *All flesh is grass.* Only the words were different.

Then Fitz noticed the smaller writing at the bottom of the poster. He pointed to it. 'Genesis, chapter three, verse nineteen.' Panhandle stared at him. She didn't get it. 'It's not a one, it's an I,' he said, disgusted at his own slowness.

He yanked open the inner door, and strode into the chapel with Panhandle right behind him. Row upon row of people stood singing. Fitz had to give Kenneth credit for spreading his net wide. There were old people and young in the congregation, women in floral dresses and women in jeans, men in overalls and men in business suits. Young and old had flocked to Kenneth Trant, including, as Father O'Ryan had said, a number of very young women. And yes, there was Sarah, right near the front, singing her heart out for the man who had told her she was special.

The Trants stood on a dais at the front, behind a table draped in a crimson cloth. Kenneth had positioned himself so that the huge stained-glass rose window made an aureole round his head. It was a clever trick, Fitz admitted: though once you became consciously aware of the resemblance it gave Kenneth to a medieval saint, it lost its power.

It was time to end this once and for all.

There was a huge, old-fashioned Bible on a lectern near the door. Fitz strode over to it. He flicked through the book, knowing that Kenneth had already registered his presence. The congregation hadn't though. They sang on.

Revelations, I Corinthians, Job . . . Isaiah. He scanned the crabbed old-fashioned typescript before he spoke. 'Isaiah chapter 40, verse 6,' he said, in a voice he hadn't used since he'd finally escaped from reading at Mass when he was a lad.

The singing stopped abruptly. Most of the people turned round uncertainly. When he was sure he had their attention, he said, 'What is it, Kenneth. What'll I find?' He didn't give

264

the man a chance to answer. ' "The voice said, Cry. And he said, What shall I cry?" ' he read. ' "All flesh is grass, and all the goodliness thereof –" '

'– is as the flower of the field.' Kenneth Trant finished for him. He glanced at the prayer book he held in his hand. As he spoke, the congregation began to sit down. 'Very good, Doctor Fitzgerald. Now, how may we help you?' He sounded calm, very much in control.

Well, that can change, Fitz thought.

Some people were still standing. Most were still looking round. A few were whispering to their neighours. It was going to be quite a show.

'She believed you when you told her she was special, didn't she?' He stuck his hands in his trouser pockets and started to saunter down the centre aisle.

'You've lost me, doctor,' Kenneth said, sounding bewildered.

Very good, Fitz thought. Oscar nomination if not the gong itself.

'You've always had a way with women, haven't you?' Fitz demanded. 'Hasn't he Norma? Mmmm?' He nodded at her, but spoke to Kenneth. 'Why didn't you have an affair with her? She's in love with you – has been for over twenty years.'

A ripple of sound – whispering, people turning – went through the congregation.

It was cruel to Norma, but not as cruel as what they'd done to Joanne. He might not be able to get Kenneth to crack, but by God he'd drive a wedge between him and the others that would drive them apart: and then they'd see who still stood by their beloved Kenneth.

Fitz moved up closer. He passed Sarah. She was pale, with two spots of colour high on her cheekbones, and she clutched the chair-back in front of her with one white-knuckled hand.

He paused next to her. 'But no, not Norma, not a woman – not a mature woman.' He didn't bother even to try and

265

disguise the contempt he felt. 'You wouldn't be equal to a *woman*.' He glanced at Sarah, and then – to make it easier for her – at another, even younger girl in the other section of the congregation. 'You need youth, young flesh.' He stopped speaking, and let Kenneth have time to make his reply.

Give him enough rope? He'd give the bastard a whole ship's chandler's, if that was what it took.

Kenneth looked beyond Fitz, to Panhandle. 'This is outrageous. Can he do this?' He sounded properly disgusted. The congregation shifted and whispered. Virginia collapsed into her seat. So did Michael. 'This is a place of worship.'

Fitz thought, if I can't have you – make my collar, as our beloved Jimmy Beck would say – I'll settle for making sure you don't screw up any more young women. He glanced again at Sarah. She was staring at the floor.

But I will have you, he thought. So help me, I will.

Time for the big push. 'Did you wait till she was sixteen?' he demanded. Norma sat down next to Michael: a tough woman, Norma, to have stayed standing through all that, Fitz thought. But he couldn't let it stop him. 'I'll bet you did. I bet, with your perverted sense of righteousness, you didn't touch her till she was of age.' It was a relief to have the gloves off, finally to allow all his pent-up rage to express itself.

Five years on, and it could have been Katie. Ten years back, Panhandle. Except, of course, they were both too intelligent – more, too smart – to have anything to do with a slimeball like Kenneth Trant. At least, he had to hope.

Aah, he thought, without letting himself stop to analyse it: the good old male urge to own, disguised as the desire to protect.

Well, sometimes it did some good, that was all.

'I'll sue you. Get out now. You leave us in peace or I'll sue you for every penny you've got.'

Fitz grinned. It was the only sane response. Try it, he thought gleefully, see what you get: tuppence ha'penny and a used Polo mint.

Virginia stared up at Kenneth. She licked her lips, and she twisted her wedding ring round and round. Norma stared fixedly ahead, apparently fascinated by a spot on the far wall. As for Michael, he was reading his Bible.

'She respected you for that,' Fitz said. 'She thought you were showing her respect.' He paused. He needed something shocking next, something to get under the skins of these so-called decent, so-called Christian folk. 'She thought the sun shone out of your arse.' He leaned heavily on the last word, and was gratified to hear a little gasp of dismay run around the congregation.

'Any teacher will tell you it is a hazard of the profession.' It sounded to Fitz like a speech Kenneth had made many times before: which, of course, he had – in his own head, as he convinced himself that what he was doing was reasonable, even desirable. He stared at Panhandle, before he went on. 'In the same way, doctor, as a patient may become emotionally attached to a psychologist. May find themselves convinced that their relationship goes beyond the professional, projecting their own fantasies onto the therapist.' And you can fuck off too, Fitz thought: just leave her out of it. Norma stared up at him, with eyes that were glazed with pain. But Kenneth's gaze was on the congregation now. 'Joanne Barnes was a lonely child,' he said to them, not to Fitz. 'Perhaps she was looking for a special relationship.' Norma looked away. Recognised herself in that description, Fitz thought, and couldn't take it. 'Perhaps she found it,' Kenneth said. 'But it was not me.'

All right, Fitz thought. If you really think their opinion is more important than mine, let's see what they think of this. Briefly, he considered telling Panhandle to play the tape. It would certainly ruin Kenneth with the Fellowship. But it would also ruin Sarah: she might live it down, but it would screw her up for years to come. And Kenneth had won enough, already. Fitz wouldn't give him any more.

Besides, this way was a bigger challenge.

'You had sex with Joanne,' he said. It wasn't a murmur

267

that rippled through the crowd this time. It was a roar of dismay and confusion. Virginia looked as if someone had slapped her. The crowd were quiet now, listening; and Kenneth tried to smile. 'She got pregnant. Was that the problem? Was that why you attacked her? Was that why you stuffed her with Paracetamol, poured gin down her, defiled her body – was that it?' Michael shifted on his seat, drawing Fitz's attention to him. He didn't just look uncomfortable, he looked haunted, as if he were remembering something too painful to bear. In that moment, Fitz knew: he'd been wrong. The others hadn't found out that Kenneth had tried to kill Joanne. They'd all been in on it. Christ, he thought: Murder on the Orient Express, here we come. Don't stop, he thought. Keep the pressure up. 'Because she was a danger to all this? Your church? Your power?' he demanded.

Kenneth appealed to the congregation. 'I drove Joanne Barnes home a few times.' Out of the corner of his eye, Fitz saw Sarah struggling to believe him. Given the most minute excuse, she would, too. 'On the basis of that, I'm being accused of rape and murder,' Kenneth finished, his voice full of injured innocence.

Rape, Fitz thought: this just goes on getting worse.

'I didn't hear any mention of rape,' Panhandle said from behind Fitz. He couldn't see her face, but she sounded thoroughly pissed off – still stinging from Kenneth's earlier barbs. Bad mistake, Kenneth, Fitz thought.

'I had no relationship with Joanne Barnes.'

'Then who did?' Panhandle demanded. Fitz swivelled round to look at her.

'You know who did – you had him in custody.'

Panhandle crossed her arms, turned away and looked at the ceiling, the very picture of boredom. Michael turned and stared at his brother. He looked as if he'd been beaten by someone he trusted – pain and shock were mingled in his eyes.

Kenneth went on, 'Dean Saunders. That vicious little psychopath.'

Michael got up. He stumbled off the dais and away down the side aisle of the chapel.

Kenneth pointed a shaking finger – fear or anger, Fitz wondered – at the congregation. 'This man,' he said. He glanced at Michael as he left, but he obviously meant Fitz. 'This man is desperate. Because he had the real killer in custody and he made a dreadful mess of things.' His voice was only just calm. 'Didn't you?' He was speaking directly to Fitz now, letting his anger and fear feed off each other. 'You drove him to his death in a police cell. Do not project your guilt on to me. I conceal nothing.'

Well, ten out of ten for the use of the jargon, Fitz thought. But for honesty? A far too generous minus nine. He grinned. 'Dean Saunders didn't write that graffiti on her. You did,' he said softly. 'But what does it mean?' He moved up close to the dais, where he could speak intimately with Kenneth. 'Hmm?' He could hear something going on to one side, but he ignored it. He'd have ignored anything short of a ground-zero nuclear attack just at that moment. 'What were you thinking of when you wrote all that graffiti all over her?' Kenneth just stared at him. So did Norma, but Virginia's gaze had never left Kenneth. 'The instant before the universe began,' Fitz said.

Kenneth stared at a point somewhere in the space behind Fitz's head. He had a look of barely suppressed terror on his face, as if by naming Kenneth's private demons, Fitz had summoned them to appear.

Fitz let his voice roll on, creating the fantasy and forcing Kenneth to live in it. 'The chaos beyond the Planck Wall – that boiling mass of space and time: no law, no meaning, no past, no future.'

Kenneth's gaze flickered over to the side of the chapel. His eyes focused, and if anything his look of fear intensified.

Mustn't let him go now, Fitz thought. 'The Big Bang,' he said, naming demons again. 'The creation of the universe. The beginning and end of life. Sex and death – your

269

obsession. You see sex in death and death in sex and beyond that . . . nothing.'

Norma's eyes went wide. Virginia reached out and took Kenneth's hand, but he didn't respond. Something was definitely going on behind Fitz, but he didn't dare turn round to find out what it was. 'That's what your equations tell me, Kenneth.' Time for the pay-off. 'You've got no belief in God.'

'Thank you, Doctor Fitzgerald,' Kenneth whispered hoarsely. He sounded distracted, rather than grateful.

There were footsteps coming up the centre aisle behind Fitz, and horrified expressions on the faces of Norma and Virginia: and wasn't that a murmur of consternation from the congregation. Fitz ached with curiosity, but he didn't dare turn to look. He stepped right up close to the dais and leaned on the table, so his head was almost touching Kenneth's.

'Let us continue,' Kenneth said. He flicked over the pages in his Bible and began to read. ' "And it shall come to pass –" '

'You're having a crisis of faith, Kenneth. A century too late –' Fitz said, over the top of the reading.

Kenneth didn't stop. ' "– that he that is left in Zion, and he that remaineth in Jerusalem –" '

There was a disturbance in the chapel behind them – talking, people moving around. Certainly no-one was listening to Kenneth.

'It's God or nothing, you can't have both –'

' "– shall be called holy, even every one that is written among the living in Jerusalem –" ' He spread his hands out wide, as if imploring his God to deliver him. 'I believe. I believe. I believe.'

Virginia joined in, then Norma. Fitz turned round at last, just in time to see some of the congregation standing up to join in. 'I believe. I believe. I believe,' they chanted. Like kids clapping their hands so Tinker Bell won't snuff it, Fitz thought.

But only some of them. The others were staring at some papers or . . . photographs. Panhandle was too. Michael was working his way round the congregation, handing them out.

'I will extol Thee, O Lord,' Kenneth said, leading the congregation, but even as he spoke, the other voices became fewer, and died away, until his was the only voice, because even Norma and Virginia were too wrapped up in their panic to speak.

Panhandle came slowly up to Fitz. She handed him the photographs: a bright summer's day, with Kenneth screwing Joanne Barnes up against a tree in some wood somewhere. Poor little Joanne, Fitz thought, with her panties down around her ankles trading her life for a few minutes of ecstasy with a man who despised her.

He hoped she'd been truly happy then. It didn't make it worth it. It didn't make it right. But at least it meant she'd had some joy in her short life.

Kenneth looked aghast. The people were starting to leave the chapel, wandering out gossiping in twos and threes, or striding out alone, looking furious.

'Michael!' Norma said.

He looked round, but continued distributing the photographs.

Another part of the jigsaw fell into place: Norma had taken the photographs, hoping to split Kenneth and Virginia up. Fitz was pretty certain of it, but it wasn't important now.

He still needed to hear Kenneth say it, so there could be no doubt in anyone's mind.

He put one of the photographs down on the table in front of Kenneth. 'Your religion is a sham,' he said. 'An act of theatre for your dreams of power –' down went another photograph. '– until one day you start to lose control and that Godlike demeanour starts to deconstruct.' And another. 'And what have you got left? A desperate grope and a hopeless shag in a Godless universe.' He slammed the rest of them down, and fanned them out.

The three remaining Trants stared at him hopelessly, while behind him the chapel continued to empty.

Kenneth's face was a mask of despair. ' "The voice said, Cry. And he said, What shall I cry?" ' Kenneth whispered. He closed his eyes. 'Oh merciful and forgiving God cleanse our sins. You are made holy by absolving me.' Here we go again, Fitz thought: the launderette version of religion – I can do anything I want as long as I say sorry loud enough afterwards. Or possibly, as long as I can convince other people I'm sorry. But Kenneth really did seem to mean it. He spoke as if the words were acid in his throat, fire in his mouth. 'Raise your spirits and forgive, forgive, forgive.'

'They cannot absolve you till you confess,' Fitz said. He stepped aside so that Kenneth could see that a few of his congregation still remained in their seats. 'Confess to me,' he said. He put just a little iron in his voice. 'I'll forgive you.'

There was silence. Come on, Fitz thought. Come on, you bastard: but he made sure his expression stayed sympathetic. Kenneth Trant stared at him with frightened eyes, all pretence at calmness and control gone.

And then Michael Trant's voice said from behind Fitz, 'I did it.'

Fitz whirled round. So did Panhandle.

Michael stumbled out of his seat near the aisle. He stood there for a moment, a pathetic figure in a rumpled suit, haloed by the light shining through the door. 'I tormented her,' he said. His voice was thick with tears. 'I disgraced her, I cleansed her and sent her to her God.'

'And Norma?' Fitz asked. He turned back to face her. She seemed numb with terror.

'Michael –' she said desperately.

'Yes,' Michael said.

'And Virginia?' Fitz didn't turn back to look at Michael. He knew he had the younger Trant brother. But the others . . . Virginia seemed past fear.

'Yes.'

'And Kenneth?' He shouted the words. If Michael backed down now, they could still lose it all.

'Yes.'

Thank you, God, Fitz thought, though he believed in God less in that moment than he ever had before.

'He's a liar!' Kenneth Trant shouted; but it was mere bluster and everyone there knew it.

Fitz smiled at him.

'And Dean?' Panhandle said.

'No!' Michael said, and again Fitz had that wonderful sensation of a piece of jigsaw falling into place in his mind. Michael had cared about the boy more than he had known: perhaps in Dean's shambling, good-hearted hopelessness, he'd seen an exaggerated version of himself. He had been able to live with what they'd done to Joanne – not easily, but he could do it. But when Dean had killed himself, Michael Trant had lost a part of his soul. After all, the boy had relied on him for most things. And then when Kenneth started talking so contemptuously of him . . . to Michael, it had been as if his brother were talking about him, calling him hopeless, a loser, a man who could never have the love of the woman he desired above all things. And who could blame Michael for retaliating with the best weapon that came to hand?

'They wanted me to dispose of Joanne,' he said. 'Package her.' Package her, Fitz thought; and then, aghast, my God, the baling machine – those whirling blades, the hydraulic rams . . . they'd have shredded her, and she'd have been alive when they started. No wonder Michael got so upset when we interviewed him at the factory. I talked about the one thing he couldn't bear to look at. 'I asked Dean to help and he let her go –' Michael continued. Something made Fitz look at Norma. She was plainly furious. '– I knew he would. He'd not hurt anyone, and never Joanne. Dean was absolutely innocent. He always was.' He stammered to a halt, and stood looking at them, obviously unsure what was going to happen next.

A better person than the others, or just weak? Fitz wondered. Maybe he really had hoped to give her a chance to escape.

'And you'd be prepared to make a statement to that effect?' Panhandle said.

Michael stared hard at Kenneth, who glared back at him. Don't lose your bottle now, Fitz thought. I'll give you the benefit of any doubt that's going, but just don't lose it now.

Michael's gaze flicked from Kenneth, to Norma – who looked at him with contempt – and back again. 'Oh yes,' he said.

It was worth all the aggravation just to see the look on Jimmy Beck's face, Fitz thought a little while after, as he walked out of the chapel with Penhaligon.

The Trants were marched to the police van amid a welter of reporters and onlookers. Sarah had long since disappeared off by herself somewhere. Fitz made a mental note to make sure she got some counselling, and to find out how many other girls Kenneth Trant had preyed on.

'What made you so sure,' Panhandle asked as they emerged into the sunlight.

'About what?' Fitz asked. They paused to watch the Trants being put into the van.

'That he'd crack?'

For a second, Fitz considered pretending that she'd meant Michael, and that he'd targeted him. But all in all, there were too many other things to be dishonest about to make it worth adding another one. 'I wasn't,' he said. 'He didn't.' Kenneth turned just before he was made to get into the van. He glared at Fitz with absolute hatred in his eyes. 'He won't,' Fitz concluded. 'He won't confess.'

They started towards Panhandle's car. 'But now that we've got the statement –' she protested.

For a hard-bitten policewoman, she had her moments of charming naïveté. 'Nah,' he said. 'He'll deny all that. He'll say it was Michael and Dean and claim it was nothing to do with him.' He started to open the car door. 'The women'll back him up.'

Panhandle leaned against the car to watch the van driving away. 'They can't.' Her tone was incredulous.

Fitz stared at her without her seeing. In the bright summer sunlight she was delicately beautiful, not something he could possibly hope to hold on to for long – not without breaking her. 'They will,' he insisted. 'They will. Such is the power of faith.' He thought about poor Joanne, shagging Kenneth up against a tree because he'd made her believe that was what lovers did. And then he thought about Panhandle by lamplight, all soft in his arms. Time, perhaps, to change the subject. 'Or sex . . .'

'Or self-preservation,' she said, refusing to be deflected. 'Michael will be testifying against them. It'll be their word against his.'

Self-preservation, Fitz thought. He wondered how long it would be before self-preservation made her give up on him. It had taken Judith twenty years. He doubted it would take Panhandle that long. 'You know what we need?' he asked, knowing she would misunderstand.

'What?' she asked.

'A miracle.'

That made her laugh, so he did too. 'You'll have to perform it yourself, Fitz,' she said.

He wondered if she'd cottoned on. He wouldn't put it past her. 'No,' he said. 'Not me. I know my limitations. What you see is what you get – imperfect.' He looked at her coyly. 'A sex god, but imperfect.'

She smiled, and Fitz's world was suddenly a little brighter. For however long it lasted.

The Cracker Writers

Jimmy McGovern

Jimmy McGovern's scriptwriting career began in the early 1980s with plays for Liverpool's Everyman and Playhouse theatres. His Merseyside association continued with scripts for over eighty episodes of Channel 4's soap opera *Brookside* between 1983 and 1989. During the 1990s he has written for over a dozen films and television series, including *El CID*, *Backbeat* and, of course, *Cracker*.

Liz Holliday

Liz Holliday is an ex-theatre director, ex-bookseller, ex-teacher (and ex a whole lot of other things, too). Science fiction is her first love, but crime will do very nicely too. In 1989 she attended the Clarion SF Writers' workshop, and found that it made all the difference. She has no intention of becoming an ex-writer. *The Big Crunch* is her second *Cracker* novel.

The Cracker Stories

Based on the original scripts, Virgin's Cracker novels add depth and detail to the televised stories and provide a permanent record of Fitz's involvement with the police and of his relationships with his wife Judith and with Detective Sergeant Jane Penhaligon.

Series One

The first three Cracker stories, first broadcast on British television in 1993, were all written by Jimmy McGovern.

The Mad Woman In The Attic
Adapted by Jim Mortimore

Dr Edward Fitzgerald, who insists that everyone call him Fitz, is a psychologist with an apparently conventional life. He teaches and practises psychology; he has an attractive wife, two children, and a big house in a pleasant suburb of Manchester. But he's also addicted to gambling, booze, cigarettes, and pushing his considerable bulk into any situation he finds intriguing. His wife Judith has had enough. She leaves him. Fitz's life is beginning to fall apart.

When one of his students is murdered, Fitz can't resist becoming involved. The police have a suspect; they are sure he's the serial killer, but he's claiming complete amnesia. The police reluctantly hire Fitz to get a confession.

As Fitz investigates, he finds that the police theory doesn't fit the facts. He discovers, in solving murder cases, a new focus for his life. And he meets Detective Sergeant Jane Penhaligon.

To Say I Love You
Adapted by Molly Brown

People do strange things for love.

Tina's parents had nothing but loving intentions when they turned her into a talking guide dog for her blind sister. Sean, full of bitterness and fury, is prepared to kill for the love of Tina. And Fitz, psychologist and occasional catcher of murderers, would do anything to win back the love of his wife Judith – if only he didn't find himself working so closely with DS Jane Penhaligon.

In this, the second Cracker thriller, Fitz can find a murderer, prevent a catastrophe, and still find time to flirt with a pretty policewoman. But he also knows only too well the motivations that drive Judith into another man's bed and that push him to the edge of self-destruction.

Compared to the complications of Fitz's own life, tracking down a team of cop-killers is simple.

One Day A Lemming Will Fly
Adapted by Liz Holliday

Everything's going to be all right. Judith is back home, Penhaligon's falling in love, and Fitz has a new problem to solve from the police.

It's an open and shut case. A schoolboy – a young, effeminate, scholarly and often bullied schoolboy – is found murdered. His English teacher – male, single, lives alone – tries to commit suicide. It's obvious: the teacher killed his pupil. The police think so. The boy's parents think so.

Everyone in the family's neighbourhood thinks so. And Fitz thinks so. It's just a matter of obtaining a confession.

But the truth is as elusive as trust and honesty, and the case goes badly wrong.

In this, the third Cracker story, Fitz reaches the crisis in his personal drama. He has to choose between Judith and Jane. And that's the least of his problems.

Series Two

Cracker's second series was first broadcast in 1994. Two of the three stories were written by Jimmy McGovern.

To Be A Somebody
Adapted by Gareth Roberts

Having argued with DCI Bilborough and abandoned Jane at the airport, Fitz isn't welcome at Anson Road nick any more. He's back on the booze, his gambling is riskier than ever, and Judith's had as much as she can take. Fitz is at a new low.

When an Asian grocer is stabbed by a skinhead, the police assume a racist motive. Fitz knows better, and as usual he's right. But he can't convince Bilborough to let him help until the murderer has struck again.

Albie and his dad, Liverpool supporters, were at the Hillsborough disaster. Five years later, Albie's dad has died. And Albie wants revenge. He'll kill anyone who makes assumptions about white, working-class scousers. But he particularly wants to kill coppers.

The Big Crunch
Adapted by Liz Holliday

Kenneth Trant is a headmaster and the leader of an evangelical Christian group. He's above suspicion. When one of his pupils and church members – a teenage   girl – is found dying, her body covered with arcane symbols, suspicion falls on the disturbed young man who works for Trant's brother. It's an open and shut case.

Fitz doesn't think so, of course, but at first there's not much he can do. Anyway, he's distracted: Judith has moved out, the house is up for sale – and Jane Penhaligon is still very interesting. And interested.

Men Should Weep
Adapted by Jim Mortimore

This story brings the second series to a shattering conclusion. The Anson Road detectives tear each other apart, and Fitz's life dissolves into chaos, as a serial rapist terrorises Manchester. This is the hardest-hitting Cracker story yet.

Publication: May 1995